MANDY

There is a doll… There is a legend…

ALSO BY
SHANI STRUTHERS

EVE: A CHRISTMAS
GHOST STORY
(PSYCHIC SURVEYS
PREQUEL)

PSYCHIC SURVEYS BOOK
ONE:
THE HAUNTING OF
HIGHDOWN HALL

PSYCHIC SURVEYS BOOK
TWO:
RISE TO ME

PSYCHIC SURVEYS BOOK
THREE:
44 GILMORE STREET

PSYCHIC SURVEYS BOOK
FOUR:
OLD CROSS COTTAGE

PSYCHIC SURVEYS BOOK
FIVE:
DESCENSION

PSYCHIC SURVEYS BOOK
SIX:
LEGION

BLAKEMORT
(A PSYCHIC SURVEYS
COMPANION NOVEL
BOOK ONE)

THIRTEEN
(A PSYCHIC SURVEYS
COMPANION NOVEL
BOOK TWO)

ROSAMUND
(A PSYCHIC SURVEYS
COMPANION NOVEL
BOOK THREE)

THIS HAUNTED WORLD
BOOK ONE:
THE VENETIAN

THIS HAUNTED WORLD
BOOK TWO:
THE ELEVENTH FLOOR

THIS HAUNTED WORLD
BOOK THREE:
HIGHGATE

THE JESSAMINE SERIES
BOOK ONE
JESSA*MINE*

THE JESSAMINE SERIES
BOOK TWO
COMRAICH

REACH FOR THE DEAD
BOOK ONE:
MANDY

REACH FOR THE DEAD
BOOK ONE

MANDY

SHANI STRUTHERS

STORY
LAND
PRESS

Reach for the Dead: Book One: Mandy
Copyright © Shani Struthers 2020

The right of Shani Struthers to be identified as the Author of the work has been asserted by her in accordance with the Copyright, Designs and Patents Act 1988. All rights reserved in all media. No part of this publication may be reproduced, stored in a retrieval system, or transmitted in any form or by any means, electronic, mechanical, recording, photocopying, the Internet or otherwise, without the prior written consent of the copyright holder, nor be otherwise circulated in any form of binding or cover other than that in which it is published and without a similar condition being imposed on the subsequent purchaser.

www.shanistruthers.com

Storyland Press
www.storylandpress.com

ISBN: 979-8-6-233-4954-5

All characters and events featured in this publication are purely fictitious and any resemblance to any person, place, organisation/company, living or dead, is entirely coincidental.

DEDICATION

To my wonderful family: Rob, Izzie, Jack and Misty – I love our travels together, especially when they involve venturing into the wilds of Canada to visit haunted dolls…

ACKNOWLEDGEMENTS

Once again, a huge thank you to those who've helped in the first book of this new series, all your comments, your thoughts, your skills and expertise are greatly appreciated. It sounds cliched, but I couldn't do this without the help I receive. So, first up, it's my usual team of beta readers: Rob Struthers (your fact checking is amazing), Amanda Nash (you made *Highgate* stronger and this too), Kate Jane Jones (I love your enthusiasm!), Sarah Savery (I know it's a winner if it gets your approval!), Lesley Hughes (a beta reader from the start) and last but never least, Louisa Taylor (also with me from the start, in more ways than one!). Huge thanks also to Gina Dickerson of RoseWolf Design, who creates all my covers and formats – a joy to work with as well as a friend, and Rumer Haven, who's my editor and also a complete joy to know. A big cheer to Richard Hardie, and all the authors from our co-operative Authors Reach, doing things our way, the *only* way, and to psychic Avril Griffiths for your thoughts on Mandy when I first started writing about her.

FOREWORD

I was inspired to write *Mandy* after visiting the actual Mandy doll in a museum in the small town of Quesnel in Western Canada, a doll reported to be possessed by a strange entity and, although on display, hermetically sealed in a glass case. Yes, there was something about her, something frightening but also a little sad. Why was I frightened, though? Was it because I expected to be, auto suggestion at play? I'm really not sure. But that question intrigued me, got my mind working, and ultimately, set me on the path to writing this novel. Whether Mandy is haunted or not is up to the individual to decide, but one thing is certain: she's a doll with a history longer than mine and most likely yours, the crack that runs down the right side of her face testament to the fact it hasn't always been a happy one (please note with my Mandy the crack is on the *left* side, this is in order to make the distinction between fact and fiction). Finally, I'm a British author but as *Mandy* and the *Reach for the Dead* series is set in America, I've written it in American English – those are not typos, honest!

PROLOGUE

"Stop crying, ya hear? I won't have it! I'll make you stop. I mean it this time. I'll make you."

Despite the old woman's warning, there was another almighty bang.

"I said enough now!"

She was shaking, angry as well as something else, something she didn't want to admit to.

"Quit that crying! That…*constant* crying."

From standing still, the woman began to pace. Close to eighty, she didn't have the stomach for this anymore, the energy to put up with such infernal behavior. The crying and the tantrums were getting worse. But why? She'd done her best by her, hadn't she? Looked after her when she'd been abandoned, given her a good home. Who else would have done that? Nobody! But she had, because…because she'd felt sorry for her. Ha! She'd been duped, more like, reeled in by a pretty face—a cracked pretty face, mind. But no more of it. Her health was declining, rapidly, and it was as if Mandy knew it, as if she were taking advantage of that fact, turning on her benefactor, determined to drive her mad. Was it any wonder she could barely remember the day of the week or what time it was? So often, night would fall and catch her by surprise.

"And it's all because of you!"

What time was it now? She stopped pacing to look at her watch, her breath coming in short, sharp gasps, her chest heaving. The dial read eight o'clock, but was that eight in the morning, or had evening come around again already? With her hands covering her ears as she padded across the room to the window, she then pulled back the curtains. Nighttime. Where did the hours go? They blurred into one another. Day after day sped by without her seeing a soul.

It hadn't always been like this. Oh no. Once upon a time, this old farmstead had been filled with people and laughter, her husband Daniel and their four children. Overlooking acres of good, fertile land in northern Idaho, their nearest neighbors had been a fair distance away, but that hadn't mattered. As potato farmers, they'd lived a comfortable enough life, working the land and letting the children fly as free as the geese in between their schooling. Lena would also see to the house and their offspring, cooking, cleaning, and teaching—not just the kind of stuff you could find in books, but about a way of life that had endured in the Dubinsky family for generations.

"Lena," Daniel would say, the pair of them sitting on the porch, savoring the sharp bite of her homemade lemonade and gazing at the sun as it melted into the ground like ice cream, "this is all of life, right here, right now. How could anyone want for anything more?"

She certainly hadn't. The modesty of their life suited her; it was what she was used to, with him and before him. Perhaps she was content because she didn't know about fancier trappings. But actually, she didn't think so. She had the love of a good man, a healthy family, a parcel of land, and a home. Daniel was right. This *was* life, and they were just so thankful.

But life could turn, and turn it did. Daniel had a cough, and it got worse. "I don't want no doctor," he'd declare when she tried to persuade him. "It'll pass."

Stubborn he was, like a mule! It didn't pass, only worsened further. When finally, *finally*, she drove into Catskill to fetch Dr Lewiston, begging him to return home with her, to knock some sense into her husband, it was too late. The cancer gave him five weeks from that visit, and it was five weeks of agony for everyone. She and the children worked around the clock to care for him, to try to ease his pain in whichever way they could, but he still left this world howling.

At the time of Daniel's death, Peter was sixteen, Paulina fourteen, Teresa eleven and Michael ten. His death scarred them. It scarred her too, but a woman had to carry on if she had a family and the fields to tend to. It wasn't the days that were the worst but the nights. She no longer slept through, opening her eyes as the first rays of dawn filtered through the curtains to illuminate the sleeping man beside her. Instead, hours and hours were spent staring into the gloom as she relived his agony, every damned moment. If oblivion came, it wasn't for long. Soon enough, she'd be spat back into consciousness and all it demanded of her.

Of Polish descent, Lena Dubinsky was nothing if not stoic. Her family had traveled thousands of miles for a better life, and, thankfully, they'd found it among the sun-scorched open plains of northwestern America. They'd settled and they'd farmed. Her grandparents had worked hard, then her parents, then she and Daniel. She'd be damned if she was going to fail them! She'd rise and she would face the day, keeping food on the table and hope in the hearts of her children, at least, who got older and wiser, who left rural Idaho to work in the cities, seizing any opportunity that came their way. And she encouraged them. Daniel would be so proud! Often, she imagined him looking down on his brood—not farmers, not anymore, but bankers, retailers, and accountants.

Everything came to an end. Lena accepted that. Even great families and great family traditions. The world wouldn't stand still, no matter how much you might want it to. Daniel had never said he wanted the kids to follow him into farming, and neither had she, hence why they'd placed so much importance on their schooling. And though it tore at her already ravaged heart when the last one, Michael, left, she stood on her doorstep and she kept on smiling, she kept on waving, right until the car that took him was a speck on the horizon.

The house and farm were bought and paid for, were hers, and so terrifyingly empty.

Over the years people had found land closer to hers and built their homes, the neighbors no longer as far as they used to be. And again, it was no matter. She liked them all. There was something in the air in Idaho; it bred decent people, but even so, neighbors had work to do, and an old lady like her was done with working now that the fields were leased out.

Dolls were what saved her. She filled the house with them and their sweet, smiling faces.

They gave her a reason to drive out most weeks,

searching for them wherever she could, in antique stores, at fairs and yard sales. The poor little angels! So many were in such a bad way. She rescued them, that's what she did, gave them all the love and attention she'd once lavished on her own family. And that's what they became: her *new* family. She'd sew and she'd knit, making the most darling outfits for them. Once they were adorned in their new clothes, she'd tease their hair into curls, which she would then festoon with ribbons. Dirty faces were scrubbed clean, a little color applied to the cheeks or the eyes to give them back their youthful beauty. And she christened them all. There was Julia, Emilia, Urszula, Wanda, Zofia, Jadwiga, Marta, Violetta, Dorota, and Stefania. It went on and on, some boys among them too, so smart, so handsome.

When Paulina visited, she would grimace. "Mom," she'd complain, "they give me the creeps!"

Lena was genuinely perplexed. "In what way, honey?"

"It's their eyes; they follow you everywhere."

Lena smiled at that. "Just like the boys at college, I'm guessing."

Paulina rolled her eyes. "I'm focusing on studies, Mom, not boys."

"Glad to hear it, but there'll come a time…"

Paulina soon met a man, as her mother knew she would. She was pretty as a picture, that girl, as well as smart, her dark hair gleaming and her eyes such a vivid shade of green. All her children were quick to couple with others, and again Lena was glad. But it also meant their visits home, infrequent enough to begin with, became less and less. Thank God for the dolls!

She didn't have favorites because, as with children, to do

so was wrong. But, oh, when she spotted Mandy in a store window in Catskill one day, she became enchanted. Perched on a shelf, the doll wore a long white dress akin to a christening gown, but it was tattered, her face grubby. Still, there was something about her. Her features were perfectly molded into that of a baby girl, and her hands were so sweet and chubby. A doll from another age, the forties, perhaps, when Lena herself had been born, maybe earlier than that. She'd stared into that window, captivated. No Raggedy Ann, no waif or stray, Mandy was something you would have ordered from the Sears Roebuck catalog, a hefty price tag attached. A gift for a very lucky, very privileged child.

And here she was, in a thrift store in rural Idaho. How life had changed for her too.

Hesitating no more, Lena entered the store. Behind the counter, Greta smiled widely.

"Well, hi there, Lena. It's so good to see you."

"You too, Greta."

"How are you today?"

"I'm good. How about yourself?"

"Mighty fine."

"Greta…"

"Yes, honey."

"The doll in the window…"

"Which doll?"

Lena had to suppress a sigh of exasperation. There was only one doll in the window, and Greta surely knew that. "Oh, she's such a beauty, Greta. She's sitting right there, on the middle shelf, next to a candelabra."

Still, Greta was confused. "You're gonna have to show me."

Lena led her onward, still surprised at her confusion and also a little angered by it. These poor dolls! Once loved and then discarded. Sitting there in pride of place in the window and then promptly forgotten about. What was wrong with people nowadays? Where was the loyalty? She might just be a doll, but she'd brought someone so much joy once. Did that count for nothing?

"There she is." Lena pointed. "She must be a new addition, 'cause she wasn't there last week when I passed."

Greta was scratching at her head. "Never seen her before."

Lena, too, furrowed her eyebrows. "But this is your store!"

"It is, honey, but…Bryan must have plain forgot to tell me about her. So much comes through the doors sometimes, it can blur a little."

Bryan was Greta's husband and business partner. Both women nodded at that explanation.

"How much?" Lena asked, keen to progress matters.

"I'll check. Wait a minute."

Greta reached into the window and turned the doll this way and that. *Be careful,* Lena wanted to shout. *Treat her gently!*

"No price tag," Greta said after a moment.

"Who decides?" Lena asked, aware of how impatient she sounded. "You or Bryan?"

"Well…we both do," Greta replied, staring at the doll with a strange expression on her face. Surely not disdain, Lena thought.

"Then how much?" she prompted.

"Erm…I…" Greta adjusted her gaze to look at Lena.

"You sure do have a thing for dolls."

Lena gave a short, sharp nod. "How much?" she repeated. "I want to give her a home." When still Greta hesitated, when still that look of hers persisted, Lena opened her purse to retrieve her wallet. Opening that too, she took out a handful of dollars. "Will fifty bucks do?"

"Fifty?" Greta said, unable to disguise her surprise.

"Yes. Will that be enough?"

"I'm not sure she's worth that much. She's…tired-looking."

"She's worth it to me."

Greta's eyes were back on the doll.

"Greta, please."

"Take it." Greta pushed the doll into Lena's free hand. "Fifty bucks is fine."

The deal was done, and Lena couldn't have been more pleased, never mind that her grocery money for the week had been severely depleted. She'd lived on beans before, and she could do it again. She didn't resent it at all. The doll was worth it.

Placing the doll gently on the passenger seat in her car, she drove her home, wondering all the while what she would call her. Having reached home and introduced her to her many playmates, she examined the doll more closely. Her face wasn't perfect after all. What she'd presumed was grime was actually a crack, running from her forehead and cutting through her eye, all the way down to her cheek and through those cherub lips of hers. No matter, Lena decided. If anything, it made her love the doll more. *I'll look after you,* she promised.

Undressing her, Lena found that the doll was soft-bodied not plastic, and, intending to clean her as best she could before wrapping her in the fluffiest of towels, she noticed something further: a name stamped onto the base of her neck, along with details of the manufacturer: *Mandy. Hayle and Co., New York*.

"Mandy," she repeated. "My, what a long way you've come."

She washed Mandy, and the soiled outfit she wore, in the gentlest of detergents, along with her bonnet and her bootees, air-drying them before redressing her and placing her bonnet just so, the molded blond curl at the front of her head allowed to peek through.

Oh, Mandy… She was sweet Mandy, beautiful Mandy, adorable Mandy, naughty Mandy, Mandy with the worst of tempers.

It had to be Mandy responsible for the chaos that resulted in every single room she was placed in. Other dolls were strewn across the floor, vases broken, and the glass in photo frames smashed to give Lena's children and husband such a strange, distorted look. The banging, the crashing, and the crying…Mandy seemed to be the source of it all. And she was clever too, because Lena never caught her misbehaving, not once, but who else could it be? Before her arrival, it had all been so peaceful. Nothing like that had happened. Nothing!

She'd tried to soothe her, love her harder than ever, shower her with affection, but it was no use. And now Lena was at her wit's end, she was… Where was the shame in admitting it? Scared.

"I'll take you back to the thrift store, Mandy," she'd

threatened so many times. "I'll...I'll throw you away with the trash if you're gonna continue in this way."

She *had* thrown her away once, tossed her in the trash can and slammed the lid down. She'd been so upset, she'd had to leave the house but returned an hour or so later. The trash can was on its side, garbage covering the floor, and Mandy had been on the floor too, staring up at her...

All she needs is love. That's what Lena kept telling herself, but it was with less and less conviction. The doll...there was something about her, just as she'd thought when she'd first seen her, but it was something not right. Greta had realized, though, and Lena had silently berated her for it. But now Mandy was moving things. She was stealing things. For a whole week Lena hadn't been able to find the keys to her car, been kept a prisoner in her own house before they'd turned up in the hallway, of all places, in the middle of the floor.

It was Mandy again.

Everything was Mandy.

Yes, Greta had sensed something wrong with her, so why, oh why, hadn't Lena?

There was another almighty crash, causing Lena to screw her eyes shut. "Stop that banging!"

Turning from the window, she rushed as fast as her years would allow her to the bedroom door. Mandy was downstairs, in the parlor, all on her own, no other dolls with her, not anymore.

You terrorize my dolls, steal my things, steal my time as well; you claw it from me. Sometimes there's no daylight at all. How'd you do it? How? And that banging...that crying!

It was a high-pitched whine that cut right through you,

dragged you with it deep into the depths of misery. A place far blacker than the night.

Why wasn't her love enough for Mandy, when it had been enough for everyone else?

"QUIT THAT CRYING!"

She'd become so incensed that she failed to see how rucked the rug was at the top of the stairs as she hurried onward, intent on one thing and one thing only: stopping Mandy. In all honesty, she didn't think to check the rug. Why would she? It had never wrinkled up like that before.

Her foot caught in it, and her arms flailed on either side but gained no purchase on the handrail.

The stairs in the old farmstead were steep. So often, she'd reprimanded her children for flying down them, warning them to be careful lest they should take a tumble. It was this and only this that crossed her mind as she began her own terrible descent.

How many times I gotta tell ya?

CHAPTER ONE

Shady. The name didn't inspire confidence, or so Shady Groves had a tendency to think. "*To be very sneaky, suspect, or have an all-around backstabbing personality.*" That was Urban Dictionary's definition of the word. But…

Shady was nothing like that—another thing she liked to think. She did her utmost to listen to people, to be kind, and to see both sides of the argument should an argument happen to occur. She was nice. People said it all the time: "I really like Shady. She's just so…nice." Which was refreshing to hear. But there *was* another side to her, and some might say it was darker. Or *fey*, as her mother described it.

"You were fey right from the get-go, honey. You just…you *know* things."

Her mother was right; she did. Shady could sense when a storm was coming, when sadness or anger sat beneath a smile, or when a place wasn't as easy as it was on the eye—when, beneath a polished veneer, it was layered with something other than pleasantness.

This particular talent of hers, if talent it could be called, wasn't something she'd inherited. Both her mother and her father would shake their heads when she'd correctly predict something.

"It's not me she gets it from," her mother would say, an

indulgent smile on her face.

"Well, don't look at me," her father would add. "No witches in my ancestry."

Witches. What a thing to suggest! She was no witch. She was just a normal, bona fide, all-American girl, trying to make her way in life.

But she had a way about her; it couldn't be denied.

"Hey, Shady, can I get a regular Coke and fries over here?"

A voice cut across her musings and Shady looked up to see a guy she recognized from Fairmont High standing across the countertop from her. It was Ray Bartlett, his red hair as crazy as ever, his pale skin freckled.

"Hey, Ray! How you doing?"

"Yeah, great. Didn't know you worked here."

"Didn't know you were still around," she countered.

"Yep, in Idaho Falls, same as you."

"Really? Haven't seen you lately."

"Been there all the same."

There was a brief silence, one filled with slight awkwardness—on Shady's part, anyway, as she was surprised she hadn't seen him. Idaho Falls wasn't that big a place.

"What're you doing, then?" she said after a moment. "Where you working?"

Ray pulled a face. "I'm in between jobs right now. A little bored, to be honest."

Shady leaned forward and lowered her voice. "Guess what? I've got a job, and I'm still bored."

Ray smiled at that, a grin that lit up his face. It was nice to see him, she decided. She hadn't in a couple of years. No, wait…longer than that. Crap, time flew. But she meant what she'd said—apart from it being nice to see him again, she *was* bored, through to the bone.

At just twenty-two, she hadn't quite secured the career path she'd wanted, but, hey, she consoled herself, did anyone at that age? Ray, by his own admission, hadn't. She wanted to go to college, but college was expensive, and she didn't want to put her parents under any more financial pressure than they already were, so she'd insisted on working for two, three, maybe four years, saving some money so she could finance her own education. The dream? Simple, really. To be a teacher, veering toward English.

Her parents' relief at her decision couldn't be disguised. They ran their own stationery supplies company, but in recent years there'd been a downward spiral in the market—competition in that area was growing fiercer by the day, people swayed by price not quality. They'd never told Shady they were worried, but they didn't have to. She could sense that well enough too. And so, her dreams were shelved while she worked at a fast-food outlet in a gas station, and not even a nationwide chain but a local enterprise called Mervin's, that decision yet more evidence of how nice she was.

Sadly for her, though, the job didn't pay much. At the rate she was going, she'd be here a fifth year, let alone a fourth. Lately, however, money had come in from other sources, unexpected money. Money that had been forced on her. Not many people knew she was fey, just a few close friends and those who sensed it too—the fey themselves, she supposed.

She'd been asked three times now by three separate

people to help them. The first two were indeed friends of hers, one who needed help finding a necklace that had gone missing and the other a ring. Each had been so grateful for her success that they'd taken her out for dinner, bought her flowers, and one had even enclosed twenty dollars in an envelope, popping it in the mailbox and refusing to take it back.

"You deserve it," Jodie, the owner of the ring had said. "Seriously, Shady, you have no idea how precious this hunk of metal is to me."

But Shady *did* know. From having handled the ring briefly, she'd felt the love that made it glow, and not just her friend's love but also her mother's before her, only recently deceased, and her father who had originally purchased it for her mother. It was an heirloom, the original token of love, having slipped beneath an edge of carpet to nestle in the darkness.

The satisfaction Shady'd gotten from helping, from seeing the delight on her friends' faces, was immense. Although, to be fair, Ray was looking pretty delighted too as she engaged in the comparatively simple act of handing him his Coke and fries.

"Thanks so much, Shady. I'm starving here."

Shady raised an eyebrow. Starving? Not if his paunch was anything to go by, and not judging by the way he stood there staring at her either, not taking a sip of Coke or a fry from the carton.

"Ray?" she prompted.

"Huh?"

"You said you were hungry."

"Oh…yeah. Sure am." She remembered now: Ray was

always awkward, always shy. He was what you'd call goofy. But he was sweet with it; he was...*nice* too. "I'd better go eat, huh?"

"Before you waste away."

He let out a bellow of laughter, one perhaps a little more generous than the joke required. "Yeah, yeah, I'll...uh...see you soon?"

"When you need sustenance, you know where to find me."

There was more laughter as he backed away. "Sure, yeah," he said again, his back crashing into the door, causing Shady to wince on his behalf. "Oh wow, jeez. Sorry about that," he muttered before abruptly turning. "Real good to see you, Shady."

"And you, Ray," she called. "And you."

Della, her work colleague, sidled over. "He's got a soft spot for you," she drawled.

"We went to school together," Shady explained.

"Huh, really? Been suffering a long time, then," she replied before heading off to wipe at a surface that was clean enough already.

Immediately, Shady felt bad. Did Ray really have a crush on her, and had he suffered because of it? Now that she thought about it, when their hands had touched briefly on handing over his order, she did get a sense of something...something deeper than his grin had suggested. But in what way? She couldn't imagine Ray suffering at all, not considering how brightly his eyes shone. But if he had and she'd contributed to it, even in some small way...well, that wasn't nice at all.

While waiting for another customer to come into this

godforsaken burger outlet on a godforsaken highway a few miles outside of Idaho Falls, she checked her reflection in the window. Her dark hair, tied in a bun, was messy, several strands having come loose. She was tall, willowy—pretty, some might say, with her dark eyes and her olive complexion, neither of which had been inherited from her blond, blue-eyed parents. Yep, pretty to look at and fey. She was also sometimes lost, she might as well admit, standing as she was, waiting for the next order of a chicken-burger combo, for her dreams to begin, for her life to go where she wanted it. An English teacher? Was that really her ultimate goal? Should she aim for something different, less normal? English was something she was good at, though.

So is being fey. She shook her head, her bun becoming messier. *Stick to the rules, Shady, play the game. Life is all about what's tangible, what you can see, what* everyone *can see.*

Still, if she was thirty before she went to college, which deep down she feared, she'd have plenty of time to change her mind, to hand over more combos, more fries, a milkshake or two…

"Miss Groves?"

"Uh-huh?"

Shady had been so involved in hosting her own pity party that, initially, she'd failed to register such a formal address. Who came in here and asked for Miss Groves? Nobody…usually.

Shady peered at the woman in front of her. She was a rhapsody in brown. Petite, little more than five feet, she had brown hair interspersed with grey, a brown coat, and brown glasses that framed brown eyes. Through those glasses, her gaze was intent.

"Hello," said Shady, perhaps more brightly than she felt, for this woman and her solemnity sent shivers along her spine, and not the good kind. "Can I help you?"

The woman nodded, a slow, deliberate gesture. "Yes. I think you can."

"Um…" Shady turned slightly and gestured to the menu that sat on LED-framed boards just above head height. "We do hamburgers, cheeseburgers, chicken nuggets…"

"I'm not here to eat."

Shady had fully realized that.

"Is there somewhere we can talk?" the woman continued.

Shady glanced sideways at Della, who was now attacking the nozzles of the slush machine, looking for something—anything—to while away the hours that stretched on forever in this joint. "We're kinda busy…" she began.

The woman kept looking at her, just looking, doing nothing else, until Shady thought she might explode under such scrutiny. Aware that Della had finally turned to scrutinize them also, Shady leaned forward as she'd done with Ray. "Who are you? Why do you want to talk to me?"

"My name is Annie Hawkins." Her accent was different than Shady's, more clipped. "You've been recommended."

"Recommended? Who by? What for?"

"Gina Dawson."

"Gina?"

Shady knew Gina well enough; she'd been the last of the three people Shady had helped. Gina had suffered from nightmares, which had come on rapidly and been very intense, full of blood and gore and terribly deformed creatures that would chase her screaming through endless darkness.

Poor Gina was exhausted. What had prompted these nightmares? She didn't watch horror films, apparently, and shunned any reading material that wasn't all hearts and flowers. Having heard of Shady via Jodie, she'd gotten in touch and asked her to pay a visit. Immediately, Shady had been drawn to the dressing table in Gina's bedroom. On it lay a handheld mirror, one that Gina had picked up from a junk store, with a faux silver frame and a long handle.

Man, that thing had given Shady the heebie-jeebies! Tentatively, she'd reached out and picked it up. The mirror might be an inanimate object, but it had *seen* stuff, had witnessed so much… Had it belonged to a woman or a man? She'd assumed a man initially, but maybe…just maybe, it was a woman. Depraved. Not what she'd done especially but her thoughts…yes, that was it…*her thoughts* were depraved, what she wanted to do, if she had the courage…what she *dreamed* of doing…

The woman had been stuck in a room. Was she ill? Disabled? Was it a prison of some sort? It couldn't be; she wouldn't be allowed to have such an object in an institution like that, surely? Something that could be used as a weapon. With that in mind, Shady concluded she'd imprisoned herself, her surroundings as cluttered as her mind, and a smell in the air that reeked. This woman…this poor woman. Shady couldn't help but feel some sympathy for her, although others wouldn't. Others *didn't*. They were disgusted by her. And frightened. The latter an emotion that dwelt at the bottom of so many negative emotions, always nagging…always prompting…

The woman would look into the mirror. She'd talk into it, in effect to herself…she'd tell it all about the thoughts that ran riot in her head, would laugh uproariously, expose the demon that ran riot too. Not just one demon, but many. They were all there for the mirror to see.

Much to Gina's amazement, and without asking, Shady had hurried to the kitchen with the mirror and held it high before smashing it into the sink there, the glass immediately shattering. She'd then bagged it all up and taken it away with her, burying it in some nearby wasteland as deep as she could, a bunch of sage thrown in with it. Sage was renowned for purifying and cleansing; Shady had read that in a book. She hoped it'd prove true.

For Gina, the nightmares had stopped instantly. Shady, however, was still curious. She'd asked where Gina had bought the mirror and visited the store, quizzing the owner as discreetly as she could, but it was no use. The mirror was one of many items that had passed through, the owner having no recollection of it at all. Whoever the woman was, she remained a mystery. One of many tortured souls, Shady supposed. The world was full of them. On the plus side, Gina had been so pleased with what Shady had achieved, she'd asked her to come over again and promptly shoved several twenty-dollar bills into Shady's hand while she stood there on the doorstep—before just as promptly turning and shutting the door on her. Glad to be rid of the mirror *and* the woman who'd been called in to help, as if somehow they were both tarred with the same brush. An uncomfortable thought, really.

That had all happened several months ago, but Gina hadn't forgotten Shady, not if Rhapsody-in-Brown was anything to go by.

"Della," Shady said, "can you cover for me?"

Della shrugged, clearly intrigued but doing her utmost to hide it, eventually turning to yet another machine with polishing rag in hand and a resigned sigh on her lips.

Removing her bright red apron, Shady walked around the counter to join Annie. But rather than Shady leading the way to the bar stools at the counter by the window, Annie took determined steps out of the door, turning left to an area that overlooked the highway, a few cars crawling by.

She came to a standstill, Shady waiting for her to speak, but Annie seemed to be composing herself. A moment ticked by and then another. Long moments. Finally, Annie exhaled.

"The reason I've come to talk to you is because of Mandy."

"Mandy?" Shady enquired. "Who's she?"

"She's a doll."

CHAPTER TWO

Annie Hawkins was the curator of a museum in a town christened Mason, about thirty miles south of Idaho Falls, in Bingham County. The next afternoon, after finishing an early shift, Shady drove there in her old but reliable Dodge Stratus to meet her, programming Google Maps on her phone as she wasn't overly familiar with the town, and for good reason. It contained little of anything.

The so-called Main Street was home to a couple of diners and a handful of stores, none of them particularly inviting. In fact, they were downright shabby, highlighting the fact Mason was experiencing hard times like so many small towns in America, fallen by the wayside and forgotten about, on the brink of abandonment.

The museum was at the end of Main Street. Shady parked her car directly outside before standing on the sidewalk to study the building in front of her. Simple in structure, it reminded her of a community hall, several stone steps leading up toward a heavy oak door. The day was a cold one for late October. There was no blue sky above, only grey with a promise of drizzle. Dressed in jeans, a long-sleeved black cotton top and a black jacket, Shady guessed she'd have to start digging out her warmer clothes soon. The minute they hit November, the rain would turn first to sleet and then snow as temperatures continued to plummet, that kind of weather on repeat all the way through to March or April.

Above the main entrance, the words *Mason Town Museum* were carved almost apologetically onto a wooden plaque. As she climbed the steps, holding on to the handrail with its peeling black paint, she noticed opening hours posted on a board behind a glass frame, just to the side of the door. This little museum, this place she suspected anyone rarely visited, was open every day of the year except Easter, Christmas Day, and New Year's Day. Shady raised an eyebrow at that, impressed. Whoever ran this concern—Annie Hawkins herself plus a team of people, surely—they were clearly passionate about it.

She turned the brass doorknob, and as the door began to open, it emitted a creak that sounded almost exactly like a scream. On hearing it, her hand froze. Was it the door or an actual scream? Whatever it was, it continued to rattle in her head as she pushed the door wider still, and the musty smell that always clung to all things old hit her. She couldn't help it; she screwed up her nose and turned her head to the side in an effort to avoid such a full-on blast, imagining the smell making its way inside her with lightning ferocity to take root there.

"Ah, there you are! Come in, come in."

Annie came rushing forward. Bereft of her coat, she had on a polo-neck sweater and a knee-length skirt, both in brown, a color she appeared very fond of. She looked harried, nervous, her hand outstretched not to shake Shady's hand in greeting but to relieve her of her jacket. As soon as Shady handed it over, the older woman rushed elsewhere—to a checkroom, presumably—giving Shady a chance to study the museum's interior.

Dark. That was her first impression. Although there were several windows, it was as if the light preferred to remain outside. Because of that, electric light was made much use of, but not narrow strip lights, which may have been more effective. Instead, in the center of the long, almost barn-like room—which was stuffed to overflowing with all manner of artifacts—a heavy wrought-iron chandelier dominated the ceiling, with supporting sconces on the walls. Weak, that's what the light was, which dismayed Shady. In here, she figured, it needed to be a whole lot stronger.

Shady didn't like museums, didn't tend to visit them a lot. The reason? They gave her a headache. Though no words were usually coherent, what seemed like a thousand voices would erupt in her head, each and every one fighting for her attention. The Mason Town Museum was proving itself no exception, as kickstarted by that scream earlier, the memory of which still made her wince. Old objects were like sponges; they soaked up energy—memories, she supposed—and although that energy might be residual, it could still kick ass.

Instead of just glancing at the artifacts, she homed in on various items. Before her were several low glass-topped displays as well as objects that hung on walls, ranging from rusted farm machinery to old wooden sleds and traditional snowshoes. There was a nod, but only that, toward the Native American history of the area, and then it was back to the white man and how he'd evolved since landing here and making his claim. There was, as far as she could see, no doll of any type, no Mandy.

Annie returned from the checkroom, still hurrying, still determined.

"Would you like a coffee first?" she asked. "Or shall we just get on?"

Shady knew which answer she'd prefer. "Let's get on."

"Good. Good. Yes, there's no time to waste. Not really. Follow me."

As Annie traversed the length of the room, Shady followed, keeping her eyes solely on the woman's back. The feelings she picked up on, the energies, weren't all cause for concern. Yes, there was a sense of forlornness sometimes, angst and weariness, but in among them were good feelings, a child's joy, for example—linked to the sled, perhaps?— and a man's admiration for a woman, the source of which could be a beautifully beaded turn-of-the-century dress modelled by a black-wigged polystyrene mannequin. Shady could also detect a mother's love for her child, courtesy of an old crib that stood in a far corner, gently rocking despite the still air.

Almost at the back of the room, Shady asked where they were going.

"Down here," Annie replied without turning.

Almost hidden—certainly Shady hadn't noticed it until she was virtually towering over it—was a metal staircase that spiraled out of sight.

"We're going to the basement?" she questioned further, any unease she may have felt upon entering the building increasing.

Annie had already begun the descent, the treads clanging as she went. "Well, yes, I don't want her up here—" she paused for a second "—contaminating things."

Contaminating? "Annie…is it okay if I call you that?" Annie nodded. "Okay, Annie, if it's causing you so much upset, if it's contaminating things, why do you have her here at all?"

Having entered the stairwell too, Shady came to a halt as Annie swung around to face her.

"You mean I should pass her on, make her someone else's problem? Someone—" again, she paused "—less equipped to deal with it? Someone vulnerable?" She shook her head. "No, that's something I can't do. It's been bequeathed to me by another museum, one in Spokane—"

"Spokane, Washington? Is that where she's from?"

"Who knows where she's from or where she's been." Annie leaned forward, a forefinger pushing her glasses back onto the bridge of her nose. "And more to the point, who she's affected along the way. The only thing I'm sure about is that she *has* affected folk."

The conspiratorial way in which they were talking caused Shady to also lower her voice. "Did they feel the same way about her at this museum in Spokane?"

"Ha!" To Shady's surprise, Annie let out a gust of laughter. "Good grief, yes! They were terrified of her. She was left to them by the daughter of a local woman on account she's very old, an antique, a piece of history. They were quite pleased with her at first, but soon things started to happen…bad things. Staff took sick. One by one, they succumbed. There was always someone ill, and I mean genuinely ill, not playing hooky. Also, things went missing, not just items on display but personal belongings too, only to turn up in the strangest of places. One staff member found a lump in her breast, and the next thing you know, she's been diagnosed with cancer. A young girl, volunteered out of the goodness of her heart, and way too young to be burdened with a disease like that. Whatever room they placed the doll in, they'd go in there the next day and something would be on the ground, like it'd been flung down in temper or even jealousy. And then there was the crying…everybody heard it at some time or other. I haven't heard it as yet, but I don't rule it out, given time. And it's not a living person responsible…it's Mandy."

While Annie had been relating all this, Shady's eyes had grown wider. Again, she had to pose the question: "If there really is a problem with the doll, if you don't want it to affect anybody else, then why not destroy it? You could…burn it, maybe?"

"Because that doesn't rid us of the problem, not really. It's a far more complex matter than that. It has to be dealt with in the proper way."

"The proper way?"

"It has to be understood."

"Understood?"

"Yes. And only then is it possible to decide on the best course of action."

"So, if not destroy it—"

"We can try and cleanse it, for example."

Shady gasped. "Cleanse as in exorcise?"

"Perhaps, ultimately. You see, even if thrown in the fire, whatever lives inside it will simply move on to the next object and take up habitation there. And so it'll continue, the cycle, I mean. It will affect people, it will harm them in whatever way it can, it will *torment* them, and we mustn't let that happen. We must do everything in our power to *stop* that from happening."

Shady forced herself to nod her head, torn between believing this strange little woman—British, she now realized—and turning tail and getting the heck out of Mason Town Museum.

"What you're saying is," she ventured at last, "the doll's possessed?" As soon as she said it, she could hear something, not a scream this time but more of a low-pitched whine, a cry.

"Miss Groves—" Annie started.

"Oh, call me Shady, please."

"Shady, that's *exactly* what I'm saying."

CHAPTER THREE

Psychometry. Often, it was described as a psychic ability, one in which a person could sense or "read" the history of an object just by touching it. These impressions could be perceived in a number of ways: images, sounds, smells, tastes, and even emotions. Of them all, emotion might be considered the most important and informative, and by far the most powerful, capable of taking your breath away. Remembering the previous owner of Gina's mirror, Shady could only agree with that description of such a skill when she'd read it; experiencing the depth of someone else's emotion was an insight into them like nothing else.

Most people accepted that evil existed, that alongside good there was bad, but most of the time a girl like Shady would amble along minding her own business, determinedly thinking nice thoughts, pretending the world was a great place to be and ignoring, as far as possible, all that was wrong with it. But then she'd get an insight, psychic or not, and damn, it was hard to shake off.

As she entered the basement, all the feelings she'd experienced at Gina's—the presence of something, the fascination too, perhaps—reached a new high. This room had no windows at all, and the electric light struggled, more so than upstairs. Mandy was a doll, only that…or she was something else entirely. The energy that emanated from her might not be residual, a hangover from its previous owner, which could often take time to dissipate. It could be that she was possessed, actually *possessed* by an entity, something harmful. *If* Annie was to be believed.

There were more artifacts in the basement, what looked to be ornaments, some ceramic, some wood, a jewelry box and jewelry too, which were curiously set apart from one another. Whatever else there was, was covered in dust sheets.

As she ventured deeper into the room, Shady stared resolutely ahead, focusing on Annie, *just* on her. She had to admit the woman intrigued her as much as Mandy. Was she a psychic? Or perhaps she was a Christian, an enthusiastic one. Was this something of a crusade for her, a battle, dealing with objects such as Mandy, intent on banishing what evil she believed lurked within them? Did the folks at the Spokane museum know that well enough? Did Annie, a bit like Shady herself seemed to be getting, have a reputation? More to the point, did Shady want that kind of reputation? Her parents didn't know about what had happened with Gina's mirror, but if they found out... They were open-minded people but *that* open-minded? They might call her fey, considering that side to her personality cute if a little mystifying, but getting involved with anything heavier than finding people's lost items might upset them. Scrub that. It *would* upset them—greatly.

The whine that she'd heard while on the stairs had long since died out. Now, as they neared the far end of the basement, there was only silence, but not an easy silence. It was one that weighed heavy, that felt loaded, that—Shady had to think hard—*waited. But for what?*

God, it was cold. Did this building have no heating whatsoever? And yet there were radiators, Shady noticed. Big old hulking things standing against the walls. Dormant. Useless. But then again, this was an old building; it had to be around one hundred years old, possibly more. And it was big. Whatever heating system had been installed, it had its work cut out.

Oh, what was she doing here? She could have done a million other things today: spent the afternoon with friends, caught up with some trash TV, read a book. Why had she so readily responded to this woman's request to come thirty miles out of her way to see a haunted doll?

Shady, you're an idiot!

The temptation to call time on this—to turn around and do as she'd wanted to do a few minutes earlier and flee—returned, stronger than before. It was cold down here, but it was also stifling, a vast space but at the same time claustrophobic. The thought of the great outdoors, where the air was fresh, was like balm on a wound. If she ever emerged from these subterranean depths, she'd make sure to breathe in great lungfuls of it, let the breeze blow away whatever it was that seemed to cling to her skin like cigarette smoke from a dive bar.

If *I emerge?*

Shady had made a few mistakes in her life, but this was up there with the worst of them. There was no way she could go through with this, no way! She had to get out, put some distance between her and that heavy, heavy silence. And she didn't have to explain herself either. This was a favor she was doing. She didn't *owe* Annie anything, or those that had been supposedly affected by a doll. It was probably all imagination anyway. People tricking themselves into believing all sorts of nonsense. She was going to do it, turn on her heel and escape…

"She's just over here, towards the back of the room."

Annie's voice sliced through her panic. Fey…nice… Shady was also usually composed in manner, laidback, taking everything in her stride. She couldn't remember a time she'd ever given in to hysterics, but right there, just before Annie had spoken, she'd been about to.

"Dear? Are you all right?"

"What? I…"

"You look pale."

"Oh…no, it's fine. *I'm* fine. Honest."

Annie continued to eye her before turning again. As her hands reached out toward yet another object covered in a dust sheet, Shady's heart began to pick up speed once more, bang-bang-banging against the walls of her chest. Pale? She felt deathly, the blood having drained entirely from her face and her hands, which were now held rigid by her side, clenched into tight fists. What would Mandy be like? What could Shady expect to see when her face was revealed? What emotion would dominate? Fear? Horror? Disgust?

"This is Mandy."

Shady hadn't realized she'd screwed her eyes shut until she had to open them to look.

There she was—Mandy—right in front of her, beady black eyes staring.

A doll, a baby doll, lying on the table. She wore a christening gown, white socks, and lace-trimmed booties. On her head was a bonnet—hand-knitted, it looked like—

with a white lace trim. Her hair, at least what was visible, was molded onto her head, a curl that sat upon her forehead. Her face…it was exquisite, so lifelike with its button nose and cherub lips, beautiful even, or she would've been if it weren't for a long jagged crack that ran down the left side of her face. What had happened to her? Who'd done that and why?

"As we discussed at the gas station, your gift is to do with handling objects. Psychometry."

Shady was still having trouble tearing her gaze from the doll. "Yes, yes, it can work that way."

"So you need to handle her?"

The thought of doing so was far from pleasant. But that's why she'd come here, why she'd remained: so that she could help—which was, of course, the nice thing to do. She hadn't been able to solve the mystery of Gina's mirror, but with Mandy she might get lucky.

"Dear"—Annie had reached out and placed a hand on her arm—"I know this may be hard, but we have to remember, it's for the greater good."

She had to ask. "Are you a Christian?"

Annie laughed again, and this time it softened her, made her seem younger than she was.

"As I said," she answered, "I believe in the greater good. I work towards it, all the time."

"*All* the time?"

"Yes. I devote my life to it."

Nuts. Completely nuts. And yet Shady couldn't doubt her, another reason she'd remained that she was only now aware of. She *believed* her. It was possible she even admired her.

Able now to avert her gaze, she looked around at other objects that remained covered. She remembered what lay above her on the first floor and the assortment of emotions she'd experienced passing by them. "Your life's work," she repeated, trying to do what was so essential here and understand. "*This* is your life's work. It's a private museum, your own collection."

Annie nodded. "Correct. I keep things safe, things that others don't want, that are unloved, that sometimes hold anger precisely because they are unloved. I provide a home for them."

"Not everything here holds anger."

Annie seemed pleased by that remark. "There are indeed objects here that hold great joy. It's about balance, you see. There has to be balance. Always. Do you get what I'm trying to say?"

Shady was surprised to find that she did. And yet at the same time it was a revelation. Annie Hawkins herself was a revelation. Shady had initially used the word *solemn* to describe her, but there seemed to be balance in her too.

"Why open this to the public?" Shady asked, her curiosity mounting. "Doesn't it put them in danger?"

"By exposing them to certain pieces?"

"Yes."

"You run that risk; I don't deny it. There are some very sensitive people in the world, people who don't know how sensitive they are, who refuse to acknowledge it. But the risk becomes far greater if you leave something in the dark to fester, because then it has an opportunity to grow, to become even more powerful. If you drag it out of the darkness, if you *expose* it, in all senses of the word—" Annie raised a hand, placed it on her chest, and took a breath "—well, then the power that's in it begins to break down. We all need the light, objects included, otherwise we rot."

"Mandy's not in the light, though. And there are things that remain covered."

"The light stays on all the time, even in the basement. Plus, they're only here until I can—"

"Understand them?"

"Yes."

Shady's eyes went back to Mandy.

"You're a little frightened of her, aren't you?" asked Annie.

Shady was, but was that just her expectation? It was hard to tell.

Annie removed her hand from Shady's arm and reached out for the doll. "Do you feel confident enough to handle her?" she asked, no reproach in her voice in case she didn't.

"Sure," said Shady, taking a deep breath as Annie lifted the doll and held it toward her, her own hands reaching out and closing around the doll's soft torso.

"I'm with you," Annie assured her. "I'm by your side. All I want is for you to help me gain some information that might prove useful. Meanwhile, I've got us both surrounded in white light."

Shady glanced at her. "White light?"

"Why, yes." Her surprise seemed to surprise Annie in turn. "Surely you do that as a means of protection? You visualize white light?"

"What…no…I…"

She couldn't say another word, couldn't even see Annie anymore or the room around her with its relentless low light and dust sheets covering other strange and unknown mysteries. All she could see was Mandy's cracked face and eyes that had never left her, not since Annie had taken off the dust sheet, boring into the heart of her. Heart? Shady had one, but this thing didn't. She was…

Excitement! Shady could sense excitement! It permeated the air. A box was being unwrapped and tissue paper and ribbons discarded to reveal something wanted, something craved. A child's delight was what she felt, at receiving such a treasure. Laughter rang in her ears, not only the child's; there was adult laughter too, the child's parents, presumably. Such joy! Was Mandy a birthday present, or for Christmas? Whatever the occasion, she was a special gift that now had a loving home and would be adored, the center of attention as she was destined to be. For this was no ordinary doll, not a poppet you could buy in just any store. She was the stuff of dreams, made to inspire devotion. She was unique.

Shady's body sagged in relief. This was lovely to see, not a horror. The doll did indeed have pride of place in the little girl's bedroom. Shady could see a crib beside the girl's own small bed and a hand reaching out to rock it gently, the soft words of a lullaby being sung. Shady's eyes drifted closed to the melody, and then she squeezed them shut tighter, tried to see beyond the doll and into the room itself. Barely managing it—the craved-for item craved something too: her attention—she nonetheless got the impression of a room that any little girl would love to call her own, with its lofty ceiling, heavy drapes, and toys, so many of them, neatly stowed. A privileged little girl, she had all she wanted, all she…demanded. And the gifts kept coming; the dolls kept coming…other dolls, just as fancy, fancier still…

Shady inhaled.

"I'm with you," a voice whispered, not anything to do with the doll. It was Annie, clearly sensing a change in Shady. "You're surrounded in light."

A cracked face appeared before her. Not Mandy's but another doll's, and then another…and another…and another. All of them damaged in some way. Malicious destruction, but by whom? The child? Yet why would the child do that, wondered Shady, remembering the sweet joy of the unwrapping. Someone was caught up in anger, though, in a web of jealousy and spite.

Your light is useless.

Shady tensed. Who'd said that? Not Annie, surely?

You're useless too.

The voice was low and rasping, inside her skull.

You can't undo what's been done.

"What's been done? Tell me."

The damage.

"What damage?"

You'll get sucked in.

"To what?"

The maelstrom.

"I don't understand."

Sucked in…so easily…

The words repeated as the visions faded, finally replaced by crying. Yes, there was definitely crying…a sound to break your heart. *But not yours, Mandy, because you don't have one.*

So, whose crying was it? The little girl's, someone else's, whose?

You cannot undo what's been done…the damage… You're useless.

Forcing her eyes to open, Shady looked at the doll, then threw it from her before finally giving in and turning to flee. All while she was running, her feet pounding the concrete basement floor and then up the spiral staircase and careering down the length of that long, long hall, words repeated in her head—not that rasping voice now but her own: *You're useless…useless.*

Something else plagued her too, something she refused to believe even though she'd just seen it with her own eyes…the smirk that had played about the doll's sweet cherub lips.

CHAPTER FOUR

"Shady? Hey, are you okay—"

Ignoring her mother, Shady flew down the hallway of their three-bedroom home—located on the numbered streets around Kate Curley Park—yanked the door open to her bedroom, and raced over to the bed. Her chest was pounding, hadn't really stopped since she'd been in the basement of Mason Town Museum. It felt like it was going to explode, burst right out of her chest. How she'd managed to drive home, she didn't know; she couldn't even recall the journey, clearly on autopilot. Thank God the roads weren't busy between towns at this time of day! Her breath heaving, she had to find some way to calm down, especially if her mother decided to knock on her bedroom door and ask what the matter was. What could she say in response?

"Well, Mom, I'm like this because of a doll, a possessed doll, you know, like in that movie *Annabelle*? A doll that's alive somehow, that's controlled by something, an entity, maybe, that stares at you through her eyes and makes you feel all kinds of weird shit. Oh, and yeah, I nearly forgot, she, the doll—she's got a name by the way, Mandy—can move her lips and grin at you."

She'd think her daughter had finally flipped—gone from fey to freaked in twenty-four hours.

Her chest gradually calming—although it took some effort on her part, having to deliberately breathe low and slow—she tried to rationalize all that had happened, to make sense of the panic that had risen up in her at the museum. She'd given in to it, perhaps because of what Annie hadn't quite said but hinted at: the doll was somehow demonic.

Demonic. Even the word was loaded. Gina's mirror was the only other incident she'd experienced that came remotely close. With the mirror it *had* been like dealing with demons but the kind that existed within everyone, the human kind, born of a tortured mind. In contrast, the voice that had rasped at her, that seemed to emanate from Mandy, sounded utterly *in*human. She could recall every nuance, every syllable, the hatred and the mockery that had characterized it, its supreme confidence that up against it she was no threat at all.

Perched on the edge of her bed, still feeling cold, her arms wrapped around herself, she did indeed feel useless.

She'd been frightened; she'd run. What must Annie think of her?

As she wiped at a tear, she sighed. *What's this, you're crying now? Shady, come on!*

When Annie handed the doll over, she'd mentioned white light. When Shady had asked her what she meant, moments before the doll and its history had forced her mind to blot out all else, she'd noticed surprise on Annie's face. More than that, actually—it was shock at her ignorance.

Shady did the math. Light was good. Light attracted people. It made them feel safe because, in it, they could see things; predators couldn't hide. Darkness was the opposite, so things *could* hide easily, strike out when you least expected them to and hurt you.

Had the doll hurt her? Quickly she examined her hands, her arms, then her eyes proceeded to travel the entire length of her body. There was not a mark on her, no sign of damage at all. And, in truth, nor had she expected there to be…not yet, at any rate. Her mind, however, was reeling.

That voice… She needed to blot it out…

"Shady?"

Her body jolted at hearing her name called.

"Shady, what is it? What's wrong?"

As she'd suspected, her mother, Ellen, couldn't keep away.

"Mom, it's noth—"

Ellen came rushing into the room. "Do you have a fever?"

"A fever? No."

Ellen's hand shot out nonetheless to press itself against Shady's forehead and cheeks. Confusion replaced concern. "You seem cool enough."

"I told you, I don't have a fever."

"Then what is it?"

"I…it's…a headache. Just a headache. I feel a little sick, actually."

Ellen sat beside Shady on the bed, her blond curls framing her face, her blue eyes similar in shade to cornflowers. Maybe it was because Shady felt so raw already that the contrast in her and her mother's coloring proved particularly poignant. "Mom, I'm not adopted, am I?"

Her mother burst out laughing. "What the hell, Shady?"

"Because look at us," she continued, "the difference."

"Oh, you gotta be kidding me. Not that again."

It was true that Shady had brought the subject up before, but always in a jokey manner.

"Is that really what's on your mind?" Ellen pressed. "Why you're so upset?"

Shady faltered. "No…I…oh, I don't know."

Ellen placed an arm around Shady's shoulders and drew her close. "You feel so cold."

"Do I?"

"Have you been out all this time without your coat?"

"I had my jacket. Look…I'm fine."

Reaching a hand out to tilt her daughter's chin toward her, Ellen looked firmly into her eyes. "Shady, you're my and Bill's child. We've told you before that your coloring is…is a throwback. That happens, you know? All the time. You only have to look at Jessie Myer's boy to realize that. He's as fair as she is dark. Besides…" She paused briefly. "You've seen your birth certificate. What do you think I am, a forger? I'm your mother, Shady, through and through."

Of course she was. Why did Shady even have to ask? It was like something inside her head demanded answers, needed to know…*everything*, because when something so senseless had happened, making sense of things helped. "Why'd you call me Shady?"

An indulgent smile spread across her mother's face. "You know why."

"Tell me again."

"Because you were born as the sun was setting, a time I love, the low light."

There was poetry in Ellen's words, and usually it comforted Shady, but today they had the opposite effect, making her feel bleaker still. Born in the low light—a time of shadows, in other words. Was she kidding herself in thinking there was romance in that?

"Oh, Mom," Shady said, leaning her head on her mother's shoulder, trying hard but failing to stop the tears from flowing.

"Shady, honey…oh, sweetheart," Ellen murmured.

There were no more questions from either of them; Ellen simply held Shady and let her cry it out. Afterward, Shady could always blame hormones for her wayward emotions. Yes, that was it, that's the excuse she'd come up with. Because she mustn't blame her mother or pay heed to more words filling her mind, looming larger and larger each time, *rasping* words, one in particular:

Liar!

* * *

Shady slept peacefully…at first. But then the dreams started, causing her to struggle repeatedly to the surface only to be dragged back down again, over and over, into the depths.

Deep but not dark…she could see only too well.

More's the pity.

There were so many images, some of them jumbled, some clear. There was her, as a child, playing in her room, her dark hair so straight and glossy, and swinging forward as she held two dolls in her hands. Barbie dolls, both of them, also with sleek straight hair, although a different shade to hers. She—the child—seemed fixated on the dolls, their hair in particular; she couldn't take her eyes from it. Blond hair, whereas hers was dark. Blond, dark, blond, dark...

Her hands, small though they were, had so much strength in them. Encircling the dolls' tiny waists, she began to squeeze. The plastic resisted at first, able to withstand the pressure, but soon that changed. It began to cave, to crumple, to melt like wax, covering her hands before remolding, turning her into something plastic too. *You shouldn't be different!* That's what the child kept telling the dolls. *You shouldn't be different! And nor should I.*

Finally, the child that was Shady examined her efforts. The dolls were mangled beyond recognition, eyes staring blankly upward, seeming to almost pop from their heads, to scream their shock. The child smiled and then started to snip, not with scissors but her fingers, as sharp with determination as she was. Snip! Snip! Snip! All that perfect silky hair. Watching as it fell to the floor, her smile widened at the heads that were now even more butchered.

"YOU SHOULDN'T BE DIFFERENT!"

The words in her head were now screamed at her. As she stared wildly around to see who was responsible, she let the dolls tumble to the ground. The bedroom had all but disappeared, and in its place was white mist, in which she was suspended. She stumbled to her feet, not so much a child now, an adult. Who the hell had said that? What did they mean by it?

"Hello? Hello? Is someone there?"

The light was as disconcerting as if it were pitch black, for in it she was equally blind, her hands held out in front of her as she tentatively placed one foot in front of the other.

Was that a sound she could hear in the distance? Low and distressed.

"Who's there?" she continued to demand.

No more distress; there were voices, like those of children in a school playground. She stopped, cocked her head to one side and listened. Shapes in the distance began to materialize.

Shady started walking again, more determinedly this time. It was cold in the mist, as cold as it had been in that strange little museum, home to all those objects from the past, home to…

No, don't say that doll's name, not here.

Shady obeyed her own instruction and focused only on the shapes. They became more distinct as she drew closer, strange shapes, soft and rounded as children should be, but their movements were far from fluid, jerky instead. Their voices had changed too, becoming higher pitched, more piercing. What were they doing, having a tea party?

"Hello," she called out. "I'm Shady. I…I don't know what I'm doing here. Can you help me?"

A sudden hush descended, and the jagged movements stilled.

She was almost upon them. Surely, they'd turn soon and answer her.

"Did one of you say something to me earlier, something about being different?"

A short giggle was quickly hushed by another. The one insisting the other be quiet produced a harsh sound, a sound that…rasped.

Shady stopped. This mist that surrounded her was so bright! There was no comfort in it, however, no warmth of any kind. And it hid other shapes too, lots of them, hovering all around her. She squinted, struggled to see. This was all wrong, wasn't it? You were supposed to see in the light. You were supposed to feel safe, not exposed and vulnerable and growing ever more frightened. "Turn around! Tell me where I am, what this place is!"

Silence. As heavy as it had been in the museum.

"TELL ME!"

The children—the shapes—began to turn by degrees. At the same time what else was in the mist, those that surrounded her, dragged themselves nearer too…

Shady looked from one side to the other, not only unsure of where she was, but she didn't know who she was either, what age, even. Those in front began to rise, so stiff and awkward.

Her fear as palpable as it had been in the museum, she tried to take a step backward but couldn't, like she was knee-deep in mud, her legs immoveable.

"Stay away from me," she cried, but her plea fell on deaf ears, as she knew it would. She shut her eyes, glad she was still able to do that, at least. "I don't want to see you. *I won't.*"

Her words had caused offense. There was crying now, a cacophony.

"Go away! Stop it! Leave me alone."

Something was in front of her. The strange jagged creatures? Dolls, that's what they were. The ones she'd butchered?

Even if it is, so what? They're just dolls!

She opened her eyes to stare defiantly.

It wasn't the dolls from earlier, but it was *a* doll, certainly.

An antique doll, wearing a white dress, cap, and bootees, a baby doll with a cracked face and a plastered cowlick on her forehead.

No smile curled her lips, but there was something else upon her face.

Recognition.

You're different.

The words exploded in Shady's head as she continued to stare.

Different, just like me.

CHAPTER FIVE

"Shady, you're going to be late for your shift."

Beneath the covers, Shady groaned. "I still feel sick, Mom. I need to sleep."

"Oh, sweetheart, really? I can call the pharma—"

"No, I just...I had a rough night's sleep, that's all."

There was a reluctant pause. "What about work?"

"I've already called and explained."

"Well...okay. Get some rest, and I'll come back in an hour."

True to her word, Ellen returned at ten a.m.—on the dot.

"Mom!" Shady groaned.

As she always did, Ellen checked her forehead to see if she was hot. When she realized—again—that it wasn't, she declared, "You don't need to sleep, Shady, you need a day out."

"What? Who with?"

"Me!"

"You? Aren't you working today either?"

"Not now I'm not. Your father can manage, I'm sure. So come on, rise and shine, young lady. Let's go shopping. That'll set you right."

Before Shady could argue further, Ellen turned on her heel and left the room.

"Damn!" Shady muttered. She really could do with another hour at least. When she'd told her mother she hadn't slept well the previous night, she'd meant it. After that terrible nightmare, she'd lain awake for what felt like hours, staring into the darkness, scared to close her eyes again, scared of the light, ironically, and being pulled back into it. Eventually, however, she'd drifted again, just as the night had begun to recede, and thankfully there'd been no more dreaming.

"Crap," she continued to moan as she pushed herself upward and swung her legs over the side of the bed. All that stuff with Mandy had really gotten to her. As for Annie, she should call her, try to explain. After running out on her like that, it'd be the decent thing to do. Later, perhaps.

Now, she had to get ready for a day out with her mother, spend some quality time together, which they hadn't done for a while, actually. Usually Ellen didn't take time off work, not even on weekends; there was always something to be done, accounting or the like, so Shady could hardly say no. She didn't *want* to say no either. It'd do her good, take her mind off the subject of dolls.

She shook her head. Okay, inanimate objects could soak up residual energy, she knew that, but it was exactly that…residual. Mandy was an old doll; Shady estimated about eighty to ninety years old, maybe more. She had history, sure, her glass eyes had seen things, they'd registered. But possessed? Shady refused to buy into it, although she had to admit, what the doll had registered had been extreme. Certainly, the emotions she'd sensed when holding her toward the end, the unrelenting violence of them, suggested that.

In contrast, she remembered what she'd sensed when she'd *first* held the doll, the little girl, the child who'd received Mandy as a gift, and how happy she'd been. Shady even forced herself to smile at the memory as she headed toward the bathroom to grab a quick shower.

Having swapped the warmth of carpet for cool ceramic tiles, Shady stared at herself in the mirror above the sink. *When did Mandy's situation change? Why?* She continued to stare. Instead of olive, her skin was sallow in color; there were dark circles of tiredness beneath her eyes and an overall expression she'd never seen before. Weariness, fear, or a mix of both.

"I'm not afraid!"

Her raised voice took her by surprise. She hadn't meant to shout, to even say the words out loud; it was like they'd been pushed out of her mouth, something inside her taking control.

"I'm not afraid," she repeated, this time more gently, running the tap and splashing her face with water, several times over, relishing how cold it was.

At last, she turned her back on the sink and, standing beneath the showerhead, she repeated those words continually under her breath and in her mind, adding to them, embellishing them.

"I'm not afraid, and I'm not different."

* * *

This was better; this was fun, just getting out and doing normal things. By noon she and Ellen must have tried on dozens of clothes in over a dozen stores.

Finally, Ellen looked at Shady with undisguised dismay. "Honey, you'd look so good in a dress. Now, hold on, hear me out. I'm not talking anything floral or too girly-girly, I know you're not like that, but a little black dress, maybe, for parties and special occasions. Come on, give it a go."

If her mother had said that once, she'd said it a million times. Ellen was desperate to see her daughter out of what she called her "uniform"—jeans and a tee shirt. "Mom, I like what I wear. It's what I feel comfortable in," she'd protest, but Ellen, in her skirt, blouse, and heels, refused to listen.

As her mother stood there shaking her head and sighing, Shady took the opportunity to study her, how pretty she was, trying to persuade her daughter to be as pretty. Even with heels, she was shorter than Shady; she was delicate, with wrists you could easily wrap your fingers around. Feminine, whereas Shady often felt more androgynous. Different. There it was again, the word from her nightmare, that she'd thought about even *before* the nightmare had happened.

Quit all this analyzing and try on a dress!

She would, if just to appease her mom. Ellen looked delighted and stunned when she agreed.

Half an hour later, Shady was done.

She'd tried on eight dresses, mainly black, the saleswoman prompted by her mother to bring more and more into the small cubicle she occupied, Shady squeezing into them, huffing and puffing as she grappled with zippers, breaking out in a sweat, becoming flustered. None of them—absolutely none—suited her. She felt like a fraud in them. Untrue to herself. An imposter.

As she paraded herself in front of her mother and the sales assistant, who was intent on giving her opinion too, their gushing compliments fell on deaf ears.

"Shady, you look stunning in that. It makes you look so…sophisticated. All you need now is an updo. Sweep that hair of yours into a neat chignon and you'll be the belle of the ball."

"She's right, miss," the assistant concurred. "Guys are gonna fall at your feet."

A sentiment expressed for *every* dress, so desperate were they.

Finally, Shady shook her head. "Mom, I'm sorry. I just need a new pair of jeans, that's all."

"But I'm buying, Shady—"

"No, really, I… Mom, try and understand."

"But what about parties and special occasions?"

"I can wear jeans to parties." As for special occasions, what special occasions? They didn't tend to happen too often in a place like Idaho Falls.

Her mother sighed deeply, stifled any further frustration or disappointment she might feel, and again resigned herself to the matter.

They continued shopping before finally heading to the mall's food court to fortify themselves with lunch, Shady opting for chicken noodles and Ellen a layered salad with halloumi cheese. Beyond a wall of glass doors, Shady could see the sun blasting down from a brilliant blue sky. Inside it was stuffy, and the light had that stark quality about it. In spite of feeling warm, she shivered. There were so many people here: couples, families, kids…

Shady stopped glancing around and focused on her food instead, but from being ravenously hungry—shopping, after all, was hard work—her appetite had suddenly blunted itself. In fact, as she messed with the takeout container in front of her, she began to see it with new eyes; it looked like a box of worms, a congealed mess, the vegetables in it barely recognizable.

"You not hungry anymore, sweetheart?"

"Actually, no," Shady confessed, placing her chopsticks down and leaning back in her chair.

With so many people came a whole lot of noise, including chitter-chatter, laughter, and even crying and screaming on occasion—such a shrill sound—children of various ages responsible.

Unable to help it, Shady lifted her hands to cover her ears.

If she thought Ellen might question her more about how she was feeling, she was wrong. Ellen had spotted a friend in the crowd, the friend had spotted her, and, as Ellen shot to her feet, they began waving enthusiastically to each other before rushing to cross the divide that separated them. Shady knew who it was—an old college friend of Ellen's who used to live close by but had since moved away. Clearly, she was back in town.

As the two friends exchanged delighted conversation, Shady also got to her feet. Glancing longingly in the direction of the glass doors again, she made her way over to the women.

"Shady," her mother said before she could get a word in,

"you remember Caroline, don't you? She's here for the weekend, visiting her folks, although"—here Ellen pulled a face as she whispered conspiratorially—"she's also here, in the mall, trying to get *away* from them."

The two women laughed uproariously at this, Shady trying not to wince as that sound also rattled in her head. Why was this happening? Why had she become so...sensitive?

"...would love it if we could spend the afternoon together..." It was Caroline talking, causing Shady to look at her, *really* look. Jeez, Ellen wasn't kidding when she said her friend wanted some time off from a family that...*oppressed* her, was that the right word? It was. Definitely. She had an overbearing mother and a strict father, time refusing to temper them; they were, in fact, the reason she'd moved in the first place. But duty called, and some felt compelled to obey. Caroline was a good woman, one of those that did what she had to do. She visited them, not often, just enough to appease her conscience, but it wasn't easy, oh no. The visits made her feel like a child again, as powerless, at her parents' mercy—made her scream, albeit silently, with utter frustration.

"Is that okay, Shady? If Caroline joins us?"

"Erm...well..."

Caroline held her hands up. "Oh, look, it's no problem if not. I know how precious mother-daughter time is. I'd hate to impose."

How precious mother-daughter time was? *No,* thought Shady, *you* hate *mother-daughter time.*

Again, Shady attempted to speak. "Look, it's fine, it's—"

"You're right, Caroline, it's just me and Shady today,

though we must get together next time you visit. Let me know in advance and I'll come rescue you."

They laughed, but their disappointment at their meeting being curtailed was all too evident. On seeing this, Shady seized her chance.

"Mom, I'm feeling kinda wrung-out again. I think I need to go home. It's been a great day, really it has, but right now I could use my bed. You two go right ahead."

"Oh, Shady, darling, I'll come with you—"

"Mom, I'm fine on my own. Just…have a good time."

"But how will you get home?"

"I'll ride the bus. I'll manage."

Ellen looked torn. "But—"

Shady held up a plastic bag as she started to back away. "I've got my jeans, there's nothing else I want." She attempted a smile. "No dresses, anyway."

Ellen smiled too. As for Caroline, she had relief written all over her face—she had an excuse to stay out longer, one her aging parents wouldn't be too happy with, but hey, she could deal with that later. With the decision made, the two women also started to retreat, already talking about a store they wanted to visit and what they intended to try on, heaps and heaps of dresses, no doubt.

For a moment Shady watched them go, and then she took a deep breath as she turned to face the glass doors. They weren't so far away, a hundred feet or so; it'd take her seconds to reach them, mere seconds, and yet…look at what stood in her way. Children, toddlers, babies in prams.

Shady didn't hate kids, far from it. She'd done some work experience in a kindergarten as a teenager and she'd loved it, creating all manner of games for the little ones to join in with. She'd found their sheer enthusiasm and excitement for just about everything so endearing, precious too, because it was so fleeting.

She liked kids. She still liked kids. It wasn't the kids that were the problem.

So what was?

It was what the kids held, either clutched in their arms or held by the hand, trailing behind the children as they, in turn, trailed behind their parents. Dolls. An army of them. They were everywhere.

I don't hate dolls either.

No, she didn't. She hadn't.

When did it change?

A question she'd just asked this morning, not regarding herself but Mandy.

That's when it had changed.

For fuck's sake, Shady! Get outta here and go home.

Despite such strict instruction, she had to force herself to move. She'd been fine this morning, hadn't much noticed those around her. She'd been focused, that's why. And she'd been with her mother. Now, in a sea of people, she was alone. She was vulnerable. But to what, exactly? What were the dolls going to do? Go all *Toy Story* on her and come alive? Start turning their heads in her direction, their beady black eyes boring into her as Mandy's had, searching, delving deep…

Shady, move!

She was trying to, but it wasn't that easy. She had to dodge people; she had to ask over and over again to be excused as that dodging turned into pushing.

"Watch where you're going!"

A man's angry voice reached her, but it didn't *pierce* her. It was like she'd thrown a wall of armor around herself, trying to focus again, this time on the end goal, that wall of glass doors.

"Miss, are you okay?"

Was somebody asking that of her? Someone with a gentler voice than the man, but still she refused to look. If she could get outside, swap stifling air for cool, she'd be okay.

"What's the matter with her?"

"Look at her, why's she in such a hurry?"

"Rude. All today's kids are."

"I wonder what's scared that one? Crap, I hope there's nothing going on here!"

Not all these words were being spoken out loud, Shady realized as she continued onward, wading through crowds with feet that felt like they were treading quicksand. She was also picking up on thoughts, so many of them, another cacophony.

All you have to do is focus.

Like turning down the dial on a radio, focusing often shut out any extraneous sound.

Damn it, girl, focus!

Thoughts, words, laughter, and crying.

Especially crying.

"Hey, come on, mind the kid, will ya?"

Shady stopped. What kid?

A burst of fresh sobs drew her gaze downward. There was indeed a little kid sprawled on her knees, her mouth wide open and wailing. "Did I…did I do that?"

The mother was angry and rightly so. "Yes, you did!

What's wrong with you anyway? Pushing everyone out of the way? Were you raised in a barn?"

"Oh my God, I'm so sorry."

Before the woman could respond further, Shady bent, intending to help the child. As she did, she noticed what was beside the small girl, and what the girl was reaching out for in turn.

Every bone in her body froze. A doll. A baby doll, dressed all in white with bootees and a cap. It was the child's doll, not Mandy. She kept telling herself that over and over—*It's not Mandy!*—unaware that beneath her hands, the child was struggling, was screaming louder than ever.

"LET HER GO! Let go of my child or I'll call the cops."

The doll's face was turned toward her, and those eyes of hers, oh, but they stared.

"I'm warning you. Help! Somebody help me!"

Run, Shady.

Just as something inside her had taken control when she'd gazed into the mirror this morning, it did so again. A firm voice, authoritative, not easily ignored.

Go, go, go!

Forcing life back into her limbs, she released the child, only vaguely aware that she had also dropped the bag with her new jeans inside. Immediately, the mother swooped in, her blue eyes wide with terror, and scooped the child up in her arms. Around her, a crowd was gathering, ready to swoop in too, for Shady this time, to grab her should she dare to touch the child again.

Shady straightened, gulping yet more apologies. "I'm sorry, I'm sorry. I didn't mean to…"

The mother's eyes remained unforgiving. There could be no excusing her. She'd made a show of herself, marked herself out as different, when all she wanted was to blend in.

Shady, leave.

She would, not bothering to retrieve her bag, skirting around the distraught child and equally distraught mother, still mumbling, still apologizing, confused and stricken by her own behavior.

Once beyond mother and child, she was determined to close the gap between her and those doors, to get out, to do as the voice urged, as the voice *ordered* her to do.

She half ran, half stumbled, blinded by tears, despite more people getting in her way and so much noise bombarding her still. Finally at the doors, her hands met with the cold metal bar and she shoved at it, falling into daylight, and not only daylight but someone's arms, which rapidly enfolded her as she clung to them, as she sobbed louder than any child or doll ever could.

CHAPTER SIX

"There you go, Shady, a caramel macchiato with soya, like you asked for."

"Thanks, Ray. Appreciate it. You got one too?"

"Yeah, sure. Americano."

As Ray placed the drinks in front of them, he took the seat opposite her, that stunned expression still on his face, no doubt, although Shady couldn't see it at the moment; she just sat staring at the table in front of her, once again trying to understand what had happened.

What a fool she'd made of herself! She'd drawn so much attention, *negative* attention, with everybody thinking what a dangerous, crazy bitch she was. *Let go of my child!* That's what had been screamed at her, as if she were the sort that would harm a child, as if she was capable of something as despicable as that, as far from nice as it was possible to get.

Tears sprang to her eyes. She didn't bother wiping them away. Ray had already witnessed her sobbing her heart out, so a bit more crying wasn't going to bother him now.

Ray. She hadn't seen him for three or four years and now twice in as many days—a moment before Annie had walked in on her life, and a moment after the consequences of that. The first time she'd been in control; if anything, he'd been the hapless one. Now the roles were reversed.

"Come on, drink it, Shady. It'll help calm you down."

Like a child with a parent, she duly obliged, lifting the glass coffee cup to her mouth and sipping, tasting its sweet warmth. In the confines of the coffee house, it was quiet, at least, just a small business on the outskirts of downtown Idaho Falls. Although he sat so patiently on a brown leather sofa that had seen better days, he must have had a dozen questions running around his head. The fact that he'd saved her, gotten her away from the mall, meant she owed him at least a few answers. Placing her coffee back down on the table between them, she wiped at her mouth.

"Ray, I'm so sorry—"

"You know, if you apologize again, it's gonna be pistols at dawn."

"What?" Shady couldn't help it; she burst out laughing. It felt strange. It felt good. It was the last thing she thought she'd do. But Ray had always been witty, a bit of a class clown. "Where the heck d'ya get that saying from?"

"Oh, I've got a whole arsenal of them. Stick around and you'll see."

She studied him; he had a good face, there was kindness in it. She'd sensed something a little deeper when their hands had touched a couple of days ago, but everybody had that side to them. No one was wholly lighthearted and happy through and through—life ensured against it. It knocked the stuffing out of you sometimes, in ways both expected and unexpected.

"Ray, I don't know what you must think of me. Shit, I don't even know what to think of me right now, but…something odd happened yesterday, something that's…had an effect."

Again, Ray remained silent, encouraging her to speak, to fill the void.

She ran a hand through her hair and scratched lightly at her scalp. "If I tell you, you're gonna think I'm crazy, and I wouldn't blame you, not one little bit."

"You don't have to tell me anything."

"Yeah, but—"

"Don't feel like you owe me."

"Owe you? I—"

"Because you don't. I was glad to be able to help."

She sighed in relief. "Thanks, Ray, thanks a bunch, but I *do* owe you." Not the whole truth, perhaps, but part of it. "That's if you wanna know."

Ray flashed a wide grin at her. "I'm all ears."

Could she do it, could she tell him at least something? Was he really as kind as he looked? She took a deep breath. *Here goes nothing.* "Ray, I can sense things sometimes. My mom says I'm fey." Shady attempted a laugh. "She always has, my dad too. I've got a kind of sixth sense, as in that film, you know which one I mean?"

His grin slipped as his green eyes focused on her. He was interested, she realized, not horrified, not amused, not even surprised, just…interested.

"Ray," she continued before he could answer, "how come we were never friends at school?"

He shrugged. "Dunno. Sometimes you just have…blinders on, I guess."

"Yeah, I suppose. I did notice you, though. I always thought you were funny."

He appeared touched by that. "I noticed you too."

Having to swallow hard before continuing, she pressed

on. "When I say sixth sense, I mean, don't get me wrong, I'm nothing like that kid in the movie. I don't see dead people or anything."

"Shame, you got my hopes up there."

Her laugh was more genuine this time. The fact that he seemed completely unfazed by what she was saying amazed her. She'd told so few people in her lifetime—or, rather, she *had* told them, but just the bare bones of it. Just as she was doing now. But that was cool, that was okay. To share even a fraction of it was a relief.

"Right after you came into Mervin's, a woman came in. Annie Hawkins. She runs a museum in Bingham County. She's got this doll, and she wanted me to go see it. Thing is, Ray, when I handle objects—some objects, anyway—I kinda sense things. It's just energy, residual energy it's called, and it's sort of like zoning into the memories of the people who once owned the object, their feelings and their emotions." She hung her head. "Sorry, is this making sense?"

"Yeah, yeah, it actually is."

"Really? Okay, that's great, well…like I said, the object she wanted me to see was a doll." She grimaced. "It had to be, didn't it? Everyone knows how creepy dolls can be."

"Maybe it's because they're so lifelike?"

"Maybe."

"They're innocent to look at, and sometimes we don't trust innocence. We know it's fake."

Shady faltered. He was right, and yet she hadn't expected such insight.

"Sorry." Ray was the one apologizing now, his face suffusing with yet more red. "It's just…my mom has a thing about dolls. She's phobic, almost. Doesn't like dolls, doesn't like clowns. That's the kinda thing she'd say about them."

"Oh, right, okay. Cool. Um…" Could she go on? *Should* she?

"Shady?" Ray prompted.

She took another sip of her macchiato, allowed it to bolster her. "This doll"—one thing she couldn't say was her name—"it's creepy for sure. It gave me nightmares."

"Uh-huh."

"And then today, well…today was going just fine. Me and Mom decided to go shopping, we spent all morning looking at clothes, and then…when we were in the food court, I dunno, everything just…fell apart. We were surrounded by families, people with kids, and those kids—"

"Had dolls."

"That's right, like…nearly *all* of them. Just like it was in my nightmare. I was surrounded by them. And I guess…well, I freaked. Mom had met an old college friend and they'd gone off together, so it was just me on my own and I freaked, simple as that. I had to get outta there."

"I was in the right place at the right time."

"You were, Ray, you really were. I'm grateful to you. Thank you, you know, for letting me cry all over you, for bringing me back to Idaho Falls…for listening."

Having offloaded, and more than she'd intended to, she picked up her drink again and drained it, clutching the empty cup for a moment before placing it back down.

"You're still scared, huh?" Ray's voice was gentle.

She nodded. She was, along with bewildered.

"You could use something a little stronger?"

"Stronger?" she asked. "What are you suggesting, we go to a bar?"

"If you've got your ID on you?"

"I have, but…"

He leaned forward. "Look, it's been nice talking to you, and if you want, we could talk some more, but those macchiato things, one's gotta be enough, right?"

"Yeah, it's nice, but ya know…"

"They go a little heavy on the syrup?"

"It's no Starbucks."

"But it is quiet."

"Amen to that."

Contemplating the offer, she dug out her cell phone from her bag. If she was staying out, it was only fair she let her mom know. About to explain this to Ray, she stopped. The screen showed more than a dozen missed calls, and all of them from Annie Hawkins.

"Shit," she exclaimed.

"What is it?"

"It's…it's okay, it's nothing. I'm just gonna text Mom quick, and then I'll shut my phone off."

"So, we are moving on somewhere?"

"Yes, Ray Bartlett, saver of sanity, we certainly are."

* * *

It was getting later and later, and Shady was getting drunker and drunker. Rarely did she drink, as it just didn't seem to agree with her; she'd spin out easily, get sick. Pretty early on she'd learned what her limits were at parties when she was way below the twenty-one age limit. Hell, every teen in Idaho Falls drank, smoked, and took all kinds of hallucinogens, and they had fun, but for her…so often, it was a no go. The noise in her head, which she could normally control, would go on a bender too, although never *ever* did it get as bad as it had in the mall.

Ray was great; he was fun. She was loving that whole parental-vibe thing he had going on, which she was cashing in on, needing to let go, relax, forget. They'd hit a couple of bars, ending up in The Golden Crown. It was full of kids like them feeding the overpriced jukebox, and her boots stuck to the floor, but it was good, it was fine, noisy, and she felt safe there.

Ray was making her belly ache with laughter. He hadn't matched her drink for drink, even though this was his idea, but he'd danced with her, striking some deliberately stupid poses, pulling all kinds of faces, and generally just amusing the heck out of her.

A clown, that's what he was. What he'd always been. Certainly, he was goofing around right now, not caring what anyone thought of him, something she admired, envied him for, really.

"You know what, Ray," she shouted over the music. "I'm having the best time."

"Same."

"I wish we'd been friends sooner."

"Same again," he replied, delight making his eyes shine.

The tunes continued to play, a curious mix from the nineties, twenty-ohs, and twenteens. The place was packed, but then it was Friday night; people were having fun, just like them. Every now and again, a rogue thought would pop into her mind, not her thought but someone else's. *When's my date gonna make a move? What does he want, a written invitation?* and *That man over there, sitting at the bar, the older guy with the thinning hair, he's creepy, gotta keep away from him. Unless…unless he's rich. Maybe I should go over, find out.*

Shady turned her head toward the bar and assessed the man this girl considered "creepy." She didn't agree; he was just lonely, that was all. Whether the girl carried out her intentions or not, was none of Shady's business, and so she quickly turned away and let the music drown everything out, which it did easily enough. Would Ray kiss her by the end of the night? Did she want him to? She hadn't had a boyfriend in over a year. No, she decided. She didn't want him, nice as he was. He was just a friend. He'd *become* a friend…at last.

The next album that came on was too lightweight-pop for her. Nodding toward the bar, she also motioned with her hand that they should go fill up on drinks.

Ray duly followed her, but at the bar, standing close to the lonely man that the girl was indeed now talking to, she noticed that Ray was shaking his head.

"What's the matter?" she asked, still having to shout to be heard.

"Maybe you've had enough for one night, Shady."

She laughed. "Who are you, my dad?" This was taking that parental vibe too far.

"I don't mean… I just think any more and your head's gonna hurt tomorrow."

"It's my head, don't worry about it."

"Do you have to work?"

"Yeah, yeah I do."

"You really wanna be hungover for it?"

"Maybe. Who cares?"

"I do, Shady. I do."

He sounded so sincere that for a moment she was lost for words. But only for a moment. "I need another drink," she said, turning away from him and toward the bar, raising a hand to summon the bartender. "Excuse me, could I get a vodka and—"

"Hey, lady, you made me spill my drink."

There was another man leaning against the bar, this one in his late twenties or early thirties. Shady had failed to realize she was standing quite so close to him.

Immediately she apologized. "I'm ordering if you want another."

The man blatantly sized her up. "You wanna buy me a drink?"

"Well, yeah, you just said I made you spill the one you have." Although, on eyeing his beer glass, it looked pretty full to her. "What are you having?"

"Ooh now…let me think about that a moment…"

Shady frowned. Was he deliberately being dumb? As he'd appraised her, she did the same to him. Lonely. On his own. Yes, she got that feeling about him too. But not like the older guy, whom, predictably, the girl had left, deeming him not worthy of her time after all and setting her sights elsewhere. *This* guy was lonely but something else besides. A predator, was that it? A regular at these kinds of establishments. Always on the lookout, always tracking. Not wanting commitment, just a one-night stand, preferring the hunt.

The man leaned closer. "The name's Gabe. And what I'd like…is you."

"Shady," Ray interrupted, "everything all right here?"

"Hey, pal." The man addressed Ray this time. "You with the lady?" He seemed amused by that fact, disbelieving of it. "Because if not—" he inclined his head, polished that twinkle in his eye "—run along home, will ya? I'm sure your momma's fretting."

"Okay, listen up—" Ray began, but Shady raised her hand.

"Actually, I'd like you to listen to *me*, mister. There's nothing else on the menu but a drink. Now, what are you having?"

"Whoa! Feisty one, ain't cha?"

If that was true, Ray was growing just as feisty. "Come on, Shady, let's leave this asshole—"

"You calling me an asshole, kid?" The man was still more amused than angry, something that made Ray angrier still.

"Ray, come on," she said, "back off."

"What? You're telling *me* to back off? What about him?"

The man's grin grew wider. "Ever think of taking a chill pill, my friend?"

Ray's nostrils flared. "I'm not your friend, okay. Don't make that mistake."

"I'm not the one making a mistake here, *friend*. You are, picking on me."

Shady had had enough. "Have you two finished behaving like kids? I've met toddlers in kindergarten more mature than you!"

Ray's face crumpled. "I was only trying to help—"

"I can fight my own battles, thanks!"

"Like I said, feisty," the man continued, his voice as smooth as a pat of butter. "Now, d'ya wanna tell your friend to take a hike so we can have that drink?"

"I'm not drinking with you," Shady said, "and I'm not buying you a drink anymore either. You had your chance."

"Oh, come on, you can't renege on a promise!"

"Shady"—although Ray's voice was still edgy, there was a plea in it—"let's just get outta here."

"We are, we're going." He was right, she *had* had enough to drink, and now she wanted out too.

She turned to go, Ray looking relieved, the man as amused as ever. As she put one foot in front of the other, trying to walk in a straight line, to appear as sober as possible, she felt the man's hand on her arm, gripping it tightly. "No hard feelings, eh?"

"None," she answered, wishing he'd get his predatory hands off her.

"But if you change your mind, want to experience a real man, you know where I am."

She yanked her arm out of his grasp. "I won't be changing my mind."

"No? Well, that's a crying shame. It's your loss…doll."

She ground to a halt. "Excuse me? What did you call me?"

"There's any number of things I could call you: sexy, cute as hell—"

"No. What did you *just* call me?"

"Shady." Ray's voice held another warning, but she ignored it, focusing solely on the man until he shrugged his shoulders—such a nonchalant gesture—and replied.

"Doll. I called you doll."

As she'd done before, she raised her hand, a wave of fury engulfing her. Pulling it back, she then released it, ramming it into the man's face, blood from his nose spraying like a fountain.

"Shady! For fuck's sake!"

It was Ray, trying to pull her away, the man no longer amused but also shouting at her, asking her what the hell she thought she was doing. Others rushed over, crowding her, standing looking at her, just as they'd looked at her in the mall, as if she were mad.

Still, Shady stood her ground. "Don't ever fucking call me doll."

CHAPTER SEVEN

She'd lost it. Completely. No longer nice, she was something else. Possessed.

No, not that; she still refused to buy it. Obsessed, then? So soon? Maybe, but not willingly. So perhaps it was a mixture of the two, possessed and obsessed...with Mandy. Whatever it was, it had almost landed her in the back seat of a patrol car. The only reason she wasn't was because the guy—Gabe O'Halloran—had finally decided he didn't want to "waste time" pressing charges against "a stupid kid." More likely, he didn't want any contact with the police, the predatory side to his nature not quite tipping the scales, not yet, but there might come a time...

Neither she nor Ray thanked him for his "grand gesture," as Ray sneeringly dubbed it, when the bar staff finally let them go. Instead, Shady glared at O'Halloran, wanting him to remember her face, at least. *Not all of us are helpless; we don't exist for your amusement. Some of us fight back, remember that.* She could hardly say it outright, accuse him of a crime not yet committed, but the message was evident in her eyes, and she knew—she could feel—she'd conveyed it well enough, that it might make him think twice. She could only hope...and pray.

Poor Ray, what else could she put him through that day?

He'd never want to see her again after this, and who could blame him? Which would be a shame because she liked him, she felt understood by him, up to a point. Certainly, he hadn't judged her, and he wasn't judging her even now as he concentrated on getting her home, helping her to sneak in so she wouldn't wake her parents, promising her that he *would* call the next day, brushing off yet more profuse apologies.

"There's no need, Shady," he replied. "There's really no need. I'll see you tomorrow."

He left her, and she not only slept, she passed out—no dreaming, not as far as she could recall, just a swift descent into merciful oblivion. But as morning dawned and she opened her eyes, her head throbbing as Ray had predicted, it was as if she'd never slept at all.

"Had a good night, huh?"

Ellen was leaning against the doorframe, "that look" upon her face, that *knowing* look. All Shady could do was groan in response.

"Wanna tell me who this friend is you were out with last night?"

"Someone from high school. Like I said in my text."

"*Just* a friend?"

"Just a friend, Mom."

"I heard you roll in, you know."

"Yeah, I know." Nothing got past Ellen. "Look…I'm not a kid."

"I'm aware of that, thank you."

They both were, and yet Shady had never felt so small.

"You have work today?" Ellen continued.

"Uh-huh."

"What time?"

"In about an hour."

"Best get up and get dressed, then."

"I will. I am."

"We can talk later."

Shady forced herself to sit up. "Talk about what?"

"As I said, honey, it can wait. Just get ready. I'll make the coffee."

She watched as her mother turned and disappeared down the hallway. A mother was a mother, and they noticed when something wasn't right. Concerning that kind of stuff, they had a sixth sense all of their own. But what could Shady tell her when she couldn't make head nor tail of it herself? She yawned and stretched. Her body ached, but her mind was screaming at her.

What's wrong with you, Shady? What the fuck is wrong with you?

She'd hit someone last night, actually *hit* him! And all because he'd called her doll. She screwed her eyes shut. Ray was right, the man was an asshole, but thank God he hadn't pressed charges; the fallout would have been immense. She'd escaped that, at least.

Shady, you've escaped nothing.

The stark truth hit home. That nagging voice within her was right. One encounter with Mandy and she was already in too deep.

A realization that made her head ache even more.

She leaned forward and groped for her black canvas backpack. It was at the foot of her bed, along with her crumpled clothes. Grabbing it, she rummaged inside for her cell phone, confused by the blank screen until she remembered she'd turned it off, just before she and Ray had gone bar-crawling, not wanting to hear from Annie or be reminded of her existence. Switching it back on, she watched as the amount of calls Annie had made to her mounted up, way exceeding nineteen. Finally, the woman had left a text: *Call me. Please.* Nothing more, nothing less, but those few words spoke volumes. Shady could sense the desperation in them, Annie hoping and praying too. If that woman had Shady's home address, she'd have been there in a flash, Shady knew it, concerned about her, wanting to question her, frightened for her.

But not half as much as Shady was frightened for herself.

She glanced at the clock. Time was ticking. She'd have to get moving or she'd be late for work. Her mom, true to her word, had brewed the coffee, its rich, pungent aroma creeping toward her. But there'd be no coffee for her this morning, and—she now decided—there'd be no work, and damn the trouble she'd get into because of that.

Despite wanting to return to bed, to pull the comforter over her head, block out the world, block out everything, she couldn't. There was only one place she had to be and one woman she had to see. If she didn't get some answers about Mandy, an inanimate object that had wormed its way inside her, to squat there like a panther, ready to pounce, she'd go insane.

Another groan escaped her, and her eyes filled with tears as she got to her feet and made her way to the bathroom, beginning a morning routine that was familiar enough.

What came after would be entirely different.

* * *

Shady had a sense of déjà vu as she stood outside the Mason Town Museum a second time, that same sense of something pending, the air as cold as it was before, and the threat of snow becoming more real with each passing day. She shivered, just as she'd shivered before, putting one foot in front of the other and climbing the steps to the entrance, reaching out, grasping the brass knob, and waiting for the door to protest as it opened, the scream that would echo…

"Shady! You came back. Oh, thank God!"

It was Annie, clearly having spied her approach and opening the door fully before Shady had a chance to. A diminutive woman still dressed in various shades of brown, she was as solemn as she'd been when Shady had first met her but also more tentative, more wary.

A moment passed, and then another before the words burst from Shady. "What's happening to me? What have you done?" And with those words came more tears, those that had filled her eyes this morning but hadn't quite broken rank. Now they did with a vengeance, pouring from her, too hard to control. "What have you done?" she repeated.

"Oh dear, dear, come inside now, come inside."

Shady wiped savagely at her eyes and sniffed hard. "I can't. *She's* in there."

"Yes, yes, she is, but you're quite safe. I'll teach you how to be safe, to protect yourself." In the midst of her own misery, Shady also noticed how stricken Annie was. "I'm so sorry," the older woman continued. "I assumed you knew how to do that already. It was wrong of me. I should have checked first; I can't believe I didn't. You did strike me as very young. I really am so sorry."

"What is she? She's not just a doll."

"No, she isn't, you know that."

"And what's wrong with her isn't just residual either."

"It doesn't appear to be."

"Who are you? A psychic?"

"I've told you I'm not."

"But you're aware?"

"All too aware."

"Am I psychic?"

Annie chanced a tentative smile. "You're certainly a lot more than fey."

"Has that doll possessed me?"

"She's affected you, that's all."

"And that's not as bad?"

"It…it can still be difficult, admitted."

"I don't know what to do."

"Come in, we can talk, I can explain, and, as I said, I can teach you."

"What if I don't want to be taught? What if I don't want anything to do with any of this?"

Annie held on to her glasses as she shook her head. "I don't think it works that way, dear. Sadly." Again, there was silence before Annie urged her yet again to step inside.

Unsure what else to do, Shady obeyed, breathing in that familiar musty smell, listening as old memories began to stir, to awaken, wanting someone to remember…

Annie closed the door and then turned to Shady. "Don't allow yourself to be bombarded. You already know that if you focus, if you streamline your mind, you can block things."

Shady blinked. What Annie had said was true, but no

one had ever put it into words before. "Where is she?" she asked.

"In the basement. She's in a box, another antique, nothing fancy. It's an old military box, but it's lead lined, which provides something of a barrier…God knows how, but it does. Come with me."

"Not downstairs." Despite what Annie had said, the thought horrified Shady.

"No, not there. There's a small private room on this floor, towards the back. We can sit and have a coffee. You could use a coffee, couldn't you?"

She could, a strong one.

"Dear." Annie laid a hand on Shady's arm. It felt…comforting, reassuring. "You need to learn."

As they walked the length of the museum, Shady was aware of more voices, but they seemed to come at her from a distance, her mind keeping them at bay, a noise that could indeed be blocked out or at the very least controlled, unlike the scream and the wretched crying before. Those sounds had set her teeth on edge.

Even the staff room, as Shady presumed it to be, was stuffed with artifacts. Annie noticed Shady looking and assured her they were all quite benign.

"But *how* do you know?" Shady asked, seating herself at a small table, one with a red polka-dot plastic cover on it and a small bunch of cheerful fake flowers in a vase. "If you're not psychic."

With two cups of coffee in her hand, poured from a filter machine glass pot, Annie sat too. "Cream and sugar?"

"No, thanks. I'm okay with black. So…?"

"I'm English, dear—"

"I'd guessed."

"And when I was a girl, my father ran an antique shop in a place called Lavenham. It's a town in Suffolk, seventy miles or so north of London."

"Okay."

"I'm not a psychic, really I'm not, but you could say my senses are well honed. Like my father before me, I knew when an object contained good energy or bad. If it was bad—not evil, mind, but erring towards the negative—Father refused to sell it on, no matter its value. Not that he'd go out of his way to buy single items like that, he didn't, but things would come in anyway from house clearances, that type of thing. He'd say to me, 'Annie, I have a duty to keep the public safe. People have enough in their lives to deal with sometimes; they don't need more,' and so he kept those particular items in another room, kept a lamp on in there too, at all times. He didn't pass judgment. He wasn't scared of them, he just…kept them separate."

"Like you do?"

Annie nodded. "Though my things are not his things. My mother and father divorced when I was eleven. It wasn't amicable, not at all, unfortunately. I loved my mother, but she had a love for…shall we say, the finer things in life, not antiques. She preferred everything to be shiny and new. In short, she was high-maintenance and demanded a good settlement. Father had to sell his business, had to sell, in the end, everything. Some of those items he kept quarantined were worth a lot. He didn't want to part with them, but as I've told you, he was forced to in the end."

Caught up in the woman's story, Shady silently urged

her on when she came to a halt.

"One specific item was quite beautiful to look at, a writing set from the eighteen hundreds. A pen and an inkwell, silver and crystal, enclosed in a leather case. It really was in exceptional condition, but who knew what it had written, what thoughts it had manifested. Father sensed it was a dangerous object, hesitated to sell it, but in the end quashed his misgivings. He had a debt to pay to the woman he'd once loved, that he'd once trusted. Father knew the person that bought it, a fellow trader. He warned him about it, but the fella laughed that warning off, asked how he could possibly know such a thing. Father couldn't answer. Like I said, he was just...*aware*.

"That same man committed suicide not two months after purchasing the writing set, and he left a note for my father, one I can still recite word for word. 'You were right,' it said. 'I don't know how, but you were. Whoever owned this originally was bad. He was evil. And in this instrument, his evil lives on. It's infected me. I can't stop writing either—not my words, his. They pour onto the page. Vile words that brim with filth and hatred. Oh God, you were right,' he said. 'You should have tried harder to stop me from buying it. I've written about my own death. It's coming, and it's your fault, all your fault.'" Annie paused again and closed her eyes briefly, her hands clasped tightly together.

"Annie, if you'd rather stop—"

"No, I can't stop. I won't. My father never got over this man's death or indeed the words he'd written, the blame that had been apportioned. He felt such a sense of...responsibility. He knew he'd done the wrong thing, that he should have been stronger, told my mother there was only so much in the coffers, and not declared everything. He was never the same after that. He just…he faded. That's the only way I can think to describe it. Soon after, he developed cancer and it was, mercifully, a short-lived illness. He died. Strangely, my mother followed him to the grave not long after. All her grasped wealth couldn't save her.

"But I resolved, on his deathbed, silently, to carry on his work. I say silently because to tell him of my intentions would have distressed him. But, as he had tried to do, I wanted to protect people. I'd inherited that same sense of responsibility. And somehow, I'd make up for what had happened, or I'd give it a good try. You see, Father called what he was doing 'acting on a hunch.' What the dealer did proved his hunch was right, albeit in the most terrible of ways. So, yes, I'd carry on his work, I'd keep alert to the dangers, and I'd refuse to marry." Here she laughed, but it was something of a forced sound. "It seemed like the safer bet."

"How did you end up here, though? In America."

"I never married, but I wasn't single. I met Donny, a man from Idaho, whilst traveling to various antique fairs. We fell in love, and I moved here to be with him. It was a whole lot easier to do that back then. I found I liked being here; it suited me. This is a vast country, and in it I could carry on doing what I do and remain anonymous. In England, especially in a small village, your business is everybody else's business too. Donny's passed now, several years ago. He never tried to stop me in my vocation. He never got involved either, but he understood and respected my reasons."

Shady frowned. "You don't charge entrance to the museum."

"Not yet, just donations."

"So, how do you…" Her voice fell away. Was it rude to ask?

Annie's laugh was more genuine this time. "Donny and I weren't married, but he left everything to me. And I'd made a fair bit of my own money back in the day. The antiques trade can be quite lucrative if you're good and you get the lucky windfalls. My fortunes were secured by a pair of rather perfect Chinese rhinoceros horn cups, of all things, items with only good cheer attached to them and, of course, a hefty price tag. In answer to the question you couldn't bring yourself to ask, I can afford to do this, for a while, anyway. I *want* to do this. I believe it to be vital."

"To collect."

"That's right, although like my father, I don't actively seek out these items. I just keep them if they find their way to me. I like to see it as fated, which"—she shrugged—"perhaps allows me to make excuses to myself for this kind of eccentricity. You know, Shady, dear, there are various people around the world with collections similar to mine. Some choose to make them public as I have, and some keep them private. Most, although sadly not all, do it for the same reasons as myself and my father, to quarantine."

"So those that don't—"

"Are not our concern. We can only take on board so much."

"But if items are possessed—"

"The term *possession* is a strange one. Like cancer, it has the ability to frighten us. But, elaborating on something else I've said to you, it's not always as simple as just getting rid of an item or trying to destroy it. If an item is possessed, it's possessed by energy, and energy doesn't die, it *transfers*. It could, as may have happened with Father's friend, take up residence in its next owner, although, of course, that would depend on a number of factors. For example, how vulnerable that person is, how susceptible, how guilty, even, of flirting with the dark side. Because that can make you susceptible too; it can open you up to it."

"I don't flirt with the dark side," Shady protested.

"I've told you, you're not possessed. You're affected."

"Because according to you I'm psychic?"

"You are, Shady. You're gifted."

And yet right now she felt nothing but cursed.

"If energy transfers," Annie continued, "it's essential it transfers correctly. If it's a soul that's trapped within or attached to an object, then they need to go home, to the light, to be urged to go there. If it's something that's never been human, it needs to return to source too."

"Are you talking about heaven and hell?"

"I'm talking about various planes of existence, some of which are much lower than others."

"Until that happens, until whatever's possessing the object leaves, what can we do?"

"It's as I've said before, we can try and understand it." As Annie leaned forward, there was a plea in her eyes for Shady to accept what she was saying, not to reject her out of turn. "Often, if we don't understand something, we fear it. Does that make sense?"

Shady nodded. It did.

"The opposite is also true. If we understand, then that fear can evaporate."

"You want me to understand evil?"

"I think you have to. Shady, you're young but your gift is developing, just as you yourself are developing. You'll be exposed to things because of it, and not all of them good. There is a very real possibility that the effect Mandy has had on you could repeat itself over and over again with other objects you come into contact with, although I tend to think Mandy is, thankfully, a rare example. If I'd realized you had no idea about protection, I would have schooled you beforehand. But I can rectify that now, if you'll let me. I can help you. You can't simply shake off Mandy; she's in your psyche now, and she'll continue to taunt you. But don't think it's personal, it isn't. She'd do the same with anyone. Mandy's energy is strong; you don't need to be psychic to pick up on that. I tend to think plenty of people have picked up on it since she came into being, so-called ordinary people, to their detriment."

"They've been affected as bad as me?"

Annie leaned back in her seat and sighed. When she smiled, she appeared younger than her years, but now, in this low light, she had once more aged.

"Annie? Have they been affected as bad as me?"

"I'm so sorry, Shady. I should have established your experience before bringing you into all this. It's just…from what Gina told me…how confident you were, how decisive…" Annie had averted her eyes, but now she looked back at Shady. "I don't quite know the ins and outs of what's happened to you since your first visit, but you're living and breathing, aren't you?"

What a strange question to ask! "Obviously, I am."

"Well then, yes, I think they have been affected worse than you, a lot worse."

"What do you mean?"

"What I mean is, I think Mandy has killed before."

CHAPTER EIGHT

"Are you ready?"

"I'm ready."

"And you remember all I've said."

"Every word."

"Envisage white light."

Shady nodded. She was to imagine white light, a column of it, streaming down from the sky above, burning bright, fiercer than darkness could ever be but at the same time so gentle, so pure. She was to draw from it, take as much as she wanted, for its supply was endless, wrapping it around herself to form an impenetrable shield that would keep her safe inside, cocooned. She was to believe in this light and all that it represented, which was love and good intent. She was a part of the light; she'd come from it, and, one day, she'd return.

It was a crash course, but, according to Annie, the lesson was simple enough.

"Good intent," she'd informed her, "really is the key to it all, along with understanding and compassion. Love is the greatest force in the universe. Do you believe that?"

She guessed she did. There'd been a lot of love in her life, and within it she had flourished.

"You're a nice girl," Annie had added, making Shady

smile.

"Thank you," she'd answered, "although I haven't been quite so nice recently."

Feeling herself flush with embarrassment, she'd then gone on to tell Annie all about what had transpired since her first visit to Mason Town Museum.

"You *are* nice," Annie'd insisted. "You're special. Keep on being that way. Keep on thinking the best of everyone and everything. Keep on being loving. That truly is your best defense."

"And try to understand."

"Always."

And so Shady had found herself agreeing. She would draw on what she'd been taught; she'd go back down to the basement and approach Mandy not with fear but with a desire to understand what she was. She might then be able to help, not only others but also herself.

"Take several deep breaths," Annie instructed, sitting across a narrow table from Shady, the doll entombed in its casket a few feet away, "in for a count of six and out for a count of six. I'm here and here I'll stay, by your side. You trust me on that?"

Shady did. This woman, who only three days earlier had been a stranger to her, was someone she'd placed her faith in. Shady didn't have the luxury of days, weeks, or even years to be trained in how to deal with her gift, not taking into account what had already happened. All she had was a couple of hours, and during that time—imparting everything she knew—Annie had taken Shady's hands in her own and clasped them gently.

Everything about Annie was gentle. If Shady was nice,

Annie was nicer, Annie was good, and that light she talked so much about—Shady could feel it pouring from the woman, sinking into her own skin and bones, warming her when she had felt so cold, clearing her mind when she'd been so confused, healing her, she supposed, or at the very least, bolstering her with positivity and hope. She could do this; she was more than capable. Never had she gotten that strength of feeling from anyone before, her parents included. It was as if this woman was a part of her, or maybe…maybe she was just her kind.

"Life leads us towards the right people," Annie said, even though Shady hadn't voiced that particular thought. "It's no coincidence that in a world of billions, we cross certain paths."

Time continued to pass, how much Shady didn't know, but it didn't matter. Within these walls time seemed suspended, or perhaps *worthless* was more apt. This was, after all, a place where the past and present collided, where both were thrown into the air to land all jumbled.

Despite asking her if she was ready, despite the urgency of the situation, Annie didn't rush to retrieve the doll, giving Shady's new awareness a chance to grow. Mandy had a hold on Shady; perhaps she'd only been toying with her up until now, but that grip would become tighter, there was no doubt about it. Shady's only defense was to do as Annie had said and try to understand her, in which case her fear of the doll should begin to dissipate, even if what was in it remained.

At last Annie went over to the box, black and lead lined as she had said, a coffin of sorts. Shady could feel Mandy's energy, but as if it was held at arm's length. As soon as

Annie opened the lid, that energy would be more like a blast, and then, when she held her…

You can do this, remember? You have to.

Annie had said the doll might have been responsible for deaths. If so, neither wanted that score to increase.

With the lid opened, Shady heard a whoosh, accompanied by a scream, a cry, as if Mandy herself was horrified at having been incarcerated.

"White light," Annie murmured, holding the doll almost reverentially in her hands, cradling her as if she were indeed a human infant, and bringing her closer all the while.

Shady nodded, frantically weaving a shield from that column of white light, a sturdy blanket that would cover her from head to toe.

Annie sat back down and took a deep breath herself before she held out the doll. As she did, the lights in the basement flickered, but only the once.

Shady reached out too, imagining her hands ablaze with the light she'd woven, a strength in them that she'd never known before, a purpose.

Her hands closed around Mandy, her molded arms and her soft body, bringing her closer, intending to cradle her just as Annie had cradled her.

The visions started immediately. "Share them," Annie had previously instructed. "Talk me through each and every one. It's better if you pass it on. It won't be as…intense."

A problem shared was a problem halved, a problem like Mandy.

"I'm sensing the little girl again. She was the first child that owned Mandy, I think."

"The one you told me about earlier?"

"Yes, yes, when we were talking. A child that wanted Mandy so badly, that craved her."

"And it's Christmas morning or her birthday?"

"I'm not sure which, but it's a special occasion."

"Carry on, Shady, you're doing great."

"This child—Kate Jane, I think that's her name…it is, it's Kate Jane—she's so happy."

"Can you see her?"

"Not yet, I can only sense her. Her parents are so pleased; her reaction is everything they wanted it to be. They're pleased and…something else."

"What else, Shady?"

"Relieved. That's it. I can see them, not the little girl but them, their faces. They're looking at each other, and they're relieved. The mother is chewing at her lip slightly. The father is sighing; his shoulders, which were tense before, are now relaxed. The child loves this doll, this doll takes pride of place, this doll is all she plays with, day and night. 'Mandy,' she whispers. 'Mandy, I love you. Do you love me too? Do you, Mandy? Do you?' It's a question she asks over and over."

"But a doll can't answer back."

"That's right, it can't, and this frustrates the little girl, it upsets her. She starts shaking Mandy, shouting at her. She starts…screaming. Her parents are beside themselves. Again, I can see just them and no one else. All they want to do is please their daughter, make her happy."

"How old do you think the child is?"

"Eight, but younger when she got Mandy, around seven or so."

"What do the parents do to make her happy?"

"They buy her more things, things they think she craves, but she doesn't. They just don't have the same impact on her as Mandy did. Mandy was a doll she'd seen in the pages of a book somewhere, a catalog…yes, it's definitely a catalog. Right away, she was captivated. She's never been captivated by something as much, either before or after."

"So, buying her other dolls doesn't appease her?"

"It seems nothing can. This child, it's like…there's a rage inside her, churning up all sorts of emotions, feelings too big for her to handle, for anyone to handle, I reckon. Her parents mean well, but they don't know how to deal with her. They're desperate. Kate Jane was something they craved too, but she hasn't made them happy, just like Mandy hasn't made Kate Jane happy."

"What era is this?"

"I don't know. But the doll was new, brand-new. These other toys…"

"Go on," urged Annie.

"There are dolls among them, prettier dolls, more expensive. Kate Jane makes Mandy sit in a corner and watch as she plays with these new dolls. Always, always, she checks to see that Mandy is watching, imagines her suffering at being excluded from tea parties, dressing up, and cuddling and kissing. 'If you want to join in,' she says, 'you have to say you love me.'"

"She refuses to accept she's inanimate," Annie mused. "Shift your focus, try and see the child."

"I'm trying. It keeps going hazy, though."

"Can you see Mandy?"

"No."

"But you know she's there?"

"Yes, because of the little girl."

"Can you sense Mandy?"

"Whether this is having an impact on her?"

"Precisely."

"No."

"You can't sense her at all."

"No," Shady repeated. "Oh wait, wait…I get the impression Kate Jane's grabbed Mandy again… She has, she's growing more and more frustrated. She's hitting Mandy. She's crying."

"The child's disturbed, isn't she?"

"Seems to be. Now she's taking out her anger on the other toys, the fancier dolls, the more expensive ones. She's hitting them too, breaking them. She breaks so much in the house."

"And it's Mandy she blames."

"She says it's Mandy's fault, that Mandy did it. She points at the doll, insists on it."

"And her parents believe her?"

"Well, Kate Jane wouldn't break things, not their perfect girl, the girl they craved. She wouldn't lie either. She hasn't been brought up to lie. She's a good girl; that's what they tell each other, what they make themselves believe. 'Kate Jane is a joy.' The mother cries but still she says it, over and over, out loud and to herself: 'If she says it's Mandy responsible for all the damage, then it has to be. There's no other explanation. That doll is…wrong. All wrong. We have to get rid of it. If we do, everything will go back to normal and we'll be happy again, like we used to be.'"

"Try to focus on the child, Shady, and Mandy as well. Try to see them."

"I can't, not right now."

"You can. Streamline your mind—they're there in the vision too."

"It's like they're hiding."

"Then drag them out of hiding."

"But—"

"If you see the child's face and the doll, then you'll understand better. If you don't, your imagination will make more of them than they are. Shady, come on, take a deep breath."

"I can't see them. I can't. I…I can see someone else."

"Who?"

"An old woman."

"Is she something to do with Kate Jane? Her grandmother, perhaps?"

"No, I don't think so. She lives alone, she…she's a collector too."

"What of?"

"Dolls. She has so many in her house; they're in every room. They're…um…a substitute, I think. This woman had a family, but now she's alone. The dolls keep her company. She loves the dolls, she clothes them, talks to them, they're her new family, she…she rescues them…yes, that's it. Any doll that's been discarded, that is no longer wanted, she gives them a loving home, a forever home. But she isn't like the girl; she doesn't demand anything back. Making them happy makes *her* happy, just as she was with her family. She's content…until Mandy." Shady screwed her eyes shut. "Oh, Mandy. Mandy, what are you doing? You're confusing me."

"What's happening now?"

"I can see Mandy now…two of her."

"Two of her?"

"Yeah."

"Okay, go with it, focus."

"Are there two of her? In real life, I mean?"

"Mandy's a manufactured doll. There would have been plenty. Tell me what you see."

"Mandy as she was, in the beginning."

"Go on."

"Mandy that was loved…Mandy that was…abused. Poor Mandy. I can see her. She's slumped in a corner, just left there, ignored."

"Not ignored, not really."

"Tormented, then. The little girl, ah, there she is! She's…a pretty girl, perfectly made, she's doll-like herself, but she's the one that's wrong…all wrong. She's wired up incorrectly; that's the only way I can think to describe it. And her parents just won't believe it, they won't get her the help she needs. Instead, they believe her. They always will. Mandy's gone; they did get rid of her in the end. But Mandy at that stage…was a doll, nothing else. Nothing was her fault."

"Who's the old woman, Shady?"

"Someone who found Mandy, in a store, a junk store, or an antique store, something like that. Poor, poor Mandy… This woman's heart went out to her. She was another to give a home to, to look after. She knew she'd been treated badly in the past, she could sense it, just like she could sense with every other doll she owned. And she'd rescue her; she'd make it all better."

"Could it be a recent owner?"

"I think so. Maybe even her last owner. Mandy cries now, and she screams. Oh, Mandy, you've changed, *really* changed. You cry, you scream, and you lash out too. You do all the things that you were once accused of. But how? You're an object, just an object. No, you've become more than that. What happened to you since Kate Jane? What have you been through? Oh, Mandy!"

Again, Shady screwed her eyes tightly shut, stopped cradling Mandy, held her at arm's length instead. "Sweet Mandy. Beautiful Mandy. Naughty Mandy."

"Are those your words, Shady, or the old woman's?"

"I'll take you back to the thrift store. I'll throw you away with the trash."

"Shady?"

"Quit that crying…that *constant* crying."

"Shady, perhaps we ought to stop now…"

"This is your fault, all your fault. You're the reason I'm so confused."

"Shady, listen to my voice, come back now. I think we've done enough—"

"I'm confused, so confused. What time of day is it? How come it's nighttime already? Where are my car keys? I put them here, on the table in the hallway. I know I did. It's where I *always* put them. Did I eat last night? Did I have breakfast? Who is she, that woman in the mirror? It's like she's…different. I don't recognize her sometimes. I don't know who I am anymore, and it's because of you, Mandy, all because of you. JUST QUIT THAT DAMNED CRYING!"

"Shady—"

"Lena, that's the old woman's name. What happened to

her wasn't Mandy's fault either, not entirely, anyway. Her forgetfulness was just so bad. But Mandy was tired of being blamed. She didn't like it; she *hated* it. Oh shit, oh fuck, I think you're right about Mandy."

"What am I right about?"

"Mandy is so angry…"

"What am I right about, Shady?"

"I think she did it."

"Did what?"

"She killed Lena. She wanted her dead."

CHAPTER NINE

The next morning, Shady's hands were still shaking as she began to pack.

"Sweetheart, there's a young—hey, what are you doing? You planning on going somewhere?"

She turned to face her mother. "I'm sorry, Mom."

"What? I don't understand. What are you sorry for?"

Hurrying over to her daughter, Ellen reached out to hold Shady's hands as if trying to keep her rooted to the spot, her eyes all the while on the backpack, staring at it like she'd never seen one before. "You didn't say anything about a vacation. What about work? You've got work."

"Mom." Shady waited for Ellen to look at her before she carried on. "I'm not going to work. I was owed some time off, and I've taken it. They're not happy about it, but—" she shrugged "—I need to go, Mom. I've got something to sort out."

"You can't just leave!"

"Mom"—Shady nodded toward the bed—"you said yesterday that we needed to talk. You're right, we do. Can you sit down?"

Exactly what she was going to say to her mother, however, she hadn't quite figured out.

A road trip, that's what she was going on, with Annie in

tow.

The second session she'd spent with Annie at Mason Town Museum had been a productive one. She'd managed to tune in to two of Mandy's owners: the first owner, it seemed, and most likely the last. What she'd seen had disturbed her but also calmed her somewhat. Annie was right: she had a better chance of dealing with Mandy if she understood her. Cold hard facts tended to stop the imagination from going into overdrive. But there could be no doubt about it—Mandy was dangerous.

Not in the beginning, though; that much had been established. In the beginning she was what she was supposed to be, a toy, something inanimate as Annie had said, a Mandy doll, hot off the production line, craved not by one little girl but so many. Hayle and Co., New York, had been the ones to manufacture her, a factory that had shut down in the early 1950s, according to Annie, who'd done some research into them.

By the time Mandy had come into Lena's care, however, she was something quite different. How? Why? What had happened to her in between? Shady had to know. It was as simple as that. Salvation was in the knowing. The doll had somehow killed Lena. Not directly, not quite that, but it had *driven* her into the arms of death, sent her rushing in desperation to the top of that long flight of stairs, blinding her to any obstacles that may have been in her way, which in turn sent her falling down, down, down to land in a heap at the bottom, to lie there for days before being discovered, her neck twisted, her eyes open, her mouth wide open.

And Mandy crying all the while…

"Mom, you and Dad call me fey. I think, though, I

might be more than that."

Although Shady had retrieved her hands from her mother's once she'd sat on the bed and pulled Ellen down to sit too, she could still sense the horror her statement had provoked.

"Shady—" Ellen began, but Shady signaled for her mother to let her speak.

"When I hold objects, I can sometimes read them. Looking back, I realize I've always been able to do it. Sometimes it's vague, but other times…it isn't. You already know I've helped friends to find lost items in the past. I've gotten kind of a reputation for doing that, but recently, whatever ability I have seems to have increased. Expanded, even. I…" She paused and had to look away, as if confessing something abhorrent, some kind of dirty secret. "I helped this woman named Gina recently. She was having terrible nightmares, which had started all of a sudden. It seemed it was all down to a secondhand mirror; it had witnessed a lot, and when I say that, I mean in a negative sense. Whoever owned it beforehand was very disturbed, and the mirror and looking into it had become a sort of focus for her. This is hard to explain, but it was like the mirror was still drenched in her energy, energy that caused Gina's nightmares. I got rid of it for her. I buried it."

"The mirror was possessed?" Ellen's expression was incredulous.

"No, not that, Mom, but it'd been owned by someone who I think had issues with her mental health. I sort of think they were undiagnosed issues, that this person had shut herself away from society, was on her own—apart from the mirror—and would stare and stare into it, at herself, hating what she saw. I mean, *really* hating it."

"What happened to Gina once you got rid of the mirror? Did her nightmares stop?"

"Immediately. I think that case is closed—"

"Case?" Ellen's incredulity was now anger-tinged. "Is that what you're calling it?"

"It's just a word, Mom. It's as good as any."

"So, what's all this got to do with you going away?"

"It's another case. And this time, it's not as easy as burying the object."

Shady never lied to her parents, but, like all offspring, she supposed, sometimes she was economical with the truth. In telling her mother about Mandy, she trod a fine line. She wanted her to realize how serious it was but not overly alarm her. The latter, however, she failed miserably at.

As soon as she'd finished, Ellen shot to her feet. "No, Shady, I can't let you go. It's—" she gestured frantically, as if trying to pluck a word from thin air "—ridiculous. And who is this Annie? You've only just met her. She could be anyone, she could be nuts, some kinda…fraudster." Ellen bent over her daughter, intent on driving her point home. "She could be dangerous. She *is* dangerous. She's nuts, and she's a fraud. When your father hears about this, he'll hit the—"

Keen to level the playing field, Shady stood too. "Mom, I'm going."

"You're not!"

"I am. I have to."

"But, Shady—"

"I'm not a kid, Mom, not anymore! I'm a grown woman, and I have to do this. But it's more than that. After talking with Annie, after being with her and hearing her story, hearing her talk about another side of life I can identify with, I *want* to do it. It's my…" Was *calling* too strong a word? Perhaps, for now, even though she had a growing conviction that this was the case. She chose *duty* instead. "I don't want Mandy to harm anyone else, or to harm me."

"Then leave the damned doll alone! Just stay away from her!"

In her fury, Ellen's blue eyes had darkened to navy. Shady tried to recall ever seeing her so upset but couldn't. Ellen was calm by nature; she was collected, and she was cheerful, despite whatever business worries nagged at her. She provided a stable home life for her family, placing herself firmly at the heart of it. Growing up, Shady had always appreciated that, she still did, but times had changed, she herself had changed, and in such a short time too.

"Mom, please listen—"

"No, I'm calling your father, see what he has to say about this."

"I'm not a kid!" How many times did she have to say it? "This isn't some schoolyard prank I'm involved in that you can ground me for! Whatever ability I have, wherever it's come from, it's increasing. And because it is, I have no choice, not really. I gotta learn how to deal with it, properly and effectively, try and manage it. I've told you that Annie says she's not a psychic, but she knows a hell of a lot more about these things than I do. She can teach me."

"She's a stranger, Shady!"

"But I trust her! When I held her hands, I could tell she

was a good person."

Ellen started pacing the room, clearly not buying anything Shady was saying.

"This isn't good," she muttered. "This isn't good at all. This is wrong." Raising her voice again, she came to a halt, her eyes as penetrative as Mandy's had been. "It. Is. Dangerous!"

"But, Mom, it might be more dangerous if I try and ignore it." Finally, she told her about what had happened in the mall and at The Golden Crown, not leaving out any details this time. "Mandy's in my head. She's trying to frighten me—she *has* frightened me. But if I know her, and what she's about, it'll help with that fear. Annie said knowledge is armor, which makes sense."

Ellen denied it. "You don't need to know more about stuff like that! You just need to rein it in."

"But what if Mandy's the start of it? What if there are worse things than Mandy out there?"

As she moved closer, Ellen grabbed her arms, her grip as tight as it had been earlier. "No, no, no. I forbid you to go or get involved any deeper. I forbid it, d'ya hear?"

As shocked as she was, Shady stood her ground. "I'll make my own decisions."

Ellen seemed to fold in on herself. Her grip loosened, and she sank back onto the bed, tears flowing from her eyes as she brought her hands up to cover her face. As Shady stared at her, again unable to comprehend such an extreme reaction, feeling distraught herself that she was the cause of it—that she wasn't being nice and giving in, that she wasn't doing as her mom wanted her so desperately to do and staying put—tears also fell from her eyes.

"Mom," she whispered, but Ellen was whispering too. Shady quieted and listened instead.

"I'm sorry," she kept saying. "I'm sorry."

Shady galvanized herself and knelt in front of Ellen. She was the one who took her hands now, who held them away from her mother's stricken face.

"Mom, *I'm* sorry," she said, but if she expected her mother to reach out, to hug her, for this argument to somehow implode upon itself, she was wrong. Ellen gazed at her for a few seconds, her eyes blurred but not softening; in fact, there was a hardness to them, a bleakness.

"The reason I came to see you was to tell you you had a visitor."

"A visitor? Who?"

"Someone else in your life I don't know about."

Shady turned toward the door. Was the mysterious visitor still here? Had they heard all that had transpired?

"Mom?"

"It's a boy, about your age. Someone called Ray."

* * *

Life leads us towards the right people. That's what Annie had said. *It's no coincidence that in a world of billions, we cross certain paths.* Perhaps you were told stuff like that at the right time too, when you most needed to hear it.

Bundled into her Dodge, the heating as high as it would go, were three people instead of two: Shady driving, Annie in the passenger seat, and Ray in the back. Oh, and there was Mandy, shut away in that black lead lined box, stowed in the trunk.

They were heading north to Spokane, Washington, to the museum that Mandy had been donated to prior to coming to Bingham County, Idaho. Annie had called ahead, and they were expected. From there, the plan was to try to find out more about Mandy, where the museum had gotten her from, who Lena was, and how Lena, in turn, had acquired her.

As Shady drove, she glanced at Ray. He was looking out the window, his red hair as awry as ever, no fear or trepidation on his face, just a kind of quiet determination.

He'd been there when she'd rushed out of the mall. *I was in the right place at the right time,* he'd said about it, ready to catch her when she was falling. And then, just as he'd promised, he'd turned up at her house, concerned about her, wanting to make sure she was okay. And, yes, he'd heard the argument, most of it, anyway. But still, he'd sat and waited for Shady to appear, and Ellen too. And he'd made the offer to go with Shady on the road trip, which had the somewhat miraculous effect of appeasing Ellen, especially when Shady explained that he was the person they'd been talking about earlier, the friend from high school she'd been out with the previous night. That was enough for Ellen, because that was a bond she could understand. In her eyes, he'd be able to step in, protect her daughter if need be.

That he was also almost a stranger, Shady kept to herself. In truth, she was grateful to Ray for his offer and found that she wanted him along. He knew all about Mandy and the effect the doll had on her, and it hadn't caused him to run in the opposite direction. He'd run *to* her, in fact.

"I'll keep her safe, Mrs. Groves, I promise."

And Ellen had smiled at that, *actually* smiled, albeit weakly.

"You'll need some clothes, Ray," Shady had said. "We could swing by your place before Annie's?"

"Sure. I'll throw a few things in a bag."

"How long do you intend to be away?" Ellen had asked, a crack in her voice again.

"Just a few days, Mom."

"No longer than that, though. You do have work."

Work? A dead-end job on a dead-end highway? She supposed so.

After sharing a coffee and giving more reassurances to her mother that she'd be fine, that she'd be careful, Shady had grabbed her backpack, and Ellen had walked them to the door.

"You'll tell Dad?" Shady asked.

Ellen shook her head. "Not all of it, no."

"What will you say?"

"That an opportunity for a vacation came up, that's all."

"I love you, Mom."

Ellen's blue eyes were like glass themselves. Finally, she'd hugged Shady, Shady able to feel the gamut of emotions within her, which fear dominated.

"I love you too, and you hurry home now, d'ya hear?"

"I will. I promise."

And now it was just her, Ray, and Annie, on another highway but no longer a dead-end one. They were on the hunt for knowledge and understanding, thirsty for it, a couple of hundred miles still from Spokane, which itself was just over a hundred miles from Canada's border, the weather growing colder.

Annie had been surprised to find Ray was joining them, but as Shady had placed her trust in the older woman, so did Annie with Ray. Readily, in fact. Just like there was something about Mandy, there was something about Ray… that something—thankfully—being the polar opposite to darkness. What role he would play on this trip, she had no idea, and most likely Ray didn't know either. But even if he was only there for support, she was grateful for it. He'd seen her at her worst, the not-so-nice Shady, and still he wanted to be her friend. And that she considered a precious thing.

The more miles that fell away, the more rural the roads, the traffic sparse. The hills that surrounded them, the normally golden hills of Idaho, sun-kissed during the summer months, had lost their glow. Soon enough, they'd be peppered with white as the first of the snows fell.

They'd been listening to music on Shady's car radio—Miranda Lambert and Keith Urban rather than Shady's playlists, as she didn't want to inflict the likes of Deftones, Dinosaur Jr. and Green Day upon Annie. Mandy may have also been occupying the car, but the mood was calm, relaxed, that lead lining doing its job. Shady was nodding her head to another track when Ray leaned forward.

"Hey," she said, "whassup?"

He had his cell phone in his hand and was pointing to it.

"Do you know this song, Shady?"

"What song? Sorry, I can't turn my head to look."

Annie had, though, curiosity on her face.

"It's a song about you," Ray continued cheerfully. "You must have heard it?"

She hadn't. "I don't know what you're talking about."

"Can I put it on Bluetooth?"
"Go ahead."
"Thanks, Shady. Now, listen up."

Seconds later, there was the sound of clapping, whatever was about to play clearly a live recording. Once the clapping died down, the twang of a banjo filled the air.

"Sounds like a folk song," Shady began, but Ray hushed her. In the seat beside her, Annie began nodding her head, as though in recognition, before uttering, "Oh yes, of course!"

The bluegrass intro continued, and then a man's gravelly voice began to sing:

Wish I was in Shady Grove
Sittin' in a rockin' chair,
And if those blues would bother me,
I'd rock away from there.
Shady Grove, my little love
Shady Grove, I say
Shady Grove, my little love
I'm bound to go away.

Shady's mouth dropped open as she heard her own name, or near enough, being repeated, slowing the car slightly so that she could more equally divide her concentration between driving and listening, the singer working his way through yet more verses.

Now I want little Shady Grove
To say she'll be my wife
Shady Grove…
Shady Grove…
I'm bound to go away.

Not just slowing, Shady pulled off the road entirely and

came to a grinding halt.

"Shady?" Annie said, turning to her. "You okay?"

"I know that song," she breathed.

"So you *have* heard it before!" declared Ray.

"Yes. No. I don't think so. Shit!" She gripped the steering wheel tighter. "I don't think I've heard it, but that can't be right because...it's familiar."

"Shady." Annie sounded as confused as Shady felt. "You're crying."

"What?" Shady lifted a hand to see, and, sure enough, her fingertips came away wet. "Oh."

Ray was clearly mortified. "Hey, look, I'm sorry. If I'd known the song was going to upset you, I'd have never played it. I just...I didn't know if you knew it, that's all."

"Ray, it's fine. It's not your fault. I don't know why I'm crying."

"It's a sad song, I guess."

"It is, but that's not why." Shady turned to Annie, trying to fight back the wave of emotion that had risen up so suddenly. "I can hear those lyrics in my head, but it's not the singer's voice—it belongs to someone else."

"Who?" Annie asked, as patient as ever. "Remember what to do, dear. Focus."

Shady closed her eyes and did just that, but the moment had passed; whomever it was that she'd imagined singing the song had faded.

"What's happening to me?" she said after a brief silence, glancing at both Annie and Ray before continuing to stare straight ahead. "Ever since Mandy, I'm different."

"You know how you said Mandy was blamed for things she wasn't guilty of?" Annie seemed to be choosing her words carefully. "This could be an example of that. What you've just experienced might have nothing to do with her. It might have happened anyway, once you'd heard the song."

"A coincidence?"

"Or a correlation," Annie suggested. "So, a little more than that."

"Shady, listen to Annie. I think she's right."

"About it being a correlation?" Shady was surprised at the conviction in Ray's voice.

He nodded. "And that it would have happened anyway. You…you're special, Shady." His face flamed bright red again. "Anyone can see that."

There was more silence, and then Shady wiped at her eyes. "Better get going, then, shouldn't we," she said, rolling back onto the road. "We've got a mystery to solve."

More than one, it would seem.

CHAPTER TEN

At the entrance to the museum in Spokane, a woman waited for them. She was as diminutive as Annie and wringing her hands in a state of agitation.

Annie was out of the car first, hurrying toward the woman, Shady and Ray behind her.

"Ruth," she said. "Is everything okay?"

So this was Ruth Judd. Annie had mentioned her, the lady in charge.

There was no greeting from Ruth; instead, she asked where Mandy was.

"In the car," Annie answered.

"You're not bringing her in here."

"No, she's—"

"That wasn't a question, Annie. I mean it. She's not coming in. Not again." Turning to Annie's companions, she held out her hand. "You must be Shady Groves?"

Shady confirmed she was. "And this is Ray Bartlett. He's…" What could she say, coming along for the ride? She wanted to appear as solemn as Annie, as professional. "My colleague."

Ray turned to look at Shady and raised an eyebrow, but thankfully said nothing.

"Is it okay if we…erm…come in at least?" asked Annie,

a hint of confusion in her voice.

Still, Ruth hesitated. She was clearly contemplating their entry too, as if just being with the doll had made them, in turn, a danger. But then she'd been with Mandy too, as had her staff…

"Ruth?" Annie prompted.

Ruth sighed with obvious resignation before turning and leading them into the building. Shady had read that Spokane was home to the Northwest Museum of Arts and Culture, housed in an impressive modern structure. By comparison, this was a poor relation, an establishment set up to celebrate more localized history. It was not, however, like the Mason Town Museum, as had been pointed out on their journey here. "It's an ordinary museum, run by ordinary folks," Annie had said, "but of course we know, and I think they're coming to realize, that sometimes there's nothing ordinary about exhibits. Sometimes you just…run into bad luck. You run into something like Mandy."

Ruth led them through a variety of rooms, all of them quite modest in size and focusing on different periods of farming history, both in a social and economic sense. Before stepping over the threshold, Shady had prepared herself for the onslaught of emotions from those long gone, but it was all quite benign. What a shock, then, Mandy must have been.

Eventually they reached a closed door, a plaque declaring it "Private." Delving into her pocket for the key, Ruth opened it, switched on the light, and indicated toward a table and chairs.

"If you'd like to take a seat," she said before pulling out a chair and seating herself.

There was no comforting aroma of coffee in the air, and no offer of it either. Ruth clearly wanted them to say their piece and go. Before that, though, she herself had something to say.

"Ever since we took that doll in, things have changed around here."

Annie nodded her head slowly, as patient as ever.

"Go on, Ruth," she gently nudged when Ruth continued to gaze, not at them but at her hands.

"You know one of our volunteers, a young girl, found out that she had breast cancer?"

"Yes," Annie replied. "We do know that."

"It isn't looking good, not at all. She's having to undergo surgery. It's...it's awful."

"But what's that got to do with Mandy?" Annie dared to ask the question that was also on Shady's, and no doubt Ray's, lips.

"Because she was fine before that doll got here! No sign of illness at all."

"It could just be a coincidence," Shady offered, but Ruth was having none of it. She glared at them each in turn before leaning forward slightly and lowering her voice, seemingly afraid that even from the trunk of the car parked outside, Mandy might somehow hear them.

"That doll came here, and she polluted everything and everyone. I've told you what happened, Annie, when she was here—the crying that *everyone* heard, at least once or twice, the objects that were moved, that were flung to the floor, some breaking, in whichever room she was placed. People got sick...not as bad as poor Lily, admittedly, the girl who has cancer, but the sheer number of headaches, the coughs, the colds, the viruses… I'm telling you, it reached biblical proportions!"

Shady couldn't help but ask, "But how can you *guarantee* any of it was down to Mandy?"

Ruth's next sigh was ragged. "Because of the dreams."

"The dreams?" Ray asked, looking as rapt—and as confused—as the rest of them.

"We all dreamed of Mandy, every one of us who works here. Collectively, she *plagued* our dreams. She certainly plagued mine. That face of hers"—Ruth's shoulders became rigid—"it was always there, every time I shut my eyes. I'd see her in the darkness, staring at me, as if…as if she could see everything deep inside me, as if nothing was sacred, her lips beginning to move, turning up at the edges, as if…as if she was laughing at me."

"But you also said she cried," Shady said. "Not laughed."

Shady's comment nonplussed Ruth; she faltered slightly, bristled, even. "Whatever she does, whether it's laugh or cry, she does it with one purpose, and that's to torment."

"Dream connection," Ray murmured, "that's really something."

"Dream what?" Ruth asked, a frown distorting her features.

"All of you dreaming about Mandy," he elaborated, "it's…incredible. It's called dream connection, I think. What did you do, come in and compare notes?"

"Compare notes?" Something flashed in Ruth's eyes. "Are you mocking me, young man?"

"Sorry, I—"

Shady interrupted. "I've dreamed about Mandy too, and believe me, it wasn't a pleasant experience. I understand.

We *all* do. We're taking this very seriously, and that's why we're here."

Poor Ray looked so contrite; she didn't think for one minute he'd been goading Ruth, but he hadn't used the best turn of phrase. It did give food for thought, though. There might just be something to that whole comparison-of-notes business, which they could discuss privately. Right now, it was more important they got the information they'd come for.

"Who donated Mandy?" Shady asked.

"Paulina Dubinsky. It was one of many dolls donated when her mother died—"

"Lena," Shady mumbled.

Ruth frowned. "Yes, that's it, that was the mother's name. You've heard of her?"

"We've done some research," Annie replied, glossing over the truth.

"Oh, yes, well, Lena Dubinsky lived about thirty miles or so from here, in one of the old farmsteads just inside the Idaho border. The house itself is empty now, waiting to be sold or, better still, knocked down; that'd probably be safest. She collected dolls, had them all around, in every room, apparently. Most weren't antiques, weren't even in good shape, although I tend to think Lena did her best by them. Made them their clothes, that kinda thing, but ultimately of no interest to a museum."

"But Mandy was," Annie said.

Ruth hung her head. "But Mandy was," she repeated dully. "And we were keen to have her. Although…even as I took the doll, I sensed something…that I was making a mistake."

As Ruth seemed to sink further into reverie, Annie took the reins. "We think Mandy is different too…" Was Shady being paranoid, or had Annie's eyes flickered sideways toward her when she said that? "That she's special. We're trying to find out what sets her apart."

"Special?" Ruth almost spat the word at them. "What a way to put it!" She tapped at her temple. "I've told you, she gets in your head, in here, she burrows her way in. I still dream about her, you know. And I'm not the only one. Lily…Lily may die because of her!"

Shady was shocked to see tears in Ruth's eyes, but Annie continued talking in a calm manner. "Ruth, you know what I do. It's no secret, not among us curators, at any rate."

"That's why I sent her to you. You'd be able to deal with her."

"Just," Annie said, her smile a little strained. "I'm only just able to deal with her. But you also know my ethos regarding these types of things."

"That if you understand something, you won't fear it."

"Exactly. Or fear it less. Understanding is key."

Ruth shook her head. "But I don't want to understand Mandy, and I speak on behalf of all my colleagues when I say that. None of us want to be…*haunted* by her."

"Then tell us where the farmstead is. Because we need to go there."

* * *

Ruth had outright refused to give them a contact number for Paulina. She'd also been reluctant to tell them the address of the farmhouse, murmuring something about client confidentiality. That was, of course, to be treated with the utmost respect, but under the circumstances, there had to be some leeway. Finally, with a frown on her face, she'd jotted down the Dubinsky address.

"You're not going to break in, though, are you? I won't be held accountable."

"We're not criminals," was Annie's reply.

Back on the road, Shady was apprehensive about visiting Mandy's last proper home and wondered what Mandy was feeling too. Despite the lead box, she could sense her, nudging at the edges of perception, but principally contained…for now.

Ray broke into her thoughts. "All of them dreaming about Mandy, Mandy being responsible for illnesses, for everything they said she was. Do you, like, believe that?"

Rather than answer, Shady looked toward Annie, keen to hear her response.

"I think Mandy as an object gets blamed for a lot," said Annie, "and she always has, as we've discovered. But yes, when you said, 'compare notes,' I couldn't help but agree with you. Auto-suggestion is a powerful thing. It can easily provoke the herd response. People *want* to identify with each other. They want something in common, even if that thing is fear."

"They bring it on themselves?"

"They do, Ray," Annie continued. "If they believe in the legend and not the truth."

Shady concerned herself with more immediate problems. "You said we weren't going to break into the Dubinsky house, so what are we going to do, just stand outside it?"

Annie smiled. "I said nothing of the sort. I simply

assured her we're not criminals."

"So, we *are* breaking in?" asked Ray, his eyes widening.

"We'll test the doors at least," Annie tempered.

"And are we all going in?" Shady asked.

"Mandy too, you mean?"

"Yes."

"That's your decision, Shady, nobody else's."

"But if we want the best results…?"

"Then it may be necessary, yes."

As they neared the house, Shady could feel the pull of it. It was perhaps the ultimate object, one whose walls were soaked in the residue of past occupants, right down to the wire.

"Weave white light around yourself. Ray, you too."

Annie's voice was so low, Shady barely caught it, but yes, she was doing just that, protecting herself. On the way over, Annie had also briefed Ray about keeping himself protected. Shady was surprised at how accepting he was, not batting an eyelid at what he was being asked to do, therefore drawing on white light, acting from good intent and good intent only, *not* seeking thrills, only there to help, to understand. "Yes, ma'am," he kept saying, almost reverently. Of course, plenty of people held an interest in the paranormal, including some of her friends, but Shady doubted if any would volunteer, as he had, to travel with a haunted doll, one capable of wreaking havoc.

They'd turned off the main highway and were currently on a minor road. There were other houses dotted around and about, away from the road, some of them fancy, with several cars in the driveway and verandas on which to sit and sip at something at the end of a busy day. They were family homes, probably, bustling with life, as Lena's had once been…Lena and…Daniel, that was it, her husband's name. They'd been at the helm of a happy, loving family for years and years. That she knew that, could sense it with their address not even in sight yet, caused Shady's breath to hitch. She'd told her mother her ability was increasing, and she was right. Mandy had unleashed something inside her, and if she could control it, then there was a chance she'd be able to control Mandy too, a theory she clung to.

"Is that it there?"

Ray was pointing to a house in the distance, the only one hereabouts, all others having been left behind. This minor road they were on, it wasn't desolate; the highway was just a few miles back, and yet it had exactly that feel, with nothing but tall trees, farmland and gently rolling hills on either side of them, stretching into mountains in the distance, an endless spine of them.

"I think so, yeah," she replied, noticing that Annie remained mute—deep in concentration, perhaps, ramping up their protection on a psychic level, at least.

Taking her foot off the accelerator, she let them cruise toward it before cutting the engine.

Lena Dubinsky's house. Mandy's house. It stood alone in fields still being tended, although on scanning the horizon, there were no workers in sight. Outside the house, a realtor's board creaked in the breeze. It was up for sale, as Ruth had said, but remained empty, and Shady could understand why. A woman had died here, a nugget of information that would have to be disclosed to potential buyers, making it so damned hard to shift. A shame, really, as it had been an ideal family home, before time and

Mandy'd had their way with it.

As she got out of the car to stand in front of the house, she could imagine well enough the children that had played here: two, three, or was it more than that? Four, perhaps? Lena and Daniel themselves would sit on the porch, watching their children, smiling indulgently, or they'd be tilling the land, back-breaking but rewarding work. A happy place. Safe and secure. It had that whole *Little House on the Prairie* vibe, a TV series Shady had loved as a child. But then Daniel had died—Shady could hear faint screams, not Mandy's this time but belonging to a man, Daniel, she was certain of it, scratching at the atmosphere, scarring it—and one by one, the kids had left home, left Lena even more alone. But Lena had been...determined. Shady sensed that strongly. She'd been a woman with a backbone of steel, and so she'd tried her utmost to remain positive, to remain useful. She'd been another collector, as Shady already knew, of dolls, dolls that she had loved, that would keep her company, ease her loneliness, filling the house again, each and every room.

Shady started to walk, Annie and Ray flanking her but remaining silent, allowing her to immerse herself in another person's life.

Lena would go out scouring local towns for dolls in need of TLC. Returning to the farm, she'd do as Shady was doing now, park just outside and hurry toward the front door, opening it, stepping inside, and welcoming the dolls to their new home, their sanctuary.

Shady climbed those same steps to the front porch, stopped in front of the same door, her hand reaching out as Lena's had. Grasping the handle, she turned it. It refused to budge. *Damn!*

"Don't worry," said Ray, "I'll go check around back."

They weren't criminals, but the level of connection she was experiencing would fade if they didn't find a way in—and quickly. A few moments later, they heard Ray calling.

"Shady! Annie! Over here."

Shady looked at Annie, saw the eagerness she, too, felt, that flare of hope. "Come on," she said.

They rounded the porch to see Ray standing next to an open window at the back of the house, one low enough for all of them to negotiate without much effort.

"Voila!" he said, grinning.

"They're a trusting lot out here in the country," Annie responded. "It's what I was counting on."

"We're doing this, then? We're going in?" Shady confirmed.

"I think we have to," Annie's said. "You and I, Shady, at any rate. Ray, it's probably best if you keep watch, in case the local sheriff happens to be out on a run."

Although clearly disappointed, he agreed good-naturedly enough.

Shady ventured closer to the window and pulled the net curtain aside, grey in color when once it had gleamed white. Beyond it was a kitchen, stripped of all the essentials, just bare cupboards lining the walls and a sink whose tap dripped intermittently. Preparing to climb through the gap, she stopped. Mandy had been here, in this very room. In her mind's eye Shady could see her, lying on the tiles, staring upward, and Lena looking down at her, horrified.

Mandy.

Alone in the car, in a box comparable to a coffin, and

crying.

Crying so hard.

The doll had shed a lot of tears here.

This was her home, hers.

Straightening up, Shady turned to Annie. "We do need Mandy. If only to stop her crying."

CHAPTER ELEVEN

Shady was right. Bringing Mandy back into the farmhouse had, for the moment, calmed her. She had about her instead a sense of anticipation or perhaps eagerness. For Mandy, this had been her last home, but for them it was just the beginning, this farmstead in rural Idaho.

Clutching the doll, Shady gazed down upon her head. "We may never know everything about her," she remarked, as much to herself as to Annie as they ventured farther into the kitchen, Ray doing as he'd promised and keeping a watchful eye outside for law enforcement.

"True," Annie replied, her voice somber, "pieces of the jigsaw may well be lost forever, but isn't that true of everything and everyone? What we may succeed in is learning enough. Now, dear, do you want me to hold Mandy? You may need your hands to…to feel your way around."

It made practical sense, what Annie'd said; even so, Shady felt a surprising reluctance as she handed the doll over, one that was…mutual…was that it? The bond between herself and Mandy was strengthening, but whether that was for better or for worse, she wouldn't like to guess.

Free of Mandy, she began to open cupboards and drawers, not sure what else to do in a room that had once been the beating heart of a home. Closing her eyes after a while, she tried to see what used to be there rather than what now took its place, which was a heart that had stilled. The present seemed so stagnant, but the past... Ah, there it was, gradually coming alive.

Where'd I put them? Oh, darn it, where'd I put my keys this time?

An old lady was turning her head from side to side, her eyes glazed with confusion.

I put them in the hall, or maybe this drawer. I'm sure I did. Why aren't they here now?

There was a sudden smell of burning, acrid in its intensity.

Not again! I...I didn't even realize I'd put food in the oven.

"Shady?" It was Annie's voice. "Are you okay?"

"Yeah, yeah, sure. I'm starting to get a sense of someone—Lena, I think."

"Okay, that's good. Do you want to stay in the kitchen or move on?"

"We can move on."

Opening her eyes, Shady half expected to still see Lena standing in front of her, a specter, a vision, a ghost, but it was just the kitchen, devoid of everyone but them.

"All okay out there?" she asked Ray before leaving.

"Sure is. How about in there?"

Shady looked at Annie before answering, at the doll in her arms. "It's fine." So far.

In the hallway, with no light bulb overhead to relieve the gloom, she got a sense of Lena rushing by, a busy woman, looking for purpose, always. That's what defined her: *usefulness*.

You're useless... Shady pushed such familiar words to the back of her mind, refusing to let them rile her. She wasn't useless, and Lena hadn't been either. What she'd done, collecting dolls, had such good intent behind it— valiant intent, Shady decided.

They turned left into what must have been a sitting room, also devoid of furniture, a fireplace at the far end, in which flames had once leapt and crackled. Shady made her way over to it, but even before she reached it or placed her hands upon it, she got a sense of how many dolls had once occupied this room where the family used to gather. There'd been legions of them, Lena's new family, whom she'd loved, all those maternal feelings inside her not having dissipated over time; if anything, they'd grown more intense. There were dolls of all kinds and sizes, baby dolls like Mandy, dolls that emulated young children, boy dolls as well as girls, each and every one christened with a name. She'd sit some beside her as she watched TV or read a book or...knitted. She'd spend hours knitting for them, her charges, her wards, the reason she continued to live.

She loved what was plastic, essentially, what couldn't die or leave her.

Ah, Violetta, I made a jacket for you, didn't I? To complement the color of your eyes. Where is it? Oh, now, where could it have gotten to? I made it especially for you.

Again, there was that sense of confusion, one that drew Shady away from the fireplace and over to the window.

It's night again? Where does the time go? It just seems to...melt.

"Annie," Shady called out. "I think Lena was ill."

"In what way?"

"She had problems with her memory, dementia or, you know, Alzheimer's."

"It happens," Annie said, somewhat resignedly.

"I don't think anyone knew. I don't think *she* knew. There are dolls…everywhere."

"What about Mandy?"

"No Mandy, not yet."

"Do you want to carry on through to other rooms?"

Shady nodded.

There was another reception room on the ground level and a more formal dining room, one she sensed was used only on special occasions, but certainly dolls had been placed in there, in various poses, some as if communing with each other, others staring blankly ahead.

They climbed the stairs, Shady shivering not only as she stood at the foot of them but also as she reached the top, having to take several deep breaths, knowing she'd return to those spots.

Dolls had also filled all four bedrooms. The woman truly was obsessed. As Shady stood in the smallest room, empty aside from net curtains at its windows, she asked herself as Lena had, when she'd stood there too, staring at such emptiness: How could life change so much?

"The dolls *saved* her," Shady murmured, "in so many ways. They gave her back what she so badly missed. But one doll, Mandy, went way beyond that."

Turning to Annie, Shady signaled she wanted to hold Mandy again. With the doll back in her arms, she imagined the white light extending to include her too.

"The light's not useless," she said—she *insisted*. "It protects and it heals." Immediately, she felt something lurch inside the doll, an emotion spat back at her and filled with loathing.

"Shady? Are you quite all right?"

Shady was aware she'd staggered, but nonetheless she held a hand up to fend off Annie. This is what they'd come here for, what they had to know.

No matter how intense the feeling, how repugnant, Shady stood her ground. "What did you do to Lena?" she wanted to know. "Why'd you hurt someone that was only ever kind to you?"

Oh, she was a dark thing, this doll, but how Lena had been taken in by her; she'd wanted to save her, this one in particular. In her mind's eye, Shady could see a junk store…a shelf…something to do with a cat…there was definitely a cat in the picture…that's where Lena had first seen Mandy. *Oh my, you're special,* she'd said. *You're a pretty thing. You're…different.*

Shady moved out of the small bedroom and onto the landing, turning toward a bedroom at the front of the house, the one that had belonged to Lena, all that she was seeing beginning to build.

This is your home, Mandy. You'll have pride of place—you can sleep with me, right here in my bedroom. I'll pop you on the pillow beside me. You'll never be alone again. Neither of us will be.

Hatred, cold and bleak, poured from this thing, but Lena couldn't sense it… She could sense something, though. What?

"Confused."

"Who? Lena?" Annie's voice sounded so far away.

"No, not Lena this time. Me."

"What about?"

"What she felt for this doll, it was…overwhelming."

Lena didn't condone favorites; no mother would. But this doll *was* her favorite. She responded to something other than the bleakness of it.

There, there, don't cry. I'll make it better. Mommy will make everything better.

Could Lena hear her crying? *Actually* hear her?

You mustn't cry so hard. There's no need, not anymore. Hush now, Mandy.

Mandy! Now come on, you have to stop it. Your crying upsets everyone, especially me.

Mandy, why won't you listen? Good girls listen to their mothers, don't you know that?

"Annie," Shady whispered, "I think Lena was psychic. She could hear Mandy, I'm certain of it."

"Others have heard her, though," Annie reminded her. "At the museum."

"Ruth said she heard her; others may have just *thought* they did."

"Ah yes, auto-suggestion."

Exactly that, prompting the herd reaction, as they'd discussed. "Lena was confused. She had problems with her memory, but with Mandy it was all crystal clear…"

Shady's voice trailed off as her mind filled with more of the woman who'd lived there.

Mandy, this is getting too much, really it is. I can't sleep anymore because of your crying, and I need to sleep, just a little. Oh, come on, let me sleep, honey.

Anger again, such patience wearing thin. *That's it! You're moving out of my bedroom. I'm sorry to have to do this,*

Mandy, but I've told you before, I need to sleep.

Not moving slowly now but with a sense of urgency, fearful that the visions might fall away and, with them, any chance of understanding this situation, Shady entered another bedroom.

Mandy! What have you done? The mess in here! Oh, poor Violetta! You've flung her to the ground. And Peter and James and Claudette. That's so naughty. I won't have it, y'hear?

Not only dolls had been flung to the ground but objects too, some of them smashing.

There was screaming, a sound that reminded Lena far too much of Daniel's screams and how he'd been dragged from this world when all he wanted to do was stay.

She'd lift her hands to her ears to drown out the sound, but Mandy would only scream louder; she'd cry harder. She persecuted this woman.

And yet Lena still tried to love her.

She'd hold Mandy, cradle her, whisper over and over that she needn't cry because she had a mother now, one that doted on her, that never again would she know the pain of abandonment.

Shady was amazed. How could she continue to love this thing? *What did you see in her?*

Whatever confusion Lena had suffered, it was getting worse. Mandy knew that; Mandy played on it. And finally, Lena resorted to blaming Mandy for it.

It's you, isn't it? You're the one that's hidden my keys?

Oh, look! You've turned on the gas, left it burning, nearly killed us all.

I put my shoes away, I know I did. You left them out so I could trip over them.

Stop bullying the other dolls. This is their home too.
Stop crying!
Please!
SHUT THE HELL UP!

Night turned into day, day into night; hour upon hellish hour passed.

Mandy was moved downstairs, was tossed away at one point, in the trash can. It had damned near broken Lena's heart to do that, but didn't she realize she'd then gone back to retrieve the doll—that it was her who'd knocked the can over, spilling Mandy onto the kitchen floor, unable to cast her aside after all? Yes, she'd grown fearful of her, but love was notorious for taking its time to vanish.

"Dear, be careful. You must be careful. Perhaps give me the doll, let me hold her for a while."

Despite Annie's request, Shady wouldn't hand the doll over. "You preyed on an ill woman. You made her worse."

Shady could hear the crying too, the relentlessness of it enough to drive anyone mad.

"Shady, please, you need to be careful."

That's exactly what you did, didn't you? Drove her all the way into madness.

Although she knew she was walking, Shady had no idea where to anymore; there was just an urge to put one foot in front of the other, that desire relentless too.

What kind of thing spits in the face of love?

Crying, screaming…hissing… It was all there, amplified, drowning out whatever it was that Annie now tried to tell Shady: "Careful…be careful… Ray…Ray!"

How could Lena have stood this for so long?

I'll make you stop. I will, I'll make you. I mean it this time.

That's what Lena had said. Because even mothers had a breaking point. So often exalted into supernatural beings themselves, the truth was, they could only be pushed so far.

I mean it this time.

Mandy had to be stopped; finally, Lena accepted that. *You're dangerous. I'll stop you! I will!*

"SHADY, NO!"

There was a hand on her, whose? It tried to restrain her. Too late, though. She was flying. Was that it? But how could she be flying? It was impossible and yet…there was no ground beneath her feet, not anymore. And where was Mandy? She wasn't in her hands anymore either because they were too busy flailing on either side of her, clutching now at thin air.

What's happening?

"It's all right, it's okay, I've got you. Shit!"

She clashed with someone, arms coming around her, and then she was falling again but not onto hard ground, something considerably softer—Ray.

He grunted as the air left him.

"Are you all right?" Annie rushed to catch up with them. "Oh my goodness, Shady, it all happened so fast. I couldn't stop you. I couldn't believe my eyes either. You stood at the top of the stairs, and then you just…*threw* yourself forwards. You hurled yourself down them."

Trying to catch her breath, Shady couldn't respond. Instead, she turned her head in the direction of that incessant crying, to where Mandy was lying on the floor to the side of them, just as Lena had lain—not intact, though, as Mandy was, but with her neck broken.

An accident. That's what it had looked like.

But it was no accident.

If she'd had any doubts before, she didn't now.

Mandy was responsible for killing Lena Dubinsky.

Shady grimaced as she shifted her weight off Ray, both of them finding it a struggle initially to sit up. Ray straightened his sweatshirt, which had ridden up to reveal such pale flesh. He looked as bewildered as Shady but not for the same reasons. Not at all.

For him it was because he'd rushed in to find Shady falling down the stairs.

For her it was because the doll's tears weren't just bitter, they were *heartfelt*.

CHAPTER TWELVE

Ray had done the math, thanks to the help of Google Maps.

"A junk store, nearby, something to do with cats. I reckon it's in Catskill, about ten miles west."

All three were back in the car, Mandy in her coffin, as Shady persisted in thinking of it.

Annie was still pale. "We don't have to go there right now. We can find a place to stay, a nice motel somewhere and just…rest."

Shady shook her head. "Let's go, get it over and done with."

"But, dear, you very nearly…" If she was going to say *died*, she clearly thought better of it.

Shady turned to her. "I'm okay, honestly." She also glanced at Ray, wincing slightly. "You sure you have no aches or pains from when I landed on you?"

"None at all. But Annie's right, it might be good to call it a day."

"Do you need to?"

Ray said he didn't.

"Do you, Annie?"

"I'm perfectly fine. It's you I'm worried about."

"Then let's go to Catskill, to this junk store. We need to know if that's where Lena got Mandy." Glancing at her watch, she added, "It's pretty late in the day, but it could still be open."

Insisting she was okay to drive, Shady pulled away from Lena Dubinsky's home, empty of everything except the memory of Mandy and all the dolls the old woman had promised not to abandon. Yet that's exactly what had happened, many of them not making it into stores at all but an incinerator somewhere, or landfill. But Mandy had survived. Mandy, it seemed, *always* survived.

There was silence as they drove, each of them perhaps, in their own way, coming to terms with what had transpired. Shady still held that Lena had latent psychic abilities, which Mandy had somehow awoken. The old woman had bonded with her, in both a meaningful and terrifying way. And if Shady was not mistaken, the doll had been upset by her passing, horrified by it, even though she'd willed her toward that death, had wantonly caused it.

Mandy, what a conundrum you are, thought Shady, more determined to chip away at her story.

Eventually, she broke the moratorium of silence in the car, having been in her head long enough and hoping they might finally process, together, all that had happened.

"You got there just at the right time," she said to Ray.

"It's a knack of mine," he said, tongue in cheek, shrugging it off though his cheeks were as red as ever.

"I did try and stop you," Annie muttered, clearly forlorn that she hadn't.

"I know you did." Shady reached out and touched her arm. "It wasn't your fault."

"We have to be more careful in future," Annie said.

"We do. We will."

"Maybe we should destroy her. Maybe it's safer after all."

Shady was stunned. "Annie, that goes against everything you've told me so far!"

"Hey," Ray said, leaning forward, "fill me in. Am I missing something here?"

"No, you know everything that's going on, it's just, well…"

When Shady faltered, Annie took a deep breath. "In extreme cases," she said, "it seems people can link to a specific object—after their death, I mean."

"Their spirits?" asked Ray.

"That's right. They become attached, or you could call it anchored. We don't know the nature yet of what inhabits Mandy. That's what this is about, trying to find out. If whatever it is, is intelligent and not residual, then that leaves a dilemma of what to do with the object it inhabits."

"Whether it's kept or destroyed?"

"If it's destroyed and what possesses it is non-spirit, there's a danger it might latch on to something or someone else, and that someone could then be vulnerable."

"And the alternative is?"

"*One* alternative," Annie stressed, "is we keep it contained."

"Okay, I see…I think. And by 'non-spirit,' we are, of course, talking about the demonic?"

"Yes," admitted Annie. "We are. Although bear in mind, it's a broad term."

"That box you've got Mandy in, though, that seems to subdue her. Why not just keep her locked away in that forevermore?"

"Because we don't last forevermore, do we? Someone else

will come across Mandy. They'll…unleash her. Someone…innocent, like Lena."

"And you really don't think it's worth burying her, like I buried Gina's mirror?" Shady asked. "Sealing her in that lead lined box and digging real deep?"

"Trouble is," replied Annie, "things get dug up, be it deliberately or unwittingly."

"So, back to Plan A. We strive to understand her," Ray said.

"Plan A," Annie mused before sighing again. "Look, I've been doing this a long time, but I'm only a collector, not an exorcist of any description. Although…I do know one or two people who could help in that way if it becomes necessary. Good people," she quickly added, "those that align themselves with the light. What I've found since I've been doing this is what I've told you both already: it's knowledge that empowers us. A simple truth and applicable to many areas in life. When you understand something, when you empathize with it, even, when you drag it out of the darkness and expose it, that's often enough for what's in it to gradually break down. It's an approach that's served me well so far. But in achieving this, I won't put your lives in danger."

"It's my choice to carry on," Shady pointed out.

"Mine too," said Ray.

If Shady expected Annie to look heartened by their response, she was wrong.

"Annie," Ray continued, "what happens when what's in an object begins to break down—eventually, I mean?"

"It returns to source."

"Source?"

"Where it came from."

"Hell?"

"Again, Ray, that's a pretty broad term."

"But your method of dealing with this kinda stuff has been successful?"

"Yes," replied Annie, "it has been." From sitting there slumped, she sat upright. "Okay, agreed, we continue with what we're doing, we give it our best shot, but *only* that, no more."

"You know," said Ray, grinning, "plenty of jobs are fraught with danger, not just this one. No need to feel bad about it."

A job. Certainly, it was one more worthwhile than plying people with burgers, fries, and Coke, Shady mused, although that stuff could also kill you in the end if you had too much of it. Whereas this…this could *save* people, from something unknown but real nonetheless. No matter how many people tried to deny it, didn't believe in anything otherworldly—Jesus, Mary, Joseph, and all the saints excepted—it was all too real.

There was so much to get her head around, but at least she wasn't alone in having to do so, not anymore. She wasn't belittling her ability either; she was beginning to believe in it.

Hey, she thought, *it was never me who belittled it. It's always been my folks.*

But it had had an effect, up until now, the *desired* effect.

A sign came into view: *Welcome to Catskill. We're glad to have you!* Shady leaned forward slightly and scanned the horizon. What lay ahead looked like any other small town with barely anything to it, just a collection of scattered houses and a main street of low 1920s flat-roofed, red-bricked stores hosting the bare essentials, including a pharmacy, café, gas station, and…junk.

There it was: The Good Old Days, still open, looking as if its insides were jam-packed.

"Shady, watch out!"

Both Ray's voice and the loud blast of a car horn sent shockwaves right through her.

"Shit!" she swore, swerving the car to the right, thankfully into an empty space.

A truck sped by, Shady catching a glimpse of the driver. Not only had he honked at her, he was gesturing too.

"Asshole," she muttered.

"Agreed on that," Ray said.

Annie was as ashen-faced as she'd been back at Lena's house. "Just be…careful," she warned again, before readjusting glasses that had become slightly crooked.

A few moments later, standing side by side, all three of them stared across the street at the store. Annie asked if they were ready.

"I'm ready," Ray said.

"Me too," Shady declared, looking both ways before crossing the road.

* * *

"Sure, yeah, of course I remember Lena Dubinsky. It was so sad what happened to her. What a terrible way to go! Thank God she was found quickly is all I can say. They're good people around here, you know. If someone hasn't shown up for a while, especially someone like Lena, an old lady living by herself, then there are those who'll take it upon themselves to check it out or notify the sheriff, as was the case with Lena. It was Sal Timpson who did that, from the grocery store. Lena hadn't been in to collect her regular order. A day passed and then a few more, and, well, he picked up the phone, God bless him."

The woman, who'd introduced herself as Greta Hollick, went on to shake her head in a rueful manner.

"Terrible thing when people end their days old and alone," she said. "It's our Christian duty to be there for each other, to keep a watchful eye."

None of the three could disagree with that.

"Forgive me for asking, but how well did you folks know her?" Greta continued. "Enough to know she had a thing about dolls, at least."

"Just a little," Annie replied, her voice convincing enough in its veiling of the truth. "It's just…one of the dolls she so loved she bought from here, didn't she?"

"She bought several from here, truth be told, but the last one, yeah, I remember it. It was about a year before she died. Didn't even know we had it in here, to be honest; it was something my husband picked up on his rounds. He sat it in the window and didn't tell me." Shady wasn't sure if Greta was aware of this, but she'd screwed up her face at the memory, and one finger started to pick at the other. "Lena was sweet on it, though. She spotted it and came right in, offered me fifty bucks—a lot, really, when I think about it. Oh jeepers…"

"What is it? What's the matter?" Annie asked.

"I shouldn't have taken that much. I feel so bad about it now. It wasn't worth it, truly. For starters, it had a crack right down its face. It was also pretty grubby; its white dress and bonnet were soiled. I just...once I had it in my hands, I had a feeling about it, you know?"

Shady straightened her back on hearing this, noted Ray and Annie doing the same.

"What kind of feeling?" Shady asked.

"That I wanted rid of it, at any cost. I just didn't want it in my store. And so I took the money she stuffed into my hands, but to be honest, I would have taken five dollars not fifty. Heck, I would've given it to her for free if she'd kicked up a fuss. I don't like dolls, do you? They creep me out. Always have, sitting there, their eyes following you wherever you go, just...staring at you. Ever heard of those reborn dolls? The ones that really do look like little babies, right down to the smallest detail? Weird, just weird. Saw a documentary on them once, sent shivers down my spine. People get so obsessed with them. Nope, don't like dolls. Never understood Lena's fascination or anyone else's, for that matter."

Shady could have told her about Lena, at least, but decided not to.

"Do you know where your husband got the doll from?" Annie asked.

Greta shook her head. "No clue, sorry. Like I said, Bryan does the rounds and I work the store. That's the way it's always been, the way it suits us." A store that was just like a museum, except everything in it was for sale. What was the saying? One man's trash was another man's treasure. Even something like Mandy was a treasure...to some. The frown on Greta's face deepened, becoming suspicious. "Why d'you wanna know about the doll anyhow? What's it to you?"

Like Annie, Greta was a woman in her later years, around sixty-five, Shady guessed. She could have been younger, but Shady didn't think so; the lines on her face were just too deep, especially around her lips—smoker's lips, clearly, all that dragging on a cigarette having made its mark. She was weathered, of average height, neither fat nor slim, and she was tough. She'd been around the block a time or two, and she didn't frighten easily, but Mandy…Mandy had given her the heebie-jeebies sure enough.

Annie was poised to answer her question, as was Shady, but Ray beat them to it.

"We're tenerologists," he announced.

Greta looked aghast, as did the other two. "You're what?"

"Collectors of dolls," he enlightened. "That's the term for it, *tenerologist*. Mandy, the doll Mrs. Dubinsky bought from you, is particularly fascinating because she's so rare."

"She's worth something, you mean?"

"In historical terms more than monetary, but that might change if we can track her history, her…um…provenance, that's it. Everyone loves a story, and those who collect dolls love it even more if they know a little about…about…the journey she's been on, like who owned her before, that kinda thing. Mrs. Hollick, is it possible you could ask Mr. Hollick where he got Mandy from? We don't mind waiting to hear, or we could phone you back for that information?"

"She might be worth something?" Of all that Ray had said, that was the thing Greta latched on to. "If she is, perhaps I didn't sell her too cheap after all." She squinted eyes that were already narrow. "In fact, she might be worth more than fifty bucks. A lot more."

"If that's the case, then of course we won't forget you," Ray said, causing both Shady and Annie to raise an eyebrow. About to interject, Shady changed her mind when Greta withdrew her cell phone and started punching a number into it.

"Hang on," she said, "Bry's only upstairs. I'll get him to come see you."

Her husband answered quickly enough, Greta turning her back on them and stepping slightly away. Annie was smiling at Ray, and Shady followed suit. *Why d'you wanna know about the doll anyhow?* That was a difficult question to answer; certainly, they couldn't tell her the truth, but Ray had fielded it perfectly. Not only that, he'd played on what was arguably a human's greatest weakness—greed. No matter how good people were, how much they might look out for their friends and neighbors, if they believed a windfall was due to them, they usually took the bait.

Silently Shady applauded Ray. She'd had no clue there was even a term for a doll collector, although perhaps she should have; after all, there was a name for most things nowadays.

"Where'd you learn the term *terrerologists*?" she whispered to Ray while Greta was busy.

"Tenerologists," he corrected her, "and I didn't. I made it up."

Shady had to suppress a grin as Greta turned back to face them. A moment later, a door opened behind her and a man walked through—Bryan, Shady presumed, around the same age and height as his wife but with a ruddier complexion and a shiny strip of baldness on his head.

"What's this I'm hearing about Lena's doll? Or should I say *my* doll before Greta sold it on."

His doll? Yes, it had been, but for how long?

Annie'd had the doll for around six months. Before her, Ruth had it at the museum in Spokane for another six months or so. From Greta, Shady figured that Lena'd had it for the best part of a year, and before that it had been Bryan's, the owner of The Good Old Days.

Shady stepped forward and held out her hand, introducing them all. Bryan shook her hand, then Annie's, then Ray's, but his impatience matched that of the truck driver who'd nearly run them off the road; he surely wanted to know if, after years of selling junk, his luck had changed in some small way. Inwardly Shady sighed. They really ought to play it down a bit, but not before they got the information they'd come for.

"Mr. Hollick," she asked, "how long was Mandy in your care?"

"My care? That's a fancy way of putting it!" He thought for a moment, then shrugged. "A few months, maybe more. She was out back for a while, in storage. Then one day I put her in the window—"

"Forgot to tell me about it," his wife reminded him.

"Forgot to tell Greta, and hey-ho, she was sold. Hadn't even gotten around to pricing her up."

"*Had* you told me, we coulda discussed it," Greta said, stonily.

"Yeah, yeah, we coulda. Anyways, Greta sold her to Lena for fifty bucks. Was that too little? Was she worth more? Come to think of it, she must have been. She's an antique, from the 1920s, I'd say, made by that big toy company…you know the one, what was it called?"

"Hayle and Co.," Annie replied.

"That's it, in New York. Jeepers, she's traveled a long way, that one, and probably a limited edition. Never seen one in circulation before."

A jolt passed through Shady. New York…New York… There was something about New York, something that hadn't clicked before. Of course, New York! That's where the little girl in the big house with all the toys was from. Mandy *had* traveled a long way; Bryan was right. Kate Jane…a cossetted girl, a girl born from craving and who was guilty of craving too, a girl who was wrong, who'd ended up…where? Not somewhere as grand as the four walls Shady had seen, far less salubrious than that. An asylum? Was that right? Destroyed, she and her parents.

Not by Mandy, though, not then.

But still there was crying, so much crying…

"Shady?"

"Miss, are you all right?"

Both Annie and Greta were asking after her. Ray and Bryan also looked concerned.

"Sorry," she said, "I…it's quite hot in here. I think I just spun out."

"Would you like some water?" offered Greta.

"Oh no…thanks. I'll be fine."

Bryan, for one, accepted her word and was mentioning the term *limited edition* again. "The more limited she is, the better," he mused.

"Bry," Greta reminded him, "she had a dirty, great crack down her face. That limits her value."

"To some," responded Ray, "to others not so much. She's antique. It's kinda expected."

"Where did you get her from?" Shady could feel her own impatience on the rise; she was keen to get going, to continue the trail.

As if aware of her eagerness, Bryan narrowed his eyes. "She came from a house call up near Montague—not far from here, about thirty miles as the crow flies. Old Mrs. Arbutt had her."

Greta clucked. "Old Mrs. Arbutt? You got the doll from *her*?"

"Uh-huh," Bryan replied before adding, "This provenance thing, is it really necessary?"

"To the enthusiast, yes." Ray was on a roll, liking this game, sounding very self-assured. "You wouldn't believe how much value these things add."

"And I'll get my cut?"

"If she's as rare as we think."

Annie butted in. "Do you think Mrs. Arbutt would mind a visit from us?"

To their surprise, Greta and Bryan burst out laughing.

"Is something funny?" Annie asked, a frown on her face.

"Oh, I'm sure Mrs. Arbutt wouldn't mind," Bryan said.

"When do you plan on going?" Greta questioned.

Not today, time was no longer on their side. They needed to find accommodation hereabouts and rest awhile.

"If it's okay with everybody," she replied to Greta, "and, of course, Mrs. Arbutt too, we could visit with her in the morning. If you have a number for her, I could ring—"

"She won't answer the phone, never does," Greta said. "Mrs. Arbutt...well, she's a law unto herself. You'll discover that soon enough. Here." She grabbed a pen from the countertop and scribbled onto some paper. "This is her address. Just turn up. She's usually in."

"And you really don't think she'll mind?" Shady checked.

"She'll be fine." Again, Bryan seemed amused. "Be interesting to see what you make of her, though. After all, if you think Lena's nuts—"

"Bryan! Come on, now. You're going too far."

In answer to his wife's admonishment, Bryan just shrugged.

Annie had clearly had enough. "Thank you so much for your help, Mr. and Mrs. Hollick. We'll visit Mrs. Arbutt tomorrow, and if there are any significant developments, we'll let you know."

Bryan's eyes were full of anticipation. "A windfall, eh? And with a doll like that. Who'd a guessed it?"

"A *possible* windfall," Shady reiterated as she and Ray also said goodbye, turning to leave.

Just before they reached the door, Bryan called after them. Not only that, he'd stepped forward, not looking excited now but more thoughtful. The sun had all but faded, and the lights in the store were no better than in Annie's museum. Because of that, half of him stood in darkness, the other half in light.

"You know, all the while that doll was out back, things happened there."

"Things?" said Annie, glancing briefly at Shady.

"Strange things. I'd put something down, and it'd go missing. Items would also get damaged. Not by me—it wasn't my fault or Greta's either." He raised his hands and gestured around him. "This is our business; it's how we make a living. We're careful. That doll..." He paused, took a deep breath. "I'd move it, return later, and it'd be someplace else, just...lying there."

"It could be coincidence..." Greta suggested, but she also looked uneasy. Shady remembered how she said she'd felt when Mandy had first been brought to her attention.

Bryan still stood there in the half light. "Strange things, dolls. Never liked 'em. Glad Greta doesn't either; I wouldn't want my house stuffed full of them. Always happy when they're sold on, when they're off my hands. That doll in particular, though, there was something—"

"About her," Shady couldn't help but finish.

Bryan nodded his head, a slow, purposeful movement, and Greta actually groaned.

"I hope we didn't do Lena a disservice when we sold it to her," she fretted.

"Thing is," Bryan said, still contemplating, "running a store like this, you come across some strange objects, ones that give you a little shiver down your spine when you hold them. You wonder about the previous owners, what they were like, you know, what kind of people they were." He shuffled and lowered his head. "I do feel bad about Lena, actually."

"Honey, you didn't sell it to her, I did," Greta said gently.

"Yeah, but I put the doll out there, when really I was uneasy about it. D'you know what I wanted to do? Just toss it away. Didn't help that it came from Mrs. Arbutt either."

Shady frowned. Just what was wrong with Mrs. Arbutt?

"Bryan," Greta said, "Lena's death was tragic, but it had

nothing to do with us. Not really."

Bryan had moved slightly; he was more in the light now, but at his wife's insistence that they were blameless, he shuffled back toward shadow. Shady also noticed, as he started speaking again, that his voice had changed. There was no longer any trace of sorrow in it, no more sense of responsibility, no more awareness either. He sounded his usual brisk, business-like self.

"Well, like we've agreed, get in touch, eh? You know, if there's any more money to be had. Keep us in the loop. Good thing I didn't toss her after all."

The darkness had reclaimed him.

CHAPTER THIRTEEN

"Hi, Mom, hi...yeah, I'm fine, it's all good here... No, nothing horrible has happened, it's all been okay. We're in a hotel now, outside a place called Catskill... No, no, not a Super 8. It's a good one, a Holiday Inn... Yes, we're safe, honest we are... Mandy? She's in the car, in the trunk... No, I'm not sharing with Ray! He's got his own room, so does Annie... Mom, it's out of season, the rooms are cheap. We're not spending loads of money, quit worrying about that too."

God, it was like being in the firing line with question after question aimed at her. And then Ellen put Shady's father on the phone, and it got worse!

"I'm not sure what you think you're doing," he said. "When your mom told me, I was horrified. We don't even know the people you're with—"

"Dad, I went to high school with Ray—"

"Ray? Ray who? I never heard you mention a Ray!"

"I didn't hang out with him, that's why, but he's not a stranger."

"The woman is! Let me tell you something, honey, serial killers don't always come packaged up like you expect 'em to, oh no. A little old lady is just as capable as—"

"Dad!" Did she have to remind him too? "I'm not a kid,

okay? And…I'm different. You know that now. I'm not just fey. This doll…"

"Is a doll! Like every other doll in the world! An inanimate object, nothing more."

"Well, that's what I'm trying to find out."

"Shady—"

"Dad, please."

"Your mom's crying. You happy you made her cry?"

"Is she? No, Dad. Of course not!"

"Look, how far away is Catskill? Why don't you get up early, head on back—"

"I'm not crazy."

Three simple words, three simple *true* words, but it stopped him in his tracks.

"Shady, I never said—"

"Then don't treat me like I am. I'm not crazy, and neither is what I'm doing. There's something about Mandy, and I want to find out what it is, because…because it's gonna plague me if I don't, and that's really where the danger lies, where my own thoughts will lead me. Dad, I can read objects. Not all the time but mostly. It's hard to explain, but I can kinda tell where it's been, what's happened to it. I can read Mandy."

There was silence, and then her father spoke again. "All I want is to keep you safe."

"I am safe," she insisted.

"And I know you're not a child anymore. I realize that. Your mom does too. You've grown into a fine young woman. It's just, honey…life's so much easier if you're normal."

Shady shook her head, her dark hair swinging. Normal.

What was that? What was it really? Was anyone in this world normal, or any*thing*, for that matter? The boundaries had always been slightly off-center with her, but now they'd moved even further, revealing a world that was new, that was full of mystery, that scared her but, she had to admit, excited her too. Whatever she was doing right now, it was better than whiling away the days at a fast-food counter.

"Dad," she said, "can you put me on loudspeaker?"

"What? Yeah, okay, sure."

When he'd done that, she spoke clearly, addressing both her parents. "Mom, Dad, I love you so, so much, but let me be who I'm supposed to be, who I think I should be."

"We're so worried about you." It was her mother's voice, trembling.

"I know, Mom, but I trust Annie and Ray. They're good people, not axe murderers in disguise—"

"Axe murderers!" Ellen gasped. "Oh, Shady, even to joke about such a thing!"

"All we're trying to do is understand what Mandy is."

"She's just a doll!" Her father remained resolute.

"Yes, she was, once. But she's more than that now."

"Oh, this is absurd!" Her father was huffing and puffing. There was no way she was going to persuade him otherwise, not right now, so she changed tack.

"Have you ever heard of a song called "Shady Grove"? Ray played it in the car today, and he thought I would know…"

Her voice trailed off as she realized her question had been met with silence, a wall of it.

"Mom? Dad?"

She might be able to read objects, but if only she had Xray vision too. She wanted to see her parents at this moment, and what was taking them so long to reply, started imagining, too, their expressions as they looked at each other, surprised or shocked—was it more the latter?

"Mom…Dad…" she said again, this time more urgently. "Have you heard of it?"

"No." There it was, an answer at last from Ellen.

"Why do you even ask?" Bill interjected.

"Because it's my name, Dad, or virtually." Surely, she didn't need to point that out? "It's like an old folk song. The reason I'm asking is because…well, I've never heard of it before, or at least I didn't think I had, but it sounded so familiar…as if I *had* heard it." *Shady Grove, my little love, I'm bound to go away.* Still those lyrics resounded in her head, those in particular. "I just…I wondered if you'd sung it to me when I was small, Mom?"

"I've never heard of it," Ellen insisted, and there was not just upset in her voice but a tightness, as if it was difficult for her to speak, to push the words out.

"Mom, I'm sorry—"

"Just come home soon, Shady," was her mother's response. "Come home safe."

* * *

The song was still in Shady's head as she slept, the lyrics on repeat, as if trying to stick there.

Shady Grove, my little love…

The voice singing wasn't the mellow, comforting voice of the folk singer, however, but someone else entirely. It was a woman, her voice high and sweet, melancholic also.

Before she'd fallen asleep, she'd done some research into the song. It was a traditional Appalachian folk song, made much use of by bluegrass and old-time musicians, even Jerry Garcia. A courting song, it revolved around the true love of a young man's life and his hope that they'd get married.

On and on the woman sang, soothing Shady, making her feel so calm, so content, so…sad.

I'm bound to go away…

Why must you? Shady wanted to ask. *Why do you have to leave me?*

In the dream she was lying in a bed with just a white sheet upon her. Slowly, tentatively, she opened her eyes, but all that surrounded her was more white, mist this time, blinding, as heavy as it had been in the other dream. Who was singing to her? Ellen or someone else?

"Mom?" she called out. "Is it you?"

Ellen's voice, though, as much as she loved it, didn't have the same melodic timbre.

"Who's there?"

Desperate to see, to solve this mystery too, she held out her hand and watched as the mist quickly enshrouded it.

The voice faltered…becoming silent.

"Tell me who you are…please. I don't mean any harm."

Shady hoped the pleading in her voice was persuasive enough.

A touch!

Just tentative, a brush on the back of her hand, but enough to inspire hope in Shady's heart.

"Don't be scared. And don't stop singing. I was enjoying it."

A slight murmur, a low hum, the touch—featherlight—back again, becoming firmer.

Shady smiled. She was getting somewhere…at last.

"Come closer," she said, her voice barely above a whisper. "Let me see you."

Oh, the curiosity in her chest was burning. *Who are you? Why do you sound so familiar?*

Her own fingers began reeling whoever it was toward her, gently, slowly.

"Let me see you."

A face appeared, a shadow in the mist with long hair surrounding it, long…dark hair.

Shady felt no fear, none at all, only delight.

"That's it, that's right," she coaxed.

This light! It was so bright! Stark, even. From the other dream, she remembered that things had hidden in the mist, those that didn't fill her with delight but horror.

Dolls.

Yes, of course, dolls. All shapes and sizes. Sentient, and in the worst of ways.

But this was not a doll. Her hand—now fully in Shady's—was made of flesh and blood, just like her own, and the face was human.

The face…

The hair…

God, she was familiar!

Just who are you?

Closer. Closer still.

Not clear, though. The mist clung to her face like gauze. Nothing could disguise the eyes, though; there was something in them—an attraction, Shady realized, as she also leaned forward. It was like looking into a mirror and seeing her own reflection there.

Is that who you are? Me? Or...a part of me?

There came the sound of humming again, more melancholic than ever, causing tears to spring to Shady's eyes, to overspill.

Her grip on the woman's hand became tighter, her other hand beginning to reach out too.

I need to know who you are...

Only inches apart, the mist suddenly cleared. Her heart leapt. This was what she'd wanted, for there to be no barriers between them. She imagined greater recognition, an answer, more joy heaped upon her, but the emotions enveloping her were the antithesis of that.

She snatched her hands back and held them close to her chest as her mouth opened wide to scream—no sound came, however, nothing that would interrupt the song the woman continued to hum, although quite how she was managing, Shady didn't know.

Because her mouth, her face, was as cracked as Mandy's.

CHAPTER FOURTEEN

"Mrs. Arbutt, hello. We've come about—"

The woman in front of them, tiny in stature, her face wizened, seemed to sniff the air. "I know what you've come about."

Annie expressed surprise. "Oh, Mr. Hollick called you?"

"Ain't no one called me, and no good if they did. Line's been dead this past month." She paused, sniffed at them now. "As you're here, you'd better come in."

The Hollicks had intimated this woman was a character, and they weren't far wrong. Thirty miles or so as the crow flies turned out to be closer to fifty when traveling by road, and they'd arrived not at a town but more of a settlement—Montague a somewhat grand name for what greeted them. Around these parts, the population was scant.

Mrs. Arbutt's residence was out on the prairie, not a house or a cabin but a trailer, occupying land filled with little more than scrub. The approach to the trailer was along a dirt road, one that stretched on and on, prompting them to repeatedly check the Sat Nav to see if it had blown a gasket. About to turn back—no one could live out here; Shady had grown quite emphatic about that—the trailer had suddenly come into view. Lonesome. That's what it was. But, according to the Hollicks, a woman *did* live here, and she'd lived with Mandy.

In the area surrounding the trailer, there was junk, plenty of it, including rusting machinery, wheelbarrows, and garden furniture thick with mold. There were even several cars, but not one of them looked serviceable; they looked like they'd been tinkered with, an engine sitting quite apart from one of them, a door leaning against the fender of another.

"Welcome to Hicksville, USA," Ray had muttered under his breath when they'd first arrived. On leaving Catskill, there'd been a slight breeze. In the wilds of Montague, however, it had picked up speed, blowing across the plains before hitting the slopes of the foothills and mountains, whipping at Shady's hair, obscuring everything from view briefly as it covered her eyes, just as everything had been obscured in her latest dream. There'd been comfort in such obscurity, though, in ignorance. Only when she'd been able to see clearly had it turned into a nightmare…

Ray had then spotted the curtains twitching. "No turning back now," he'd added, leading the way.

After they'd been ushered into the trailer, Mrs. Arbutt pushed the thin door shut. Some trailers were cramped, and some were vast—this erred toward the latter. If Shady had expected it to be as messy inside as it was out, she was wrong. Certainly, in the room they now stood in, a living room, it was cluttered but neat enough, no signs of a partner evident.

The older woman walked past them, and they followed. Closed doors on either side concealed who knew what as they traipsed through the narrow hallway into a kitchen that was gloomy but also neatly kept, the only view from the window more of that scrubland.

They were offered neither coffee nor water. Mrs. Arbutt simply stood there by the kitchen table, a look in her eyes that highlighted well enough the fact that she, despite her diminutive size and how ancient she might be, was not someone to mess with.

"This is about that doll, isn't it?" she said.

"Mandy? Yes."

"Mandy?" She snorted. "Called her many things, but it was never that."

"Do you mind if we sit, Mrs. Arbutt?" Annie asked.

"Please yourself. And call me Cora. I ain't got time for formalities."

As chairs scraped against faded linoleum, Annie did the honors in introducing them too. "The doll—" she continued, but Cora interrupted her.

"There ain't nothing you can tell me about that doll I don't already know." Although clearly reluctant, Cora also sat, a slight wince on her face as her bones eased themselves into a seated position. All three looked at her and she looked at them, her gaze holding such gravitas before she continued. "I had the doll for many years. Bryan Hollick tell ya that?"

"No, no, he didn't," Shady replied.

"Kept her out of harm's way."

Ray's eyes widened. "So, you think she's dangerous too?"

Cora turned her head toward him, a fierceness in her eyes. "I don't think, sonny, *I know*."

"What is it that you consider wrong with her?" Annie asked, her voice calm and even.

Cora's steely gaze next fixed on Annie. "Where you

from? Not these parts."

"I live in Mason, Idaho. I run a museum there. Originally, though, I'm from England."

"And you ended up here, with Mandy. More fool you. Where is she? Where you keeping her?"

"She's in the car, contained."

"As much as you can contain a doll like that."

Annie seemed to straighten somewhat, a gesture of defiance. "I do my best on that score."

Cora fired up. "Don't judge me, lady, for getting rid of her! Ten years I had her, and it weren't no easy ten years neither. It was hell. That doll cost me a lot, including my job, my husband, and now my health. She leeched everything from me, sucked me dry. No more of it! I've done my bit."

Ray shook his head. "Ma'am, why'd you keep her if she caused you so much heartache?"

For a moment—just a split second—Cora looked lost, as if she couldn't figure out the reason either. Quickly enough, though, she rallied, stabbing at the table with her forefinger. "Nothing and no one gets the better of Cora Arbutt, not least a damned doll!"

Shady worked hard to conceal her surprise at this response. Instead, she forced herself to focus, grasping the edges of the table as surreptitiously as she could, hoping she could read something of the woman who sat there day in and day out. If only she could close her eyes and tune in properly...

Just focus, Shady.

Cora was a proud woman; that was obvious to anyone with eyes in their head. A woman who didn't like to be beat. She liked to be in control. Even when Mr. Arbutt was alive, it was Cora who'd ruled the roost. Fear. Yes, Shady was sensing fear too. Hence the need for Cora to remain in control, hinting at a time in her life when either she or events she'd been subjected to had been so far out of her control that it had marked her deeply, scarred her. She never wanted to be vulnerable again, at the mercy of others and whatever cruel whims they cared to visit upon her. She may have dominated Mr. Arbutt, but it had suited him. He hadn't been a bad man, but he'd preferred to be guided rather than steer the boat himself. Their marriage had suited them both; there'd been a degree of contentedness between them as long as each had let the other be who they'd wanted to be. And then Mandy had come along, and another fight had begun…a battle of wills.

Shady had indeed shut her eyes, albeit involuntarily. When she opened them, Cora was staring at her, livid. "What're you doing? Why're you sitting there like that?"

"Sorry, I—"

"Don't be sorry. Just tell me what you're doing!"

Shady swallowed. "How…how did you know we'd come to see you about the doll?"

"How? Because *everything's* about the damned doll, that's why."

"Does she…still haunt you?"

"Haunt?" A bellow of laughter escaped Cora. "I don't believe in no ghosts!"

What? She didn't believe in ghosts, but haunted objects were another matter…?

"I don't understand," Shady admitted.

Cora was only too keen to enlighten her. "I've never seen

no ghosts. Heard plenty of people talkin' about them, but we've got an imagination, haven't we"—she started to tap the side of her head—"and that runs away with people, that fools 'em. No, I ain't never witnessed no ghost in this home or any other home I've lived in, and if I can't see it, then it ain't there. It's as simple as that. But I can see that doll, and I can sense trouble when it's brewing. People laugh at me, they call me Crazy Cora who lives all by herself now, out on the plains. They think I don't know what they call me, but I do. Oh yes, I can sense trouble, and that doll, that *Mandy*, she was that, all right."

"You kept her because you wanted, in effect, to break her?" Annie was clearly also trying to make sense of a woman like Cora Arbutt. "Is that it?"

"Always liked a challenge. Why d'you think I live out here?"

There was a short silence before Shady spoke. "You think it's Mandy that's responsible for the bad luck you've had since you've had her, that it's all her fault?"

"I know it for a fact."

"How?" Shady was forced to ask again.

"I've had some shit in my life, let me tell you, but with the arrival of that doll, that shit turned several shades darker. I shoulda known she was bad news the minute I saw her, and yet…yet I was soft on her." There was a distant look in her eyes that she quickly chased away. "Never had kids. I couldn't. Maybe that's why I got tricked. Don't have a thing for dolls, usually. But that one…"

Cora climbed to her feet, her face contorting with the effort. She walked over to the window and stood looking out of it as she continued to speak. "Never had much in life, never wanted for much neither, but what I had she destroyed. I don't believe in ghosts, but one thing I do believe in, that I've witnessed too many times for my liking, is evil. And that doll is evil. It's found a home in her somehow, and she wanted to make me suffer, just as others have made me suffer, but I wasn't having it, not this time. I was gonna show evil it couldn't use Cora Arbutt, not no more."

As she spoke, several clouds raced across the sky, covering up what little blue there was and stealing yet more light from the kitchen.

"Each time something bad happened—we lost money, we lost a pet, I got ill, or Mick got ill—I'd look at Mandy, and I could see she was loving our misfortune. Heck, she *thrived* on our misery." She swung back around to face them. "And that gave me the push I needed to carry on, to show her. I made certain we bounced back. I'd tell her, 'Looky here, now, I can beat you.' But then"—were those tears in her eyes, Shady wondered? Certainly, they were glistening—"something else would go and happen, the *worst* thing. Mick died, that's my husband if you ain't guessed. A while back, he just…plain died on me. I tried to carry on, but enough's enough. I was getting rid of stuff, and that included her. I've fought enough now."

"You didn't just think to destroy her?" Shady had asked that question of Annie, and the answer she'd given had made sense, but she wanted to hear Cora's own reason for not doing so.

"I couldn't. I just… Maybe it's her being a baby doll or something. I tried, but…it was easier to call Bryan."

"Do you know how she got the crack down her face?"

Cora became defensive again. "Wasn't me, if that's what you're thinking!"

"No, no," Shady said, raising her hands in appeasement.

"You're right, though. Why didn't I destroy her? I shoulda. Damn it! When did I get so weak? Where is she, that doll? She's in your car, did you say? Is that where she's hiding?"

"Cora," Annie said, maybe trying to distract her, "how did your husband die?"

"How? I'll tell you how! He choked—on his damned cereal, of all things. I was out at the time, fetching groceries, came back to find him slumped on the table"—she pointed to where Ray was sitting—"right there. About as dead as dead can be. But who dies eating cereal? He was a grown man, for God's sake, been eating it all his life. It was her. It had to be. I see him all the time in my dreams, grabbing at his neck and choking, his face red, his eyes bulging, and I can see her too, laughing and crying and screaming, driving me mad with her racket."

"In dreams?" Annie asked. "You can hear her in dreams?"

"Uh-huh."

"Only in dreams?"

"Dreams is bad enough!"

When Cora started to stride forward, Annie rose too. "Cora, where are you going?"

"I shoulda put an end to her. I really shoulda."

Annie and Ray made to follow her, but Shady shifted around to the right of the table, where Ray had been sitting, where Mick had died, apparently, and quickly placed her hands on the table. Was Cora right, was Mandy responsible for his death too?

Focusing, she tuned in—a man, a big man, obese, some might say. He was sitting and eating cereal just like Cora had said—Lucky Charms. Oh, the irony of it. He was laughing to himself, chuckling away, his wife the cause of so much amusement, Cora and her crazy ways. Yeah, yeah, okay, she was crazy, he conceded, but he loved her, and he loved her because she was good at heart. She'd suffered, and he wanted to take care of her…no one else had ever taken care of her. Shame she wouldn't let him, although he couldn't deny it: he liked being taken care of by her well enough.

Oh, Cora, Cora. Her big, tough ways hid a world of hurt, and he saw that about her, not that she liked that he could, or did she? Yeah, yeah, course she did. He saw and yet still he loved her, that's what made him unique in her eyes, but that doll, that poor doll. She blamed it for everything. Then again…no doubt about it, it inspired her too. It kept her the way she was: tough and determined. Whatever got you through the madness of life, he had no argument with, and there'd been some stormy times recently.

Crazy Cora and that crazy doll. If he was allowed to have his way, they wouldn't give it houseroom. It was a horrible thing, the way it looked at you, the way it stared… He was laughing again, at how carried away he was getting—a doll couldn't stare at you, not with any intent, no matter what Cora said. She was just a doll. A stupid, ugly doll. As he thought that, he inhaled, a big lump of something catching in his throat. Immediately, he started to cough, doing his darndest to dislodge it, coughing harder, unable to catch his breath at all now, choking, a glimmer—just a glimmer—of disbelief setting in before he pitched forward and it all went dark. A freak accident, but an accident all the same. So, who was laughing so hard, who was it that was crying?

"Mrs. Arbutt, stop that! You can't!"

Hearing Annie's raised voice, Shady forced herself back to the moment and began racing down the hallway, out the door, and into the junk-filled yard. The sight that met her made her gasp. Cora, with something akin to a crowbar in her hand, was about to attack the Dodge.

Shady added her protest to Annie's. "Cora, don't do that. Ray, stop her..."

Ray didn't need to be told—he'd already lunged at Cora, lifting his hands up, ready to wrestle the crowbar out of hers. Elderly and wizened she might be, but she had physical as well as mental strength, and the crowbar came down, down, down, all the way onto Ray's head. Shady shut her eyes and screamed, having to turn aside and screw her eyes shut, imagining far too vividly the crunch of his skull as metal met bone. "No! Oh shit, no!"

The ensuing silence forced her to open her eyes, to look back at what she was sure would be nothing less than carnage, with blood everywhere. Why had she yelled at him to stop her? Why hadn't she told him to get away from her instead, to protect himself? She should have just let it be, let Cora have her way with Mandy, the doll that she, like so many others, blamed for her misfortunes. And yet...like Cora, she could no longer bear the thought of Mandy being destroyed. She wanted to save her, *actively* wanted it. But at Ray's expense?

The first thing she noted was the complete absence of

blood. At that, the breath left her body in a whoosh. Next was Ray, looking as stunned as Shady felt, his hands covering his head, unable to quite believe his skull was still intact. Annie had drained of color entirely, but Cora, having relinquished her hold on the crowbar, having come to her senses and thrown it to the side at the last minute, was on her knees and crying, great big sobs that set her torso heaving.

Annie, too, fell to her knees and put her arms around the woman. "Oh, Cora, we're sorry. So sorry."

Shady caught up with them and also moved closer to Cora, as did Ray, lending her their silent support. Eventually, Cora stopped crying and wiped at her eyes with the back of her sleeve, dragging the skin there. Instead of looking at them, she returned her gaze to the trunk.

"No more tears," she said after a while. "Always found 'em useless anyway."

"Would you like to stand?" Annie said, helping the older woman to her feet.

Cora still stared at the trunk but didn't say another word, not until Ray asked her a question, picking up on something she'd said earlier that Shady had quite forgotten about.

"Um…Mrs. Arbutt…you said Mandy was bad news, and yeah, we agree. But…you also said you shoulda known that the minute you saw her. How come?"

At last Cora was able to tear her gaze from the car, scrutinizing the three people in front of her instead. "That doll when I got her reeked of smoke."

"Smoke?" repeated Shady. "You mean—"

"She was in a house fire, over the border in a place called

Grand Forks, but she survived it unscathed. Just needed a bit of TLC, that's all, and me, fool that I am, tried to give it to her."

"A house fire?" It was Ray repeating Cora's words this time.

"Uh-huh. No one wanted what was left of the family's stuff, and so it found its way to various rummage sales hereabouts. That's what the guy I bought her from told me, anyway."

"Did you know the guy, his name?"

Cora shook her head. "Had no reason to ask."

"But he told you about the fire and the family too?"

"He sure did."

"And?"

"Every single one of 'em—ma, pa, and two kids—perished in the fire. But as you know, not Mandy. Oh no, that doll just goes on and on." She paused, bit her lip. "Does that answer your question well enough? D'ya see now why it was I shoulda known?"

CHAPTER FIFTEEN

Scorching heat and smoke filled her lungs, obscured everything, just like the bright light filling Shady's dreams would shroud everything. The family was in here…all of them…but they were separate too, lost from each other, only a few feet separating them, but it might as well have been canyons. All that could be heard were shouts and screams, a crescendo of panic, and, of course, the relentless rush of flames as they consumed all that lay in their path.

This had all happened so long ago, more than a decade, and yet the spot on which the house had stood, in the suburb of a small city, had never been built on again. The house may have been razed to the ground, but not the memories. They were—for Shady, at least—as vivid as ever.

"Shady, if this is too much—"

After yet another near brush with death, Ray's this time, Annie had shown yet more reluctance to continue with their journey, Shady again insisting. They'd gotten this far, against the odds, it seemed. As Ray had said on the approach to Cora's trailer, there was no turning back.

And so, she'd driven them through border checkpoints and into the Canadian town of Grand Forks, the vastness of the terrain that lay on either side of the highway continuing to amaze her. This was a land of such startling contrasts.

She'd rarely traveled north of Idaho Falls; it had always been south, down to the sun-drenched beaches of California or the theme parks of Florida. Family holidays were a constant source of good memories, a pool from which she'd regularly draw on, something to put a smile on her face when she was standing at the counter of the fast-food outlet, remembering carefree, happy, lazy days filled with love.

But heading north, as they had now, and certainly not under carefree circumstances, she'd realized again that a whole new world was opening up to her—quite literally— one in which she'd be a very different person. Was a changing world, a changing personality, something to be scared of? Despite what had happened, Shady didn't think so, but it was one in which she'd need to tread carefully.

Don't fear what's different. Those words formed in her mind, behind them a wisdom she suspected it'd take a lifetime to understand. *Don't fear yourself.* Perhaps it was meeting Cora Arbutt and seeing how fear had shaped her life that caused such thoughts. Yet she'd also learned fear wasn't something to be derided, not completely. It could inspire as well as derail you.

A shaken Cora had finally been persuaded away from the Dodge, returning to her trailer. The surname of the family who'd died in the fire had also been persuaded out of her— the Wynn-Carver family. A quick look at Google and enough details had been obtained to make a visit. Had Mandy somehow been instrumental in causing the fire? That's what Shady was trying to find out.

Because the residual energy was still strong where the Wynn-Carvers' home once stood, there was no need to get

Mandy out as she'd done in Lena Dubinsky's house. She could stay in the car for now, Ray standing by the trunk, guarding it somehow, just as Shady had wanted to guard her when Cora was intent on attacking her. She'd wanted only to keep the doll safe, a fact that wasn't lost on her, that squatted enquiringly at the edges of her mind—an urgent need to protect.

Come on, let's see what else we've got here, Shady thought as she continued to wander the perimeters of what had once been. Sally and John Wynn-Carver had had two children, Laura and Sam. The doll must have belonged to Laura, so, with that in mind, Shady focused on her, Annie keeping a respectful distance, ready to intervene if need be, a comfort blanket in human form.

More images began to form, but they were frustratingly slow at first, fragmented almost to the point of nonsense. She wanted to zone in on what had happened before the fire, not during it. Certainly, it was the fire and the fear and the agonies suffered that was most ingrained upon this land, but so was a time when the Wynn-Carver family had *lived*, not died.

A little girl, Laura, and…another girl? Ah, so Sam was a girl, not a boy. When Shady had read the name, she'd assumed it was a boy, and the article had said nothing to dissuade her on that. But Laura and Sam were two little girls—more than that, they were…twins. Identical. Shady sighed. Of them both, whom did the doll belong to? Laura…no, Sam…no, Laura…

She's my doll!
She's not! Mommy bought her for me.
But she didn't! I saw her in the window first. It was

me!
She's our doll, then. You have to share her.
I don't!
But we share everything.
Not her. Not this one.
Mandy was being fought over, yet another negative situation she'd found herself in. But while she was culpable for some of that negativity, could she be blamed for all of it? Not in the beginning, not with Kate Jane, whom these little girls were reminiscent of—not because they were mentally impaired, they weren't, but they were as spoiled, as indulged, their parents as blind.

Nine years old, that was their age, born in the month of December and later dying in that month too. Life coming to an end so early, and in such a horrific way, wounded Shady. An image of the girls' parents reared up, like scenes from a movie this time, their bewilderment over their daughters' obsession with an antique doll, one they'd purchased… Shady couldn't see where—another thrift or antique store, no doubt, or a yard sale.

The twins came back into view. The mood between them had changed, their attitude…

I don't like her anyway. She's ugly.
Ugly? She isn't. You are!
That's stupid, that's like calling yourself ugly. Besides…my face isn't damaged like hers.
She's still pretty.
No, she's not.
She is—
She's not. How can anyone be pretty when their face is cracked?

Shady tensed. Her face had been cracked already? She'd

half expected to see these girls tugging and pulling at Mandy, involving her in an ever-increasing struggle of ownership, and that was how the crack had appeared in her face. Evidently not. The damage had been inflicted elsewhere.

The mood grew darker still.

She is ugly, isn't she?
Told you so.
She's just…junk.
Not like our other toys, our new toys.
I don't want her anymore. Here, you can have her.
I don't want her either! Why would I? I never wanted her.
But you did! You said—
I never said anything.
You did!
I didn't.

There was a brief pause before the twins began speaking again.

What should we do with her?
Throw her away.
With the trash?
Uh-huh. It's where she belongs.
Yeah, let's do that. No one would want a doll like her.
That's right. No one would.
We *don't want her.*
We don't.
We hate her.
We do.
We hate her.
We hate her.
We hate her.

And Mandy had listened to it all. She'd soaked it up, she'd—*focus, Shady, focus*—been both delighted and dismayed by it. Shady paused. Was she reading that correctly? Mandy had been so upset and yet she'd fed upon such feelings—again, was *fed* the right word to use? Shady couldn't find an alternative so stuck with it. The twins' attitude had both revolted and nourished the doll.

What are you Mandy? Such a mystery, like the woman in the dream. *What did you do?*

Children shouldn't play with matches—that was the saying, what the twins were always told, what Shady herself had been told when she was younger. "Don't touch the matches, honey," Ellen would say. "Matches are dangerous."

But these children had felt compelled to touch them; they'd been *encouraged* to.

Go on, a little voice kept saying in their heads, *fire is pretty, fire is nice.* If they hesitated, there was more prompting. *It's no lie. See for yourself how pretty it is.*

Whose was that voice, their own or Mandy's? Certainly, it was in *both* their heads, the same words, repeating and so seductive.

It was the father who smoked. Not a massive habit, but after a busy day, it was how he liked to unwind, smoking a cigarette and drinking a beer. His wife, Sally, didn't like that he smoked, but she didn't say anything. Stress was the biggest killer, and if smoking alleviated that somewhat, enabled him to relax, well…perhaps it was the lesser of two evils.

Evil.

Another word that wound its way through Shady's

mind. A word that Cora had used to describe Mandy. *That doll is evil. It's found a home in her somehow.*

Either the twins had started the fire, listening to voices in their heads that were their own, or it was Mandy, urging, urging, urging...

Alone in the room they shared, one twin had looked at the other, and the other had gently nodded. *Do it!* One opened the box of matches—Shady could see this all so clearly now, as if Mandy *wanted* her to see, every last detail. The child retrieved a match and struck it against the side of the box. *Don't,* Shady wanted to shout, and perhaps she did, because there was a light touch on her arm, Annie's hand, most likely, although she didn't open her eyes to check. *Don't do it! Don't listen to Mandy.* Mandy who hated them as much as they hated her. Who wanted to destroy them before they had a chance to destroy her, to throw her away yet again.

Mandy, leave them alone!

They set fire to the curtain, both of them watching wide-eyed as flames quickly took hold, dancing as gracefully as ballerinas around the edge of the curtain before shooting right up the length of it, making the girls giggle, it was so spectacular. *Like fireworks!*

Shady shook her head in despair. *Not like fireworks, far deadlier than that.*

The other curtain caught fire too, and then the carpet upon which the curtains rested, encircling the girls, trapping them, wonder turning to fear...at last.

Where were the parents? Why wasn't a fire alarm sounding?

And finally, why wasn't Mandy in the bedroom too,

because if she was, she'd have been destroyed. Was she outside already? In the trash? A humiliation but also her saving grace.

There were no more images, no more facts; the world turned black behind Shady's eyes, and it stayed that way no matter how hard she tried to tune back in to what lingered in the air, to see not the inevitable—she didn't want to see that; what nice girl would—but to backtrack through those images to when Mandy had first been spotted by one of the twins, what thrift, junk, or antique store it was, to get a sense of whether it was nearby, a few miles away, or somewhere far from home, purchased while the family had been vacationing, perhaps, or visiting relatives. They could scour stores in the local area, they could spend days and days doing that, but who'd remember a doll from over ten years ago? Or more to the point, who'd be trying to forget her?

It was no use. The link she'd forged was gone. And there was a feeling of cold glee about that, a satisfaction, not emanating from her, of course, but from Mandy.

Shady opened her eyes. "Damn it! You love being an enigma, don't you?"

There were no more answers. Not with all four members of the Wynn-Carver family dead and Cora having no idea of the name of the man who'd sold the doll to her.

On the site of a house that had once burned, the trail had gone cold.

CHAPTER SIXTEEN

"Hi, Mom… Yeah, I'm fine. Just letting you know I'm coming home first thing tomorrow."

"Oh, thank God! I'm so glad to hear it. So glad that this…this…"

Shady tensed. Was she going to call it nonsense?

"…*business* is over. What have you done with the doll? Do you still have it?"

If her mom wanted her to say she'd tossed it in a dumpster, then she'd be disappointed. Despite Annie's brief wobble after Lena's house, all three were in full agreement that you couldn't get rid of Mandy that easily—in both real *and* psychological terms.

"The doll will return with Annie to her museum, Mom."

Again, her mother sighed in relief. "Good, because I don't want it here."

Who would? Even a doll *perceived* as haunted?

They'd been away three days—not a lot of time, but at least some progress had been made in terms of Mandy's history, although certainly plenty of gaps remained. Yet as Annie had said, they didn't need to know everything, just something *significant*—primarily when Mandy had changed, to become what she was now. It was this they'd failed at, so far, anyway.

In a last-ditch attempt, Shady had indeed suggested they visit any possible stores Mandy could have been purchased from by the Wynn-Carvers within a reasonable radius, but no one, *no one*, remembered a doll such as her. They'd resorted to bringing Mandy into the various stores and showing her off. All, without exception, from the young to the old, male or female, flinched upon seeing her, that sixth sense that very few people believed in coming to the fore.

Finally, in the lounge of another generic hotel, nursing their respective drinks, they decided that what they did know about the doll would have to suffice—for now. Mandy was dangerous; Mandy was insidious. She invaded your mind, your thoughts, your dreams, and she twisted things.

"It's so frustrating!" Shady lamented once she'd gotten off the phone with her mom, her head in her hands and fingers rubbing at her temples.

Ray and Annie's silence was evidence they agreed.

"I had another dream," Shady continued.

"When?" asked Annie.

"A couple of nights ago, and it was about her…but it wasn't, if that makes sense." Seeing their baffled expressions, she elaborated. "There was the same blinding white mist that was in my first dream, but there were no dolls this time. Instead, there was a woman. She leaned forward out of the mist, and although she was a stranger, she also wasn't, not quite." Shady took a sip of her beer, not ice-cold anymore but lukewarm. "Oh God, it doesn't make sense, does it, what I'm saying."

"Just tell us about it," Annie replied.

Shady took a deep breath before explaining. "She had

long dark hair like mine, but wasn't a young woman, maybe in her fifties, something like that. Her eyes were dark too; looking into them was like looking at my own in a mirror, and yet she wasn't me. She was someone totally separate. A familiar stranger, I guess you could say." More reluctantly, Shady added, "There was something else familiar about her."

"What?" Ray asked, his green eyes intent.

"Her face was cracked, just like Mandy's."

There was a brief silence before Annie commented, "A dream is a dream. Things get skewed."

"Or it's Mandy that skews them."

"Don't do it, don't fall into that trap," Annie warned.

"What trap?"

"Always blaming Mandy."

Shady rolled her eyes and laughed, albeit wryly. "It's so easy to do, though, isn't it?"

They'd sat for a while more, and then, when Annie had finished her drink, she rose from her chair. "It's been a long day. I'm off to bed. Shady, when you're ready to sleep, remember to envisage white light and ask the universe for protection. I'm sure you'll rest peacefully enough."

As Shady watched her older companion make her way through the lobby to the elevator, a slight stiffness in her movements, she felt a surge of emotion. Annie was a diminutive woman, unassuming to look at with a penchant for the color brown, but within her lay the heart of a warrior. Even if their journey had ended prematurely, it had brought Annie into her life, and she was grateful for that, for Annie *and* Ray.

"Hey." Ray leaned a little closer. "You okay?"

"Yeah, why?"

"You've got a tear running down your cheek."

Shady lifted a hand to wipe at it before smiling at him. "I'm a bit tired, that's all. And I'm thinking about Annie…what a remarkable woman she is. I'm glad to know her."

"Me too."

"And I'm glad to know you as well, Ray."

"At last," he said, grinning.

"Yeah, at last."

"I've said it before, no harm in saying it again, you're pretty remarkable too, Shady."

"Me?" She could feel her face flame as red as Ray's hair.

"Yeah. Not just your intuition but how determined you are, how focused."

"Well, what about you? I'm amazed you're not fazed by any of this."

"I am…a little," he admitted. "But only a little. You see—"

The bartender's sudden presence made them both jump.

"If you want to order more drinks, now's your chance," the man said, looking wholly uninterested as to whether they actually would or not. "Bar closes in a few minutes."

"Really?" replied Shady. It was barely nine o'clock, but maybe this side of the border, they stuck with the old ways, going to bed earlier and rising with the sun.

Both ended up declining a drink but decided they weren't quite ready to follow Annie's example just yet, so they went for a walk instead, Shady hoping to stimulate tiredness to the extent she'd fall asleep as soon as her head hit the pillow.

Outside it was cold and fresh, the night sky packed with a thousand stars. Together, she and Ray wandered, not too far from the hotel and not too deep into the woods behind the building either, not wishing to encounter any of Canada's famous carnivorous wildlife.

It was strange being alone with him; she hadn't been since that day at the mall, which had turned into an evening at The Golden Crown. Always, someone else had been with them, mainly Annie. She felt nervous suddenly, not in a frightened sense, but in a way that made her acutely self-conscious. Ridiculous, really, because she saw Ray as just a friend, and hopefully that was how he saw her too. That boy-girl thing, however, was capable of kicking in regardless.

"Ray, you were about to say something before the bar guy came over. What was it?"

"No, nothing. It's…stupid, really."

"Hey, you haven't judged me, I'm not gonna judge you!"

"Seriously." His face was pale in the moonlight. "It's nothing."

Walking farther, the Dodge came into view—an object, inanimate unless revved into life. Is that what someone had done with Mandy? Revved her up somehow, switched her on?

"What will you do when you get home?" Ray asked. "Go back to your job?"

"I'll have to, I guess. Not that I like the idea. It seems so…dull."

"In comparison to this, I guess it is."

"But how do you make *this* pay?"

"No idea."

Just before the car, they came to a halt. There weren't too many other vehicles in the parking lot as it was too early for the skiing season, but she'd bet in the summer months it was also busy, a nearby lake perfect for boating. Again, she eyed the trunk, a shiver running through her that had nothing to do with the cold air. "But if we're right, if the doll's dangerous and we're somehow trying to contain that danger, it's just…it's gotta be done, right?"

Ray seemed to shiver too. "Hey, I agree, but to make money from it, to set up…I don't know, a paranormal investigative team? Is the world ready for that?"

"You don't think so?"

"I think, just like you do, there's a whole lotta people who scoff at this kinda stuff."

"And yet there's a whole lot who'd be afraid of a doll like Mandy, afraid of the rumors, at least."

"We're strange, aren't we, humans? We don't believe in ghosts, yet we believe in gods and the *Holy* Ghost." He pointed to the sky. "We think we're the only life-form, and yet there are other planets out there, maybe other universes. We think we're superior to other animals, but are we? I don't see other animals ruining the world like we are." He shook his head. "Ever wonder what it's all about, Shady, this existence? Why we live, why we die, and what comes after, heaven or hell, and the reasons they exist too? Ever wonder, 'cause I do…all the time."

"Ray?" Shady reached out and put a hand on his arm. She couldn't help it. He appeared not just curious but stricken by why so much remained mysterious, the deeper side of him that she'd suspected was there coming to the fore. "I do wonder, yeah. Now more than ever. I think about the strangeness of this world we live in, all that we consider normal and all that we don't. How reluctant we are to accept what's different, why it is that it frightens us."

From gazing into her eyes, he lowered them slightly. "Do you think Mandy's demonic?"

She shrugged. "Like Annie said, it's a broad term. Is it just something otherworldly, because I can think of a few people who could be called demons too."

"Same."

"Ted Bundy, for one."

"Charles Manson."

"Edward Theodore Gein."

"Who's he?" Ray asked, laughing.

"The inspiration behind *Psycho*."

"Oh, really? I'll have to Google him."

"Google is our friend, eh?

"We have the world at our fingertips."

Shady grew serious again. "In answer to your question, though, I think Annie's now veering toward that theory, but me? Not entirely, no."

"Huh? What do you mean?"

"That's just it, I don't know what I mean. Not exactly." Her gaze returned to the trunk as she at least tried for an explanation. "I've sort of realized I don't want Mandy destroyed. Cora didn't either, and neither did Lena—she threw her away, but she couldn't go through with it; she retrieved her. What Kate Jane did doesn't count. Mandy was Mandy in name only back then. She was just a doll. As for the twins, they *did* throw her out with the trash; that's how she survived the fire, but in one of them, at least, I sensed a despair that she'd done that. See, there's something that draws people to Mandy as well as repels them, and some people…well, some people feel both those pulls. I guess I'm one of them. When Cora was trying to get to her…"

She trembled at the thought, something Ray must have noticed. He stepped forward and put his arms around her, held her close. She was glad for his warmth.

"We're a good team, aren't we?" she whispered.

"I like to think so."

He released her, leaving Shady wishing he hadn't, not quite so soon, anyway.

The night growing colder still, they walked back to the hotel and entered the lobby, the man at reception not bothering to glance up at them. "We could be anyone," Shady whispered to Ray, "coming in here, escaped convicts or on the run from the local psych ward…"

"We could be demons," Ray countered.

Shady shook her head. "Not that. Not us."

"We just keep the demon safe."

"As well as the public, remember?"

"In true *Buffy* style."

"Used to have a little crush on Spike."

"You like the bad guys, huh?"

"Maybe."

"I liked Willow."

"Willow? Yeah, she was cute. Ray, I've never asked, you have a girlfriend?"

He grinned. "Kinda like I am with jobs, I'm in between with them too."

"Same here with the guys," she replied, happy enough

that it was so.

As they reached the elevator, Ray spoke again. "After this, after Mandy, what then?"

"So many questions, huh?"

"I just...I don't want it to end, that's all. Like we said, what we're doing has purpose."

She didn't want it to end either. But it had. They said goodnight and returned to their respective rooms, just across the corridor from each other. Exhausted, Shady did indeed fall asleep just minutes after she'd climbed into bed, and, thankfully, a peaceful night followed.

In the morning they met in the breakfast room, where they filled up on pancakes and maple syrup, the good stuff, the real stuff, not the Karo her mom filled the cupboards with. Back in the car, they headed toward home, some of the mystery surrounding Mandy solved but not all of it, not by a long shot. *Ah well,* thought Shady, *at least Mom's happy, and Dad too.* Despite that, the mood in the car was somber, each of them battling their own disappointment and sense of defeat.

Glancing at the digital clock on the radio, she figured they'd make it into Idaho Falls before it got too late—it was a long drive, but the roads were largely empty and progress was good. If she got tired, Ray had offered to take over, but so far she was doing fine. Before going home, they would, of course, transfer Annie and the doll to Mason and...that would be that.

A cell phone rang—Annie's.

As she retrieved it from her purse, she muttered, "Oh," piquing Shady's interest.

"Hello, Ruth," Annie greeted, "how are you?" There was

a brief pause, and then she said, "Right, I see. Sorry, Ruth, do you mind if I put you on loudspeaker? I'm with Shady and Ray."

"Not at all," came Ruth's response, the connection not as clear as it could be, her voice tending to fade in and out slightly. They'd already crossed the Canadian border and passed through Washington, heading toward Missoula in Montana, then Butte, then home in Idaho. Slowing to a cruise, Shady concentrated on what Ruth Judd had to say. Something about a kid, a *dead* kid.

"I'm not saying this child has anything to do with anything, not at all." And here she paused, the air filling with expectation, Shady glancing at Annie, Annie glancing at her, Ray leaning forward slightly. "And also, this is going back some. I'm talking years. I don't know how many for sure, but it's got to be at least twenty. It was up in Canada, in a place about as remote as you can get."

"Do you know what it's called?" Annie asked.

"Dupont, in the Saskatchewan province. The nearest big town's probably Saskatoon. There was a house in the woods there, or there used to be, where the child lived. Look, this is hearsay—"

"Hearsay?" Ray asked. "Wasn't there media coverage?"

"No," Ruth answered. "Maybe…maybe because there was no murder as such."

"Okay," Ray muttered, frowning a little as he inclined his head to the side.

"So, what do you mean by hearsay?" Annie probed.

"It's local knowledge, or a story—you know how it goes. My colleague Isobel told me about it a day or so after your visit. We'd been discussing you folks, you see, and what you intended to do, though as she was telling me, I kind of remembered it too. I've heard the story of this little girl before. Again, it was a long time ago, and…well, I guess I'd forgotten."

Another pause followed, one seemingly filled with sadness on Ruth's part and perhaps a little guilt, but for the rest of them, it was with sheer curiosity. Shady could even imagine Mandy bracing herself to hear it—or, rather, something *in* Mandy.

"The reason I think the story sticks in people's minds is probably to do with the length of time the child lay dead before she was found," Ruth continued, her voice echoing the gravitas of Annie's when she'd first met Shady, when she'd walked into Mervin's and asked, *Miss Groves?* "It was three years. Three whole years. A little kid like that, no more than six or seven. No sign of a parent, a caregiver, nothing. She was just…left alone. It was thought she'd died in the winter and that she couldn't get out to tell anyone she was in trouble because of the snow, assuming there were neighbors close by, that is. I expect the cause of death was starvation."

"Oh, that poor soul!" Annie whispered. "Did they ever find out why she was left alone?"

"I don't think any trace of her mother was ever found. From what I remember, her father had already died. He was a logger, apparently, got involved in a work accident."

Ray cut in. "And there was *actually* no media coverage? Even though the kid wasn't found 'til three years after her death?"

"No," Ruth replied, her voice sounding small suddenly.

"Okay," Annie concluded, "as sad as this is, as

horrendous, what's it got to do with Mandy?"

"Well…" Ruth stretched the word out. "As I've already said, it might have nothing to do with her, but…and again this might be hearsay, rumors, you know…"

"What could?" Annie prompted when Ruth continued to hesitate.

"She was found with a doll by her side, and Isobel happened to say, 'I wonder if that doll was Mandy.' Normally, I'd have dismissed it; after all, why would it be her? It could be *any* doll. I'd have shrugged it off, but…I couldn't. And it's been playing on my mind ever since. What if Isobel's right and the doll *was* Mandy? What if that child's the reason she's haunted?"

The minute the words left Ruth's mouth, Shady slammed her foot on the brakes, the car screeching to a halt.

"Hey!" yelled Ray, swinging his body around to check behind him, no doubt expecting a car to slam into their fender. Thankfully, there was nothing, which was pure luck because Shady hadn't checked the road before she'd stopped; she'd just reacted. Slowly, she eased the car over onto the shoulder and parked there.

"Saskatoon," she breathed. "How far is it from here?"

Annie was also quite breathless. "Not sure. Two days' ride, probably. Shady, do you think—"

"What was the child's name?"

"Erm…Ruth," Annie asked, "do you know—"

"Emma," both Shady and Ruth said at the same time.

"It was Emma Moore," Shady continued, her hands beginning to shake, her head beginning to pound, and her heart…what was her heart doing? It pumped furiously, not just with fear but something else too…could it be hope?

And what was that noise she could hear? The sound of crying? Ever so faint, but it wrenched at her guts all the same.

"Like I said," Ruth was taking pains to reiterate, "whether or not the doll found with the child really was Mandy, I don't—"

Again, Shady interrupted. "It was. I know it was."

With that stated, she put the car into drive, hit the gas, and headed back toward Canada.

CHAPTER SEVENTEEN

"I'm not crazy. Honest, I'm not."

"No one's saying that, dear," Annie assured her.

"And I know there's no actual proof, that all of this could, as Ruth says, be rumor," Shady continued, her hands gripping the steering wheel, eyes fixed on the expanse of road ahead. "I also know that there are millions of dolls in the world, in America alone, in Canada…millions."

"True that," Ray murmured from the back seat. "Likely more dolls than people."

"The doll that was found with Emma could be *any* doll."

"But…" Annie prompted.

"It could also be Mandy."

"Is that what instinct is telling you?"

"Yes."

"Then that's good enough for me. Ray?"

"Good enough for me too," he said.

What Ruth had told them could represent a breakthrough, but what about Mandy, what did it represent for her? Was she aware that they knew? Would she push back somehow, react, and, if so, how violently? They'd need to remain on their guard, not let it down, not for one minute.

Ray was in charge of the music and thankfully not

playing any more folk tunes that tugged at Shady's memory in ways she couldn't understand—or, rather, one folk song in particular. This time, he favored Taylor Swift and a selection of her greatest hits.

Shady smiled to hear the iconic American singer belt out her first tune. "Hey, I didn't know you like Taylor Swift!"

Ray blushed to the roots of his hair, but he also smiled. "Got a little crush going on with TayTay as well as Willow. Sorry."

"No need to apologize. I like her too. Annie, can you bear it, though?"

Annie looked affronted. "Bear it? I'll have you know I'm also a fan. Pop music isn't solely the domain of you youngsters!"

The camaraderie between them not only felt good, it felt essential. If they were going to do this—continue to try to understand something outside the realm of normal, the *para*normal, Shady supposed, citing the true meaning of the word—there had to be balance, as Annie had taught her, a counterpoint. Moments such as these, rolling toward who knew what, provided exactly that: the three of them, trepidatious, no one would deny it, but also enjoying a sing-along to "Shake it Off," reveling in their newfound if rather unlikely friendship.

Dupont was way too far to make it in one hit, and Shady eventually gave in to tiredness, knowing that Annie and Ray were tired too. They stopped in Shelby, another small town not far from the border—a railway junction and truck stop, really, a fuel point around which had grown a handful of motels and diners.

Shady had already texted her parents earlier to let them

know there'd been a change of plan and that she would call them to explain. That call had come and gone, and, understandably, her mother had been furious...furious *and* distraught. Just how much of both had shocked Shady, something she was struggling with while alone in the darkness of her motel room. Why was her mom reacting this way, and was Shady doing her a cruel injustice in being so bemused by it? It was Ellen's insistence that it *was* madness, what she was doing, that most troubled her. She'd seemed just so damned certain of it.

Shady stayed awake for as long as she could, trying to find at least something on Google about a child who'd died in the Saskatchewan province of Canada and who'd remained undiscovered in her cabin for three years. There was absolutely nothing, so was it legend or fact? *Trust your instinct, Shady,* she kept telling herself. *You're not crazy. You're not.*

Her eyes growing tired of staring at her phone, she switched it off and watched CNN instead, soon losing interest in that and reading a magazine, one she'd picked up in the motel lobby, her eyes taking in every word, from cover to cover, trying to zone out again, to exhaust herself...

With massive relief, the next thing she knew it was morning. She opened her eyes to see twin shafts of light filtering through the curtains, bathing the room in a welcome glow. She yawned, she stretched, she quickly showered before joining the others to grab breakfast and get on the road to Dupont, which was still another seven hours' drive.

As they reconvened, Ray pointed out how ominous the clouds looked. "They reckon snow's gonna fall later today.

If we're gonna get there, we'd better not hang around."

It was to be breakfast on the go, then: cups of coffee and blueberry muffins, Ray cursing that Dunkin' Donuts hadn't yet made it to the northwestern states for occasions like this.

Taylor Swift was reinstated on the radio as more miles were eaten up, Ray driving the first leg of the journey this time, giving Shady more of a chance to marvel at the landscape, which was breathtaking despite the lowering clouds. Canada felt different to America; it felt…raw, home to only a few people along the way in various settlements, some evidence of farming going on, a gas station here and there, but otherwise untamed and majestic, a land where nature dominated.

She not only loved it, she felt at home, in this place that she'd never visited before, that her family had always shied away from. This might be her first visit, but she'd already resolved it wouldn't be her last. She'd come here again and hopefully to do something a little more innocuous, hiking, perhaps, conquering at least a fraction of the wilderness. She'd immerse herself in its heady vastness with no haunted doll in tow, no ulterior motive other than to enjoy.

With Shady back in the driver's seat, they entered Saskatoon and exited on the other side. It was a nice enough city, but by that time she was too enamored with the wilderness surrounding it to be impressed by anything man-made. In fact, she found a mild loathing developing within her for any place so inhabited, probably heightened by the sudden transition from land and forest to crammed housing, as if entering a fenced-in encampment. This country was affecting her in all sorts of ways, and this trip…it truly was changing her.

Around a hundred miles from Dupont, the clouds that had been threatening the entire length of their journey finally delivered. The snow wasn't heavy, not initially, but it was set to increase.

"We need to find somewhere to stay," Annie said, agitation in her voice.

Ray immediately retrieved his cell phone. "I'll Google motels around Dupont." After a few minutes, though, he sighed. "I can't seem to find any."

"There has to be something," Shady said.

"Only one way to find out, I guess."

"And what's that?"

"We keep going."

"Annie?" Shady asked. "That okay with you?"

"Yes, yes, as you say, there's got to be a hotel of some description. Or…we turn back."

"Hole up in Saskatoon, you mean?" Ray asked. "I suppose we could check government archives there, see if there's anything more we can find out about Emma Moore."

"You know that name," Shady said, "I've been thinking, there's gotta be a hell of a lot of them."

"Yes," Annie conceded. "I'm sure there is."

Emma Moore…Emma Moore… It was almost too *conveniently* common.

Ray spoke again, his worry evident. "We've been away for the best part of a week now. If we head back to Saskatoon, we could be stranded, waste days there."

It was a fair point. None of them wanted to be stranded for days, especially miles from where they needed to be. Plus, they had commitments. Old lives couldn't be put on hold indefinitely.

"So, we press on, take our chances?" said Shady.

This time, Annie didn't hesitate. "We're so close."

"Do it, get the job done," Ray concurred.

With her foot on the gas, the miles disappeared and, as predicted, the snow got heavier.

* * *

None of them could believe it. There was *nothing* between Saskatoon and Dupont, absolutely nothing. The breadth of this place was astonishing, its emptiness too. The sense of unease in the car had nothing to do with Mandy this time but at the decision they'd made to press on under such conditions. One good thing: they'd reached the town of Dupont, no real commercial enterprises visible, however, apart from a store and a bar, both of which unfortunately had "Closed" signs slapped in their windows. There were a few homes, at least, the likelihood of knocking on a stranger's door and begging to be taken in becoming all too real.

As Shady stared at a land now covered in white, she shook her head in disbelief. How had it come to this? They'd underestimated the weather and their location in equal measures; they'd compared it to their own state when really it was nothing like it, a world apart. They'd been naive, and that worried Shady. What else had they underestimated?

Silence reigned now as Shady concentrated, the only sound to break it that of the wipers struggling to maintain some semblance of visibility. That trepidation she'd been feeling? It sat like a stone in her chest. She felt so small up against the elements, both natural *and* supernatural.

"Shady, we'll be all right." Ray's soft voice punctuated the silence.

"What are you, a mind reader?" she said, attempting a stab at joviality.

"At least there are some signs of life," Annie further consoled, referring to the homesteads.

"I wonder where in Dupont Emma Moore lived?" Ray mused.

"In the woods, Ruth said." Shady's eyes widened as she said it, maybe because there was so much forest up here, stretching for eternity, crossed only by logging roads. Where to even begin looking, and they didn't know that Emma had actually lived in the woods, not for sure. It was all hearsay, as Ruth had also said. And yet…it was something else Shady was convinced was true. But it could also be the case that the child's house, just like the twins' home, was no longer in existence. It may have been destroyed years ago, leaving nothing behind but scarred land. Would that matter? Would she still be able to detect something as she'd done at the Wynn-Carvers'? The answers they needed?

She could definitely hear crying. It was so, so faint, but it was there. It had been ever since they'd started the return journey—barely noticeable, easy to ignore, but constant.

"Shit!" Her outburst betrayed her agitation. "We need to find shelter."

It might look picture-postcard pretty out there, but it was as treacherous as the Antarctic. No way could they spend the night in the Dodge; they'd freeze to death. They needed a log fire, blankets, and thick, thick walls.

"Keep going, Shady," Ray urged. "Next house we see, I'll get out and knock on the door."

"I'm sorry," she said.

"What about?" Annie asked, turning to look at Shady.

"We should have holed up in Saskatoon after all. I didn't realize—"

"None of us did," Annie countered.

The road was still drivable, but how much longer before it wouldn't be? She'd loved her surroundings earlier, but now that love was on a downward slope. Who would willingly live so far from civilization? The fact the child had lain undiscovered for so long didn't seem quite so improbable now—this was a land that could hide you forever.

That crying, oh, that crying, faint as it was, was irritating her.

Stop crying, ya hear! I won't have it! I'll make you stop. I mean it this time. I'll make you.

Lena's words, not hers, but they were there in her head, on a repetitive loop. They had to turn back, find one of the houses they'd already passed, bang on the door, insist…

"There! Over there!" Ray was pointing up ahead. "On the edge of the forest, to your right."

On the edge of the forest… What if…what if…

Shady stopping thinking and started to act. Carefully, measuredly, she turned the car to the right, up what had to be a dirt track, although the snow was making it sparkle.

The cabin ahead certainly looked rustic, but there was a light on in one of the rooms, and smoke puffed out of the chimney. Not Emma's house, she knew, not abandoned but very much lived in. Parked outside was a truck as beat-up as her Dodge.

As she came to a standstill, Ray opened the door and jumped out, emitting a "Whoa" at how cold it was. "Stay there," he said. "No sense in us all freezing. I'll do the honors."

Shady and Annie stared after him, Shady for her part fretting how successful Ray would be. If three strangers appeared on her doorstep begging to come in, she'd direct them to the nearest hotel, but then you could do that in Idaho Falls. Out here, that wasn't an option.

"Please," she found herself whispering, "please, please, please."

She held her breath, pretty sure Annie was doing the same as Ray knocked on the door of the cabin. The moments ticked by with such slowness, moments in which the door remained firmly shut. Shady closed her eyes briefly, continued to pray. As her eyes opened, so did the door, again with such slowness, inch by inch. A man? Was that a man she saw, standing opposite Ray? Certainly, his bulk suggested so, but his hair was long. All that mattered was that on seeing Ray, he hadn't slammed the door. In fact, they were speaking, Ray turning at one point and gesturing to his two companions, the man with long hair peering over Ray's shoulder to see.

The snow was falling so hard, piling up on the windshield, the wipers complaining, threatening to no longer do their duty. Her eyes flickered upward, toward the sky. Would there be any letup? The thought of being inside that cabin, that log fire, some hot drinks and warm food…

Ray turned and walked back toward the car. Behind

him, the door had closed.

"Fuck!" Shady swore. He'd been turned away. Annie kept quiet, but her sigh was ragged.

Having reached the car, Ray bent down until he was eye level with Shady. As he peered through the glass, he wore his trademark grin.

Grab your things, he mouthed. *We're in.*

CHAPTER EIGHTEEN

It turned out that folks living in the depths of Canada were very different from folks in Idaho. As they followed Ray up the path, he assured them that the man with the long hair—Keme, his name was—had at no point indicated he was frightened of them or that he would turn them away.

"He seems like a real nice guy," Ray continued as the light in the window drew them like a beacon. "A native, you know."

"Native American?" Shady asked.

"Well, Native Canadian," Ray said.

Shady nodded. "Of course."

"I told him just the basics—we're on a road trip, we got caught out by the weather, there's no accommodation around here, that kinda thing."

"Uh-huh, good," Shady said. If he'd told him the whole truth, that door would have probably shut and remained that way, bolted from the inside.

The man was standing in the doorway, waiting for them. He was pretty ancient, judging by the lines on his face, although his back was ramrod straight. Ushering them in, he pointed at the fire. "Warm yourselves," he said, and to Shady's ears it sounded like a command.

"Thank you," she muttered as she passed him. "Thank

you so much."

Annie, too, was busy thanking him as she dropped her bags and followed Shady to the fire.

Holding her hands out to warm them, Shady looked around her. The interior reminded her of something she'd only seen in Disney films, a cozy log cabin with rifles on the walls and a moose-head trophy. There was also a rocking chair, a settle, some framed family photographs on shelves, a colorful rug on the floor, its edges fraying slightly, and animal pelts hanging out to dry. Her eyes once more on the guns, she told herself to rein in her imagination, that *of course* a man would have guns in a place like this. He was a hunter, the moose head and animal skins were testament to that; he lived life the old way, the real way.

She was aware Keme had noticed her studying the guns. Able to drag her eyes away from them, she held his gaze instead, tried to read him. The word *thunder* came to mind. What did that mean, that he had a thunderous personality? Maybe so, but there was also kindness in his eyes, which were dark, almost black. There was sadness too. This man had lost people precious to him, and, looking around, she noticed no sign of anyone else other than those in the photos. Above all, however, his eyes held wisdom, a wealth of it; in comparison she felt like a newborn, as if she'd lived a few days rather than twenty-two years, as if she really was at the start of it all.

"Sit down." Keme broke the spell his gaze had on her and, again, as if he'd issued a command, she, Annie, and Ray immediately obeyed. "I'll get you something to eat."

The room was like a void after he'd left it. A bear of a man, he had filled it so completely.

"You okay now, Shady?" Ray asked, tufts of red hair having stiffened into peaks.

She nodded. "Yeah, I'm happy." She meant it—she was, happier than she'd ever been, more *alive*, all fear, all trepidation put on hold the minute she'd walked in here.

Annie, too, looked relieved. "As in Idaho, they know how to deal with these conditions in this country," she said, taking off her glasses to wipe at the lenses, "which is more than I can say for England. There, you get a few flurries and everything grinds to a halt. Heck, you get a leaf on the rail track and it grinds to a halt! Here, though, tonight, the snow ploughs will be out in force, and by the morning all roads will be usable again. We can knock on more doors, ask for information." She lowered her voice. "You never know, Keme might know about Emma too."

Keme was back, a tray in his hands upon which sat three mugs, steam rising from them.

"It's broth," he said, offering them the tray. "It'll warm you up."

The broth, compete with chunks of meat and vegetables, looked dubious and grey but tasted delicious. As they ate, he left the room and then returned once more, this time with thick slices of bread—homemade, Shady presumed, as was the soup. Certainly, both were heartier than anything she'd ever had before.

Joining them, the man sat on the rocking chair, the three of them occupying the settle, which had more brightly colored rugs covering it. There was silence as they consumed what had been offered, grateful silence, *companionable* silence. Shady thought she might feel the need to fill that silence with chatter of some kind, more expressions of gratitude, at the very least, but was surprised to find that words just wouldn't come. Instead, it was as if they sank into peace, all four of them, that it was sacred somehow, something to be cherished, Mandy and even the little girl Emma put on hold for now as simple pleasures took hold.

Despite being hungry, food was savored not hurried, the flames of the fire continuing to crackle, drowning out that nagging crying in Shady's head until it was an intermittent whimper.

Their broth finished, Annie placed her cup on the floor and leaned back against the rugs. She was exhausted, barely able to keep her eyes open. Not an old woman, only in her sixties, she nonetheless wouldn't have as much energy as her two younger counterparts, and Shady felt for her, wondering where they were going to sleep, in a bedroom or right here on the settle.

Keme stood. "Come," he said to Annie. "You need to rest."

"I'll be all right," she protested, but in the next minute changed her mind, heaving herself upward and following him as he left the room.

When he returned, he was carrying blankets. "You two will have to sleep here."

"Fine by me," Ray said, the expression on his face one of pure contentedness.

"Me too, of course," Shady said, taking the blankets from him. "These are such pretty colors," she commented, eyeing the reds, blues, and greens that knotted around each other.

"My wife made them," Keme answered.

"Your wife? Is she—"

He nodded. "A long time ago now."

"Do you have children?"

"They left, as children do."

"Where are they?"

"They're far flung, in Australia and New Zealand. Living good lives."

"Oh, I'm sure," Shady replied. "But you stayed."

"This is my home. It will *always* be my home."

"Well, from what I've seen of your home so far, it's beautiful."

There was a slight pause, and then Keme asked where they were from.

"Idaho," Shady told him, noticing that Ray had closed his eyes, leaving her alone to talk with Keme, a man she didn't know but who'd taken them in, who hadn't even faltered when asked, according to Ray. If this was America, she'd feel nervous. With her colleagues both asleep, she'd feel vulnerable too. But she didn't. Not one bit.

With seemingly enough questions exchanged for now, Keme had returned his gaze to the fire, giving Shady a chance to study him. His long hair, once black and glossy, she imagined, was now all but grey. She'd love to know how old he was; he could be sixty, ninety, or anywhere in between. It was impossible to tell and too rude to ask.

His name, though, like hers, was unusual. She could ask him about that.

"It means thunder," he said before she had a chance to. "Just as you thought."

If Shady could see herself, she knew she'd be a picture, her jaw having fallen open.

"How did you—"

"Because I'm attuned."

"Attuned?"

He nodded, his long hair swaying slightly. "And so are you."

"I don't under—"

"Like calls to like."

Like calls to like?

Looking at Keme, at Ray, thinking of Annie, she had to ask herself: Is that what had happened? They'd been *attracted* to one another? A theory that compounded what Annie had said about whose paths you crossed in life.

"The world is mysterious," Keme continued, as if he'd heard that thought too. "The spiritual world even more so." His words, and the heat of the flames, held her mesmerized. Beside her, Ray was gently snoring, his chest rising rhythmically up and down. "But we are exposed to both, to what we can see and what we can't see, what we can hear and what we *think* we hear. The latter many people will dismiss; they bury their suspicions. Put simply, they refuse to attune themselves. But those voices, when they come, are the most important of all. They belong to our ancestors, who are guiding us, leading us, warning us. You must learn to listen to them."

Shady could only nod. "I am. I do."

"Don't be afraid, but be wary. It is always wise to be wary."

"To achieve balance," she said.

A slight smile graced Keme's face. "Yes, in all things. The elder, Annie?"

"Yes, that's it, that's her name."

"Listen to her. Be willing to learn from her."

Shady nodded.

"You *must* learn," he reiterated, and this time, if Shady wasn't mistaken, there was slight agitation in his voice, quickly concealed. She assured him again that she was willing to do just that, to learn about the spiritual as well as the material, the mysteries that enshrined them both.

Keme appeared satisfied. He leaned back in his rocking chair, and silence resumed, Shady also leaning back, beside the sleeping Ray, wondering when sleep would come for her too.

"Who named you?" Keme said after a span of time.

Shady hesitated before answering, although she had no idea why. "My parents, my mother."

"Your mother?" He seemed to question that.

"She said I was born as the sun was setting. That's what gave her the idea."

"Shady." Keme tested her name. "And yet you walk in the light."

Shady gulped. "Do I? I hope so. I try to."

"Good," he muttered. "That's good."

After a while he asked her the question she knew was coming.

"So, what's the real reason you're here?"

With the fire continuing to flicker, she told him about Mandy.

* * *

What was that? A noise of some kind? Where was it coming from?

Shady grimaced as she forced open her eyes, having fallen asleep again without realizing. A shot of fear ran through her. Where was she? She had to work hard to remember. She was in a log cabin. In the woods. Someone had provided them with shelter from the weather. It was Keme's house. Of course it was. Nothing to be worried about.

So why did worry linger?

She sat up and rubbed at her arms. It didn't appear to be morning yet. The fire was still alight, but it was now only embers, the cold creeping in as the warmth receded. The noise… Initially it was inside the house, maybe a person moving around, but there now came a transition—a crunching sound, like boots on snow. Whoever it was had gone outside, to do what?

"Ray?" she whispered, but his slumped form told her he was still in the grip of sleep.

Too curious not to investigate, Shady eased herself to her feet, adjusting the blanket so that Ray was covered with hers too. Pulling her boots on, she made her way over to the window as silently as possible, barely even catching her breath, and rubbed at the condensation on the glass before peering outside. Against the white snow, bathed in the silver light of the moon, a figure could just be made out in the darkness. Moving toward the car. She could see it was Keme. What she couldn't see so well, what she had to squint at, was what he held in his hand. It had a long handle and something on the end of it. An axe?

"Mandy!"

With no more hesitation, Shady flew to the door and yanked it open, a blast of cold air succeeding in only briefly paralyzing her. There was no time to find her coat, to wrestle it on—she had to get out there and stop Keme from doing what he intended, which was to destroy Mandy.

When she'd told him earlier about Mandy, he had listened. Simply that. He hadn't passed judgment, hadn't nodded his head in contemplation; he'd sat as still as a statue while she'd related as succinctly as she could everything that had happened since Shady had first met Annie. It was only when she'd mentioned her dreams that he'd shifted slightly. But still, he'd said nothing.

And then she'd fallen asleep and woken to this…Keme marching out to the car with an axe.

"Keme! Keme!" she called, but if he heard her, he gave no indication. There was no breeze, though, and the snow was now settled. He *must* have heard her. "Keme! Wait! Please."

She picked up speed, striding through the powder. This was where youth won out, as he wasn't hurrying, perhaps couldn't; his wading was steady as his body turned from side to side to push through. She'd be able to catch up with him and stop him.

There was a howl in the distance, nothing to do with Mandy; it was a wild creature of the night, but Mandy might be howling too if Keme had his way.

He'd reached the car and positioned himself in front of the trunk, lifting the axe above his head. She reached the car too, her hands latching on to him. "Stop!" she continued to beg.

Thunder. That's what his name meant. And now she could see why. Gone was the mild-mannered man of earlier, and in his place was a warrior, yet another one.

Her voice shivered with shock as well as cold. "You can't do this to Mandy."

"There is evil in her."

"Maybe. But you still can't destroy her. If she's evil, I have to try and understand why."

"You're too young—"

"Too inexperienced? Maybe, but I have to learn. You were insistent about that before." She dared to take one hand off him as she gestured toward the trunk. "This is *how* I learn."

Her words had the desired effect. Slowly, slowly, he lowered his weapon.

As well as Mandy, she'd told him the story of Emma Moore that night. She hadn't asked if he knew about her, because she'd figured he'd say so if he did. She'd been disappointed, then, when he'd shown no knowledge of the child, as it meant they would indeed have to ask elsewhere to try to find something out, but how long that would take—and, in these conditions, how possible it would be—was anyone's guess. She supposed that somewhere between falling asleep and waking up she'd resigned herself to temporary defeat, admitted they had no option but to get back on the road to Idaho when morning came, returning to Dupont another time, during a milder season. They'd just have to keep Mandy restrained until then, and Shady would have to restrain herself too, be patient. But as she and the old man stared at each other, hope resurfaced.

"You know about the child, don't you? You know where Emma lived."

"Not Emma," he replied.

"What?"

"Not Emma. That wasn't her true name."

"What was it, then?"

"Hurit. It means beautiful. Her mother's true name was Wapun, which means the dawn."

"But…I don't understand," Shady confessed. Why had they used aliases?

"They, as I am, are part of the Woodland Cree, the native Canadians, the First Peoples. Some keep our true names, some don't. They don't because it is easier to fit into your society."

"Yes, yes, of course." Shady knew something about Native history; she was aware of how they'd been persecuted and that, to a large extent, they still were, shunted onto reservations and treated as second-class citizens, worse than that, even. "So, you knew her."

"I knew *of* her. Everybody does around here. That she lay dead for so long undiscovered, that a doll lay with her. If it is this doll, then I am right when I say it is evil."

Still Shady struggled to understand. "Why?"

"Because like attracts like. I've told you this!" The patience he'd displayed earlier in the evening was no longer in evidence. "Death, when it occurs like that, in such…terrible circumstances, in such *lonely* circumstances, attracts a particular energy."

"Negative energy?"

"Yes, and it will feast. It will find a home. It will grow."

"Find a home? In the doll, you mean?"

He nodded, raised his hand again, the one that gripped the axe. "And so it must be destroyed."

"Keme, Keme, listen to me. Annie said we can't destroy the doll. Doing that would be too easy. If you're right, if that negativity, that energy, *has* found a home in the doll, then destroying its vessel won't destroy *it*. All it will do is release it, and it will find—" the cold made her catch her breath once more "—a new home elsewhere."

His hand stilled.

"But there's more, Keme. Much more. Annie's talked to me a lot about balance. I've talked about it with you too. I think…I've got this hunch…Mandy isn't completely evil. Somehow there's balance in her too. And she was just a doll once upon a time, she really was, nothing more, an inanimate thing. But even so, the thing is, negativity has *always* surrounded her, and whether sentient or not, she's soaked it up. She's dangerous, but"—how many times had she said this, not just to Keme but to herself and others?—"there's something about Mandy, and as much as people fear her, they want to protect her too, me included. And *that's* what I have to understand. I don't know when she changed for sure, but from everything you're saying, everything that I feel, it has something to do with Emma…Hurit. If you destroy Mandy, I'm never gonna find out."

"Annie is a wise woman," Keme declared.

"She is. I want to be like her."

"You?" Something in his eyes shone. "You'll be greater. You know who you are, don't you?"

"Who I am? I'm Shady—"

"No!" He was emphatic. "You're one of us."

"Attuned?" Is that what he meant?

He shook his head, even more thunderous. "One of us! One of our People!"

Shady was about to refute that, but he started to speak

again, and so she fell as silent as the land around them.

"Sometimes I am not so attuned." As quick as a heartbeat, his voice had gone from impatient to gruff, a crack in it. "About Hurit, I never knew... I was concerned only with my own family, and yet...there seemed no need to worry. I encountered Wapun only a handful of times in the town, at the store, and each time Hurit was with her. Her husband was a logger, and he'd died when the child was very young, but mother and daughter gave the impression of being devoted to each other. And then...then I didn't see them any longer, and I failed to ask why."

"God, you knew them, you actually knew them!"

He nodded, such a sad gesture. "If I recall correctly, I think Hurit may even have had the doll with her on one or two occasions, holding it tight. It was all such a long time ago." With Shady remaining quiet, he continued to speak. "The doll was just a doll. The child just a child. The mother just a mother. A family who'd suffered tragedy but who carried on, who endured."

Shady's own eyes were beginning to well at the sentiment of what he'd said.

"But then it changed"—he wasn't gazing at her anymore but into the distance, the moonlight reflected in his eyes— "as all things must."

"Keme," Shady whispered, "tell me where Hurit's house is."

There was only a slight hesitation. "I will tell you. I'll take you there, tomorrow. But I won't go in with you. I'll come back here, and I'll wait."

"That's fine. You don't have to come in. I'll go—*we* will, Ray, Annie, and me." She reached out to touch his arm.

"Thank you…for leaving Mandy alone. For allowing me to continue on this path."

On his cheek was a solitary tear. "A man has to know when to stop," he said, not bothering to wipe it away. "And a woman has to know when to begin. I'll wait for you, and I'll pray."

CHAPTER NINETEEN

That Shady managed more sleep that night was something of a miracle, but she did, to be woken in the morning light by Keme handing her and Ray a mug of strong black coffee each. Annie had also re-joined them, the exhaustion of last night wiped clean away. Shady's two friends were oblivious to all that had happened just a few hours previously, and she decided to leave it that way, explaining only what was necessary: that Keme knew where Emma had lived—or Hurit, as her real name was, being of Woodland Cree descent—and that he'd agreed to take them there.

"The house still stands?" Ray asked.

"It's a cabin, like this, and yes, it does."

"And it's only a few miles away?" Annie, too, was trying to get it straight in her head.

"Farther into the forest," Keme answered.

That it was so near, that they'd succeeded in finding it, caused Shady to shake her head in wonder, that same emotion evident in Annie's eyes and Ray's too. What other emotions it provoked, she buried for now. They were *meant* to do this.

Keme left the room only to reenter with an armful of jackets, gloves, and hats, all of them far more heavy-duty than the ones they owned. "The smaller sizes belonged to my wife and children, so they should fit you two. Ray, you can take one of my jackets."

None of them protested, glad of the prospect of extra padding. The autumn and winter months could be bitter in Idaho, but they didn't compare to this.

Without further delay, they piled into Keme's Chevy Blazer—Shady in the back with Ray this time and Annie riding beside Keme. The sky wasn't as ominous as it had been the day before, there were some patches of blue, but Keme warned them that more snow was forecast; what was debatable was how heavy it would be. He also told them in spite of the weather, he'd return for them. They just had to call him. If he didn't hear, though, he'd return anyway before nightfall.

All three had made sure to charge their phones fully, Annie turning hers off to conserve the battery should the cold run the other two down more quickly than normal. Shady had groaned when she'd checked her cell phone this morning. Ellen had called dozens of times, leaving texts as well as voice messages, all saying roughly the same thing: *Shady, you're to quit what you're doing and come home! I know you're an adult, I respect that, but respect is a two-way thing. You need to take my feelings into account too. Come home, Shady. Please… Come home.*

Keme had noticed her frowning, had muttered something beneath his breath when he'd handed her the padded jacket she now wore. "You're no quitter," it sounded like, and she'd glanced at him curiously, but he'd turned away by then, handing out gloves and a hat to Annie.

Trussed up, all of them, and none quitters.

Mandy had been moved from the trunk of Shady's car to the rear of Keme's truck, and Shady had noticed him bristle as he watched her carry out the task, those powerful hands of his still eager to destroy, perhaps, but aware that Annie's reasoning was valid. The Natives were renowned for their deep respect of the natural world and also the world beyond that, but there was faith and there was absolute knowledge. No one, but *no one*, knew for certain what was beyond the veil that separated life and death, how thick that veil was, or what caused it to thin on occasions. What was it that the English playwright, Shakespeare, had said about such things? Shady thought back to high school, to a quote from *Hamlet* that had always resonated with her: "*There are more things in heaven and earth... Than are dreamt of in your philosophy.*"

Balance. For Shady it all came back to that, the light and the dark. How much darkness would they encounter this day?

Keme's Chevy negotiated roads that had indeed been ploughed in the night, his tires gripping steadily enough the snow-impacted road beneath them. The miles fell away all too quickly, with no one speaking a word, simply preparing themselves for what might or might not be revealed.

Just before they reached the cabin, Annie let out a gasp. "Look! Oh, look!"

They all turned their heads toward where she was pointing. Ray inhaled too, as did Shady. Keme simply chuckled. "*Moswa*," he said. "Moose."

"Never seen one before," Ray said. "Not in the flesh."

"Nor me," replied Annie.

"Incredible." Shady accompanied her remark with a sigh,

watching the animal as it stood and stared right back at them, a noble creature, majestic, a sight to treasure, to make your spirit soar. That this could happen considering their destination, their intent, gave her the boost she needed.

Eventually, Keme brought the vehicle to a stop, and both Shady and Ray ducked their heads to look out the windshield. There was indeed a cabin ahead that screamed abandonment.

Shady screwed her eyes shut, almost in pain. This area was just a few miles from Keme's house, a good man's house, and yet it felt so isolated.

"Shady?" Ray's voice forced her to open her eyes. "We're here for you, every step of the way."

She nodded. "But who was here for Hurit?" Or rather *what*?

Keme's voice reached her from the front, although he didn't turn his head to look at her. "Wapun was a good woman. She loved her child; it was obvious. She wouldn't have just left her alone." Now he did turn, his gaze piercing. "There are things you need to know. Canada is a beautiful country. I took my first breath here, and I will take my last—that is my choice and my right. So far, I've been left alone to live out my life, but not all our People are as fortunate."

"Keme?" Annie prompted when he fell silent. "Tell us more."

After a second or two, he obliged. "It's been reported that over the past thirty years in Canada, as many as four thousand indigenous women and girls have either been killed or gone missing. The true number is likely to be much higher. The government has failed us. Despite promising over and over to investigate this matter, they don't. You see, *that's* how a little girl, a little *Native* girl, could lay dead for three years with no mention of it in the media, her memory kept alive only by word-of-mouth, nothing more. As for her mother, no one knows where she went, and no one cares. I tried to make amends for not being neighborly enough, for not checking up. I told the authorities she was a good woman, a good mother. My concerns have never been acted on."

As all three sat listening to him, Shady's heart growing heavier and heavier to learn there was a sinister side to such a stunning country, Keme turned back toward the cabin.

"There was evil there, but there was also love. Both sides of the coin. Remember that when you go in. There were both sides of the coin."

Leaving the car, Shady followed Keme around to the tailgate. He opened it, but she was the one that leaned in, still fearful he might change his mind and snatch the doll from her.

He did no such thing.

"Thank you," she said, "for everything."

"I'll return before dark."

"I know you will. And, Keme, I'm sorry. For what your People suffered."

"Your People too. Remember?"

"But—" How could she tell him he was wrong?

"And because they are, I'm letting you do this. Because you *can*."

"We need answers. We need to understand."

He nodded. "It is right to strive for understanding. If only others would, there might be hope for this world.

Understanding and…tolerance too."

Their gaze held for a moment longer, then Keme returned to the driver's side of the car, climbed in, and reversed for a few yards before making a turnabout and driving away. The three watched him until he was out of sight, Shady having to take a deep breath.

"This is it," she said, the casket in her arms. "Showdown time."

* * *

As they ventured forward, Shady couldn't shake the feeling that she'd had yesterday: that they'd been drawn here, lured. It was a trap, a web that would entangle them, never to let go.

Rein it in, Shady.

She would. More to the point, she *could*. She'd been given the tools to do that by the woman who walked to her left. Visualize white light, practice good intent, and have faith that, in some way, you were helping. Light existed. So did the darkness. You had to choose your side.

Inside the casket all was still, yet she had a sense that the doll was struggling in there, something in it kicking out, both in protest and excitement. Both sides of the coin, as Keme had said. Just a shack, that's all this was, a modest cabin in which an ordinary family had lived. And then something *extra*ordinary had occurred, and on many levels.

A few yards from the door, they stopped.

"Shady," Annie checked, "how are you feeling?"

"Determined," she replied, smiling at her and Ray.

"Even so, if it becomes too much, we pull out. Ray and I

are here to ensure you don't become overwhelmed, because that in itself will achieve nothing and may cause harm. We're only here to try and understand, because knowledge, as we know, will help us."

Shady nodded. "This is one heck of a journey, isn't it?"

"It is," agreed Annie, "and we're all at different stages of it, including Mandy."

There was a moment of silence, perfect silence. Mandy had stopped her struggles, aware of the gravitas of the situation, perhaps, weighing up her position, contemplating it every bit as much as they were. The snow had managed to subdue everything, absorb what was there before, covering it up in layer upon layer of white. The clouds above threatened another deluge, but it was what lay in between land and sky that Shady focused on—not just a whole load of nothingness, she realized. Instead, without anything to dilute or distract from it, the air was filled with energy. It was just so...*alive*. The earth's energy, there for all to harness.

"Can you feel it?" she said, hearing the awe in her own voice as she woke up to this simple, ancient fact. A fact she knew the Natives were all too aware of.

"The energy?" Ray said, tuning in as much as her.

"The *gathering* energies," Annie elaborated, and she was right, for there was plenty gathering here, energy that could recharge you but also deplete you, maybe even destroy you.

There was no more time to contemplate, to wonder—not for her and not for Mandy.

Placing the casket on the ground, Shady levered it open.

There she was, the doll, lying inside, her glassy eyes staring up at Shady through a face that had known violence at some point, that had witnessed all that was wrong with humanity, the flip side that had imbued it, and yet it wasn't just fear and loathing she felt for it, not any longer.

"With Kate Jane you were just a doll. But with others, with me, you were something else."

She reached in and slowly, gently, closed her hands around the doll's waist and lifted. Annie and Ray stepped forward, lending her their strength and energy.

A cry…a scream…faint, but both would grow stronger the minute she stepped inside the cabin. From thereon in she would start to see, and understand.

Shady cast a final glance at Annie and Ray, noted the worry on their faces but also the pride.

This was a journey; they'd all agreed on that. Would there ever really be a conclusion?

CHAPTER TWENTY

"Hurit, hush now, Daddy will be home soon. He can read to you. You'd like that, wouldn't you. He'll read your favorite book, the one you love so much."

Shady knew that she would see, but this clearly? It was as if the people in front of her were truly here, Wapun and Hurit, the latter so small, so pretty with hair and eyes that were practically raven. It was clear whom she'd inherited her beauty from. Wapun was lithe and graceful, with a sweetness about her, maybe even naivety. A happy woman, but there was conflict within her. She had nothing but respect for the enormity of her heritage, yet she also desired to fit in with an ever-changing, more modern world, and for her child to fit in also, for life to be…easier.

Where was Wapun's husband, the child's father? At work, Shady supposed. He'd been a logger, had suffered an accident and died, but on this night, he was expected home.

Although she was aware that Annie and Ray were close by, they were the ones who'd faded, who'd become nothing more than shadows; only Wapun and Hurit were substantial. As for her and Mandy, they were caught somewhere in between, both of them observing.

When they'd pushed their way into the cabin, Ray having to heave his full weight against the door to open it, a surprisingly large space had greeted them, a former living room with a hallway leading off it to other rooms, similar in layout to Keme's home. It was bare inside, all contents long since removed along with the girl's body—finally—and then the house shut up, not to be vandalized by curious youngsters, graffiti sprayed upon the walls, something moronic along the lines of *Look out, look out, there's a demonic doll about.* That sort of thing might have happened in the city where she lived, but not here. Here, a site such as this was left alone to decay in its own time, nature gradually moving back in to reclaim it.

Where had Hurit's body lain? Not in the living room but elsewhere in the house. If she sought that spot out immediately, though, she might miss out on the bigger picture, and so she resolved to do her best to avoid it until last. Holding Mandy tight, the struggle inside the doll was intensifying, although her limbs remained static.

The living room was warm and cozy, with a log fire burning and brightly patterned rugs adorning both the walls and the floor, heirlooms possibly, the nimble work of ancestors.

And there was humming…humming that reminded Shady of another woman, the one in her dreams. *Kanti*— she who sings. It was a word she'd never heard before, another Cree name? Yet it had formed vividly. A woman who sings, who'd sung to her—*I'm bound to go away.*

Don't get distracted, Shady.

She mustn't. This was not about her, or some dream she'd had, this was what had truly happened.

The door opened, and someone walked in. A man, tall, as broad as Keme, his skin a shade or two darker than his wife's. The husband, it had to be.

A family scene, striking in its normality. What went on here was exactly what happened in millions of houses all over America, Canada, and the world. People were just people. They had different cultures, different beliefs, different talents, but they were essentially part of one big tribe: the human race. But differences were still differences—*You're different*—if only people would accept them, celebrate them, instead of being fearful of them, intent on ostracizing them, destroying them, even. What Keme had told her about the indigenous genocide of the Canadian First Peoples had shocked her. Why would anyone want to harm people like this?

The book that had been promised to the child was being read by the father. Shady was surprised to find she recognized it, a book she'd also had read to her: *The Velveteen Rabbit* by Margery Williams, a British author. It dated back to when? The 1920s or something? Just like Mandy, it had endured, becoming something of an institution.

The father's voice was soft, the child gazing up at him as he related the tale of the rabbit who arrives at a nursery one morning, only to find himself snubbed by the other toys. Soon, though, he makes friends with one toy—the Skin Horse—who explains to him how toys can become "real."

A sweet story, a story Shady had loved too, and yet at this point she shuddered, refusing to look down at Mandy in her arms, to give her that satisfaction.

"In the story they only become real if they're loved enough," she said, her voice a whisper even though the family in front of her would never be able to hear. "*Only* if they are loved."

No sooner had she uttered those words than the scene was swept away, as if by a sharp breeze, another swiftly replacing it. A slightly older Hurit, around four, was sitting in front of the fire, clutching the same book and crying. From another room came the sound of sobbing, a woman—Wapun, no doubt. Shady swallowed. They'd lost him, then, the husband; the accident had happened. The child's bewilderment and the sheer, raw pain of the mother were so abundant, they filled this little cabin in the woods, a physical expression of two potent questions: How do you recover from such a tragedy? Where do you find the strength?

Another scene: the child on a chair in front of the fire again, the mother on another chair opposite. The child still clutched something to her, but it wasn't a book this time; it was something else, a doll. She was holding that doll as if her life depended on it, a new source of comfort, one perhaps not as painful as a book that still held her father's soft voice. A toy that had nothing to do with him, which might help her to move on.

The doll was Mandy—no crack down her face and something innocuous, one of many "Mandy" dolls produced. Not new, oh no. Kate Jane had had her when new, and that was many, many years before. Yet she was still a doll that had been made for a child, to inspire love in that child, but hadn't always hit the spot.

Had a child ever loved Mandy, *truly* loved her? A love born from purity rather than obsession?

Shady peered closer. Hurit looked like she loved her, looked so proud to have her.

There was a scream in Shady's head—so much anguish in it, so much…pain.

Mandy, are we getting somewhere with you?

She had a feeling they were, and the doll both hated and wanted it.

Not just a scream—a hiss and words that rasped, *Your light is useless here.*

We'll see, Shady shot back. *We will see.*

"Shady, do you want to go through to another room?"

It was Annie asking, her voice far more welcome to Shady's ears but still so far away. Was this what it was like to be caught between two worlds? The material and the spiritual? The in-between, as she'd thought of it earlier. She must ensure she trod carefully, kept the balance.

"Lead the way," Shady replied, her own voice sounding distant too.

Ray stepped forward, took her arm, and guided her.

There was no bed in the next room they entered, no physical bed, but Shady could see one nonetheless, and the woman lying on it, still sobbing, still heartbroken. Lost. Scared. Constantly berating herself. She should have the strength to bring her daughter up, she should! And yet…the despair within her was only increasing. She tried, Shady could see that, to keep the child's life as normal as possible. She had bought her that doll, just a junk doll, not the kind any modern kid would want, right at the bottom of a basket of dolls in a thrift store, but Hurit had dove into that basket, pulled that doll out, and coveted it.

Money was tight; all Wapun could pick up were menial jobs, jobs that allowed her to bring Hurit along, whom she was always careful to call Emma in public, and herself Carol

Anne. Menial jobs meant lousy pay, with nothing left over for luxuries, for that doll, but oh, to see the child smile like that when she'd found it! Wapun was so relieved. And, if she was honest, a tiny bit jealous, something else she was angry with herself for. But to feel joy again…just a hint of it… Violently the woman shook her head. No, there was to be no more joy, but she'd continue breathing, for Hurit's sake, even though all she wanted was to curl up and follow her husband into the realm of spirit.

Oh, she mustn't keep crying for him, she mustn't! Her grief might tether him to the material world, and that was unforgiveable. After the fourth sun had set, she should have dried her tears. But there'd been so many settings of the sun since, and enough tears to form an ocean.

Although part of an ancient People, there was no family to call on. On the contrary, they'd moved here to escape family—not their parents, they were dead, but brothers and sisters and cousins who'd chosen a darker path, who'd allowed bitterness to claim them. Dupont was supposed to represent a fresh start, one where they could start a family of their own, not end up alone! Stupid, stupid accident! But he'd been tired that day. He'd worked hard to give them material things, when really all they'd needed to thrive was each other.

Yet again, Wapun cursed her tears. She had to be strong, she had to call on the strength of her ancestors to help her through. Yet she'd done that. And all that met her was silence. A wall of it.

Her little girl…her poor little girl…she deserved better…

"Shady." Once more, Annie's voice drew her from the

scene, stopped her from immersing herself too deeply in it, from becoming Wapun... Because that's what it felt like: she was losing her identity and taking on the woman's, feeling every emotion that exploded in her chest.

"It's okay. I'm fine," she responded. A lie, because she wasn't fine; how could she be when witnessing such misery? And what was that misery doing? Entrapping them further.

Wapun, listen to your own advice. Drag yourself out of the pit you've fallen into. You've still got plenty to live for. Please, don't do this... Like calls to like. You don't want what this attracts.

Again, the scene dissolved, revealing what in actuality was there, a room quietly rotting. Wondering if that was it, if that was the extent of what she'd experience, Shady was about to explain all to Annie and Ray when she heard voices from another room. Turning toward the source of them, she left the bedroom and went into what had once been the kitchen, some cupboards still intact, but on others doors were hanging off hinges or missing entirely. She made her way over to one of the cupboards and leaned her forehead against it.

A woman's voice, Wapun's... *That's not her name! Not anymore.* The voice in her head was adamant, and swiftly Shady made the adjustment. She was Carol Anne again, she was *only* Carol Anne, and the man she was talking to— Shady squinted—was a white man. She was talking to him and she was laughing, she was drawing comfort from him, the way Hurit drew comfort from Mandy, or at least Carol Anne was trying to, she was forcing herself to.

And Hurit, aged five or so, sat not in front of the fire but at the kitchen table, clutching Mandy still and gazing at her mother and this new man, and she felt something…something like fear because this new man wasn't like her daddy, not at all. And yet her mother loved him; she'd said so. She'd said that *Emma* should love him. That he'd look after them, save them.

"We need a man," she'd told the child after one of his earlier visits to the house. "You understand that, don't you? Money is so…tight. It's hard to get a job, to keep a job. He can look after us; he's promised to. No one will replace your daddy. No one! But…we need him."

"Oh God! Oh shit!" Shady said.

Quickly Ray responded, "What is it?"

"There was a man here, not Wapun's husband but someone who came after him. He brought the darkness, and the child…the child knew it."

Carol Anne was a good person; Keme had said that. But good didn't always mean strong, as the woman herself was only too aware. Not weak, no. Shady wouldn't say she was that either. But she was vulnerable. She was prey. And where there was prey there was often a hunter.

This man brought food to the table and clothes for their backs; he paid off accumulated debts and even proffered gifts. What he wanted in return was Carol Anne's attention, all of it. Again, Shady could see Carol Anne tried to include the child when she could, but his ways were subtle, they were insidious, his threats low-level at first. If she didn't comply, if she didn't give him what he demanded, the gifts would stop, the food, the "bankrolling," as he began to call it. And Emma was all right, he said. "She just plays with her toys, with that doll. She don't need nothing else."

And Carol Anne would convince herself he was right.

Emma *was* happy, as long as she had Mandy. That doll, not the man, had been her savior.

Low-level threats, however, rarely tended to stay that way; they got worse, more insistent, more demanding. What Shady saw was a man's obsession with a woman rather than a child's obsession with a doll. Emma was nothing to him, he barely even noticed her, but Carol Anne—she was *everything*, and, in turn, he wanted to be everything to her.

And finally—*finally*—Carol Anne realized the weight of his obsession.

"I want you to leave," she said. "You have to. I'm sorry, but this is a mistake. We can't go on."

Shady winced as he struck her across the face for saying such things, for refusing to succumb to his will anymore. He hit her not once, but twice, so many times, breaking her spirit, her will, which became his new obsession, reducing her to dependency any way he could.

But one look at the terror on her child's face as she witnessed this and Wapun dug deep, surprised to find there was courage there when she had doubted it so much.

"You need to leave!"

If only Shady didn't have to see this play out in order to understand, if only she could switch it all off. Throughout, one other thing was apparent: Mandy was still just a doll.

The violence he inflicted upon Carol Anne was systematic and brutal, often sending her flying across the length of the kitchen, or smashing her head against the wall, his face close to hers, spittle flying from his mouth as he told her if she tried to force him to leave, he'd kill her and no one would care, because no one did, not about her kind.

"It's one less," he said.

Another day, another beating, but this time it was different—this time the child intervened. As young as she was, she tried to stop him, she begged him, she pleaded. So, what did he do?

He took the one thing he knew was precious to the child, Mandy, and, holding her soft cotton-stuffed body, he lifted her up, enjoying further pleading from the child, further begging, before he swung the doll's head against the wall, just as he'd done with the child's mother, and then threw the doll back at her, its face not intact, not anymore, a crack running down its left side.

Shady inhaled…Shady waited…Shady clutched both Annie and Ray.

Was this it? Would this moment trigger something in Mandy?

The child cradled the doll in her arms, tears falling from such sorrowful eyes to land on Mandy as if she was trying to wash away the damage, as if such a thing were possible.

And still Shady waited.

From Mandy there was no response at all.

CHAPTER TWENTY-ONE

Shit! Shady really thought that when the violence in Hurit's household had extended to include the doll, causing the child yet more distress, something would happen. That, prompted by this act, whatever energies had gathered there would accumulate further, using Mandy, taking up residence within her, forcing her into sentience, into something destructive too.

But she was wrong.

The visions she'd experienced faded, adding to her frustration. "I don't understand!" she yelled, the doll in her arms and her arms only, the crack more pronounced, the lips curling, if only in her imagination, laughing at her, so damned gleeful. "You are *not* an inanimate object. You're something more. When did it change? When the hell did it change?"

Annie reached into her pocket and retrieved her phone, switching it back on.

"What are you doing?" Shady asked, frowning.

"This is becoming too much for you."

Shady could feel her face contort as she frowned. "So, what are you doing?" she repeated.

"Phoning Keme to come and get us."

"No!"

Ray intervened. "Shady, look at you. You're shaking, you're shouting. I don't know what you've seen, but—"

"Not enough! I still haven't seen enough. Annie, don't ring Keme. Give me more time."

"Shady, I'm responsible for you."

"You're not."

"I am!" Annie insisted, her voice rising too. "If anything happens to you…your parents…" She shook her head. "Perhaps this needs to be done in stages. Some things can't be rushed, not when we don't know what we're dealing with, truly dealing with, I mean."

"Well, that's the whole objective, isn't it? To find out."

"As much as we can, that's all. No, I'm sorry, I'm phoning Keme."

Shady looked at Annie, looked at Ray too; both of them seemed resolute. "I don't understand. This is what we've come all this way for, and we're close to finding out. We honestly are."

"Shady, look around you," Ray said. "Do you see how dark it's gotten in here? How cold?"

"It was always dark and cold."

"Not like this. Something's happening. Something's…building."

She almost snorted. "Are you the psychic one now?"

"No, I…well, yeah, because I can feel it. Annie can feel it. How come you can't?"

"All I know is I'm close to the truth. Go ahead, call Keme if you want, but I'm not leaving."

"Oh, I am going to call him," Annie retorted. "Don't worry on that score. I thought we were all in agreement about the lengths we'd go to. I can't put your life in danger, or anyone else's."

"I'm not a kid." She'd said it to her parents, and she said it to Annie. "And I'm close. I am."

It was perhaps her certainty of that that caused Annie to falter. "I just...I don't know. Ray's right, something's happening in here. The atmosphere's...shifted. Tell me you can feel it too."

Damn right she could, so hard it almost took her breath away, something she quickly concealed, so as not to alarm them further. She would not, *could not,* leave here without knowing the full story. All along, this journey had been about Mandy, but it had led them into the lives of others, the deaths of others too, and none more mysterious than Carol Anne's and Emma's.

Ray reached out to Annie. "Okay, let her do it. Give her a few more minutes."

"That's all I need. I promise."

It took another moment, but at last Annie nodded, holding on to the phone but not dialing. Shady knew where she was going next, the only room they hadn't been so far: Hurit's bedroom.

She'd have been lying if she'd said she wasn't scared when she entered that particular room; she was. Here, the energy was even more intense, so alive it was crackling, that sound, like Mandy's crying and screaming and hissing, only audible to her ears. Still holding the doll, she walked to the far side of the room, the side where the child's bed would have been, a single bed, layered with blankets and a fur pelt, its metal frame rickety, a table beside it on which there would have been a lamp and a book too, *The Velveteen Rabbit*, not cast aside after all.

"Oh, Hurit," whispered Shady, seeing the room the way it used to be. Such a bruised heart the child had had, and yet still there'd been room in it for the book and Mandy.

Without further comment, she dropped to her knees in the place where the bed had been and then lay fully on the floor, on her side, fetal-like, the doll beside her.

This was where Emma had died, the *way* she'd died, in this position.

But what had death created in its wake?

* * *

In the cabin everything was grey, like the sky outside was grey; there was a mist that swirled around and around, never clearing, always there, as heavy as a cloak. The maelstrom?

The child stood there, only briefly glancing back at the body that lay on the bed—and the doll.

She'd died. She understood that. At some point, with her beloved Mandy beside her, she had breathed in and never breathed out. But the spark within, the great spirit, remained lit.

Dead…but alive. And—except for Mandy, *always* except for Mandy—she was alone.

Tentatively, the child placed one foot in front of the other. She could move forward, just as she always had, but it was with a new lightness.

She turned her head from side to side, and that was easy too. She knew where she was: at home, in the cabin—this was her world, after all, what lay beyond, far beyond, always such a mystery. There was nothing to see, however, but this mist, thick in some places, thinner in others.

"Momma, where are you?"

Had she said that or just thought it? She couldn't tell. Everything was different now, yet in many ways it was still the same. Where had her mother gone? What had happened to her?

Something bad.

Yes, that was it. Something bad had happened to her. She was scared to remember, but she had to try, be brave and force herself.

There'd been a struggle and shouting. *Him* shouting at *her*.

Their life had already changed, but it had changed again with this man's arrival. She could still remember so vividly her true father and how he'd sit and read to her, how he would talk to her afterward until she fell into the depths of sleep, his voice so soft, so kind. And then he was gone, and her heart had become heavy, but not as heavy as her mother's heart, which had seemed to tear itself in two as she'd lain awake night after night and cried—not just cried sometimes but howled.

When she'd come home with the other man, there'd been laughter on her face once more, but not laughter such as Hurit had ever known it, because her eyes had retained their sadness. His eyes, though…even now, the child shuddered to remember them. They were blue, a bright shade, but they were…empty somehow. And yet…and yet…at the same time, they were so focused, on Wapun, always on her, her beautiful, broken mother. She was all he could see.

Her mother had said he was going to look after them. "Everything will be all right now."

Yet, as those days and weeks and months passed after her father's death, hadn't they already reached a new level of "all right," just she and her mother, *Nikawi,* as the child called her, the Cree word for mother, *Nohtawi* the name for her father. Sometimes Nikawi would teach her words from the ancient language, "but just for us to use in the house and with each other," her mother would say before pointing to the window. "Out there we speak their language, always."

With her mother a little stronger, they would venture "out there," the child accompanying her to her jobs, watching as she scrubbed other peoples' cabins and houses while theirs remained just a little messy. They would also drive to the store in town in the truck that had once belonged to Nohtawi and buy food, which they would eat in silence in front of the fire.

And then one day her mother had bought her something special—she'd bought her Mandy. They hadn't eaten as much that night, the dregs of some leftover stew and a bit of bread that was already going stale, but Hurit didn't mind because she'd had something to take care of now, and she would; she'd look after her. Because Mandy—the name stamped on the back of the doll's neck, such a funny name, a name that made her laugh—had known loss too. She must have to end up where she had. Hurit knew *exactly* how it felt. As between a mother and a daughter, the bond between the child and the toy was special. They were kindred spirits.

And it was Mandy that had kept her company when he'd demanded her mother look at him and only him, that she put the child to bed early so that he and she could have their "special time" together, that she get her daughter and that "stupid doll" out of the way.

At first, the child had stood her ground, wouldn't run and hide simply because he wanted her to. This was her home, hers, Nikawi's and Mandy's.

"Don't call me Nikawi," her mother would say, "not in front of him. Just call me Mom."

She'd ignore that too, continue to call her by the Cree name, even Wapun sometimes instead of Carol Anne, referring to herself as Hurit instead of Emma. After all, what did Emma mean? She had no idea. It was another strange-sounding name. Hurit meant beautiful. Her father had chosen it. She was proud of that name. It was nothing, *nothing* to be ashamed of.

Her defiance had soon been turned against her—or, rather, her mother. The man who had made Nikawi smile had now made her cry again. If she didn't do as he said—if *they* didn't—when he said it, his blue eyes would become like flint.

Bewildered, lost, hurt, Nikawi had become all those things once more, but perhaps…perhaps a person was only willing to suffer so much, because eventually her soft brown eyes had begun to harden too. She wouldn't jump at his every command, not immediately, not anymore; she would make him wait, she'd answer back, she'd even refuse. Defiant. And the child had been proud to see it, relieved. She'd stand there with Mandy and silently encourage her: *Don't let him hurt us anymore.*

But he had.

He'd taken Mandy and destroyed her first, grabbing her

out of Hurit's arms and smashing her head against the wall. "Get that doll and that child out of my sight!"

He'd broken Mandy and then he'd broken her mother, and by degrees he'd broken Hurit too.

Still, she kept calling.

"Momma, where are you? Please answer. Nikawi? Where did he take you?"

Because he'd taken her *somewhere*, she realized. They'd been arguing, her mother insisting again that she wanted him to leave, screaming at him, telling him that if he went near her child, anywhere near her, she'd call the cops. Oh, how he'd laughed at that.

He'd hit her mother, both she and furniture crashing across the floor. Terrified to hear it, cradling poor Mandy in her arms, Hurit had crouched in a corner of her bedroom, all bravery having deserted her, the hurricane he was creating too strong a force to reckon with.

Perhaps it would be all right, perhaps another force greater than him would intervene, would somehow save them. She was just a girl, clutching a broken doll, hearing her mother begging the man she was supposed to love to leave her alone, to not kill her.

There'd been the sound of a door slamming and then…silence. All was quiet.

Eventually the child had moved. She'd padded across to the door, opened it, and peered outside into nothing but darkness, into an abyss, it seemed. She'd returned to her room, cowered there again, beginning to cry. When morning came, she forced herself to explore other rooms in the cabin, moving quietly, her hands tight around Mandy, the only comfort she had. There was no sign of Wapun and no sign of him either. Where had they gone? What had he done to her?

Hours passed. Daylight faded. In the living room she built a fire from leftover scraps of wood and tried to keep warm. She ate what was in the fridge and the cupboards. It was very little but enough to keep her going for a short while. Because Nikawi would return. She wouldn't abandon her. She'd return. If she could.

Please, please, come back.

Day turned to night, night turned to day, over and over. The fire had grown cold and the cupboards empty, but still she waited, having taken to her bed now, cradling Mandy, trying to nurse her, assuring the doll as her mother had once assured her, "Everything will be all right." She was grateful for Mandy, precious Mandy; no one could take her away, no one! Nobody had wanted her when she was perfect, so nobody would want her now, only Hurit, remembering the story of *The Velveteen Rabbit*, that if you loved something hard enough, that's when it became real. And she *did* love Mandy hard enough. She loved her with all her heart.

If it wasn't for Mandy, she'd be completely alone.

Come back.

Those had been the words on her lips as she'd died. Words that remained there in death as she wandered these empty rooms, still no escape and the mist churning, always churning.

Words that had become more desperate.

Someone come for us! Don't leave us here alone!
Someone…something…please…
Please…
Something…

Anything…
Please!
Come for Mandy and me.

In the darkness, in the mist, something *did* come. Finally.

And Mandy changed.

CHAPTER TWENTY-TWO

Hurit, what have you done?

As if Shady was thrown out of sleep, the connection was severed.

She sat up, stared with horrified eyes at Mandy, and then pushed her away.

"Annie, Ray, help me up! Help me!"

Annie and Ray had always stayed close; they knew when she needed them, kindred spirits of her own. So why weren't they responding?

"Where've you gone? Come back, please."

Her breath caught. She sounded like the child, *just like her*, repeating the same words.

She realized something else: the mist from the dream, from the vision she'd experienced, hadn't cleared. It was churning, as it had churned before, making it so hard to see.

"Shit!" She was awake, wasn't she? It felt like she was awake. Maybe she wasn't.

Raising her hand, she pinched at the skin there. "Ouch." It hurt.

If she was awake, then the balance had been tipped. She wasn't straddling the material and the spiritual anymore, she was caught deep within it. Somewhere she shouldn't be. Beyond a state of alpha. A no-man's-land. Delta.

Trapped.

Just as she'd feared.

With Mandy, a conduit.

"No, no, no." She had to get away from the doll, find the others.

Climbing to her feet, she stood with her hands held out in front of her as she endeavored to negotiate her way through the mist, fearing, as she had in her dreams, what was hiding in it, praying it was only her colleagues. But why would they hide? And should she hide too?

Of course you should!

What the child had called upon, what had listened to Hurit, the *only* thing that had listened—that had been lying in wait—she didn't want to encounter again, the agonizing darkness of it.

"Ray! Annie! Answer me if you can."

Wapun had been killed by the man masquerading as her lover; Shady was certain of it. Killed and her body dumped somewhere out there in that vast wilderness, the man also condemning the child to death as he closed the door behind him, albeit a much slower, more torturous death.

He had brought evil into the house, and evil remained. Not an entity as such, not a shape in human form as he had been, but an energy that made her sick to think of.

She wouldn't hide; she had to get out of the cabin. Maybe that's where Annie and Ray would be, on the path, waiting for her. Safe. Oh God, she hoped they were safe.

As she continued to stumble forward, she attempted to forget, at least for a short while, what someone like

Wapun's boyfriend could set in motion. She did her utmost to visualize only white light and positivity, but her mind wouldn't play ball. It was as if that, too, had become shrouded in mist, leaving her yet more confused, a stench rising up to blind her further, that of old things decaying.

Where the hell was the door to the bedroom? Considering the number of steps she'd taken, she should have reached it by now, or a wall at least, from which she could feel her way along. It wasn't as if the cabin was a big space. Even so, there was nothing, absolutely nothing.

It's as much a wilderness in here as it is out there.

And she was lost in it. Alone. She shook her head. Not alone. If only she was. That would have been the better choice.

"What's that? Who's there?"

There was a shuffling sound, a scraping.

"Annie?"

Silence returned.

"Ray? Is it you?" Twice he'd caught her when she'd been falling, something he'd said he had a knack for, being there at the right time. If that was so, he should be here right now.

Laughter! Was she imagining it? There was laughter instead of tears, nothing delightful about it, though; it was cruel. Her plight such a wonderful source of amusement.

She spun around. "Stay away from me! I'm warning you! If it's you, Mandy, stay away!"

Crying.

A sob.

"Oh shit, who's there?"

The nightmares she'd had, at some level she knew they

were just that—she'd wake up and they'd be over. This time, she knew nothing of the sort, not where she was, what she was doing, or even why she'd been so eager to understand. There was no understanding any of this, the sheer depths of depravity, the mercilessness of it, the insatiable hunger…

She'd been wrong, and white light didn't work. *Your light is useless here.* If only she'd listened to her mother and stayed home, worked her dull job, remained fey—just that, nothing more—helping people to find lost items now and again, using her intuition that way, *clamping down* on her intuition, even, not using it at all. As her father had said: *life's so much easier if you're normal.*

Different!

Someone had spoken. No, not spoken, they'd *spat* that word at her, a voice that was rasping.

"I'm not! I don't want to be!" Surely that was her choice?

Useless.

How it wanted to drive that point home.

Screaming.

Her ears hurt to hear it. There was a world of pain in that screaming, pain that would reach out and inflict itself upon her, tear the flesh from her body and consume it.

"STAY AWAY FROM ME!"

The doll had to be destroyed before it destroyed her, but where was it? In her confusion she'd wandered away from it, and now it was out there, in this strange and sinister landscape.

Her and what else?

"I've got to get out," she muttered, hating how small her voice sounded.

Determined to claw back some control, desperate to, she started to walk properly. There was a way out, and she'd find it. She was taking so many steps, an impossible amount, but she refused to acknowledge it further. Everything she thought she knew had been torn apart, all boundaries and parameters removed. This world between worlds was new to her, but she had to learn to negotiate it and fast. *Keep walking. Just keep walking.*

Find sanctuary, somewhere she could rest, where she could make sense of this madness.

I'm not crazy. That's what she'd said to Annie and Ray when she'd raced them back to Canada. They'd believed her, but perhaps her mother was right when she'd told her that if she persisted with this matter, madness would ensue.

As she continued walking with no sign of any doorway or cabin walls, she certainly felt something akin to madness. The edges of her mind becoming even more vague, those sounds she could hear—the crying, the laughter, and the screaming—vague too but enough to stop her in her tracks every now and then, to keep her yelling out, "Who's there? Who is it?"

Another scream resounded: her own.

Someone had touched her; she was sure of it. It had reached out of the mists and laid its hand, no matter how briefly, upon her back—a touch that was cold and reptilian, not human at all. And yet it *seared* her, left its mark—as if branding her.

Her breath fast and shallow, she peered into the mist. What did it hide? Mandy was there, but what else, dozens of other Mandys? Evil, but on a mass scale and surrounding her.

Mandy's unique! Desperately she tried to convince herself. Not all her kind were infected in the same way. What had happened to her had been exceptional, negativity like a magnet, attracting more and more, that energy then congealing. There were definitely shapes in the mist, things on the move. This time, she didn't call out, not wanting to alert them further. Whatever they were, they weren't dolls. What if they weren't hiding either but biding their time, waiting to strike, to reach out, to mark her again? The things that roamed were beyond ugly, because evil always was, and if she looked upon them, if they found her, she'd wither and die.

Wither and die…

What had happened to the child? Where had she gone when further evil had come calling?

Had she flown or had she hidden?

If the latter, Shady had to do the same. There was no choice now. This dream, or this nightmare, this *reality*, was without end. Out here, she was as vulnerable as Wapun and Hurit.

There must be a place to hide. There had to be.

As something had touched her, she touched something. Immediately, she snatched her hand back, but whatever it was didn't blight her with the coldness of before. It was something more solid. A wall? It was! She'd found some sort of boundary at last. Hope returned. *Trace the wall, find a door, something, anything.* She corrected herself. No, not anything. A haven was all she wanted until Annie or Ray found a way to reach her. *Have faith that they will.*

A doorframe! *Thank God!* And within it a door. Flailing for the handle, she grasped it, immediately pulling it open.

It led not into a hallway or another room; instead, it was some sort of closet. She hesitated, fearful of being trapped again. But when something shrieked behind her, the sound cutting her to the quick, she fled in there and pulled the door shut.

A small space, she had to shuffle around to face the door. It was dark, but there was no mist, and her eyes adjusted soon enough. It was indeed a closet, and in it she crouched low, praying that it would offer some respite.

The tears that she'd held back began to fall. She tried her hardest to be quiet, but sobs burst from her, her eyes streaming, her nose too, which she wiped at savagely.

Fear turned to despair, its twin emotion, perhaps, a tsunami that engulfed her, that she was powerless to stop. *Madness...* Why hadn't she listened to her mother, to the urgency in her voice? What she was dealing with here was simply too big for her. And she was alone. The child was nowhere to be seen, nor Annie or Ray. She'd been abandoned.

Another sound cut through her sobs, but not one that increased her terror. Instead, it was soothing. Humming? Was someone somewhere humming?

"Who's there?" she whispered, but no reply came, and certainly she could see no shape materializing in front of her. It was just a gentle song she heard, and familiar.

"Shady Grove."

That was it. The song she'd first heard when Ray had played it to her. *Do you know this?* he'd asked, and she'd had to pull the car over as the memory of it engulfed her.

What memory, though? From when?

You were called Shady because you were born as the sun was setting.

Her mother had always said that. But when Shady had called her and asked about the song, she'd denied any knowledge of it, dismissed the curious fact it was so similar to her name. *Vehemently* dismissed it. And yet Shady herself knew it. Someone had hummed it to her as they were humming now; someone had tried to soothe her, not just this time but long ago.

Wish I was in Shady Grove
Sittin' in a rockin' chair,
And if those blues would bother me,
I'd rock away from there.
Shady Grove, my little love
Shady Grove, I say…

She began humming too, singing the words, such sweet words…most of them.

Shady Grove, my little love
I'm bound to go away.

Who was bound to go away? To abandon her too?

"Tell me your name."

Abruptly, the humming stopped. She'd asked whoever it was to tell her their name, but instead, it was her own name being called. "Shady!"

Someone was out there, hollering for her! Her heart leapt. Could it be Annie? Or Ray? She was about to leap to her feet, shout back, open the door, even, but then she stopped. The voice calling didn't sound like Annie or Ray; it didn't contain the gentleness of the person who was humming either. She inclined her head to one side. There was a strange tone to it, that *rasping* tone.

Fresh horror rising, she listened as the voice continued to

call, as it drew closer.

"Shady. Sweet little Shady. Born as the sun was setting. Born into darkness."

Inside the closet, Shady shook her head.

No. That latter part wasn't right. She'd never heard that said before.

"Born into darkness," the voice repeated, *insisted*. "Pretty little Shady."

It wasn't true. It couldn't be. Keme had said she walked in the light.

And yet where was she? In the darkness, all right, a dank place, stuck there.

"Go away," she whispered. "Please go away."

A pounding on the closet door made her yelp.

"Shady, sweet Shady, *nice* Shady."

Go away!

"Shady!" The rasping grew rougher as whatever it was pounded harder and harder.

She looked up at the door, prayed it would hold against the force attacking it, that it wouldn't be torn off its hinges to leave her exposed.

"Come and play, Shady. Play with Hurit and Mandy too."

"Leave me alone!"

"You *have* to come and play."

She couldn't do this; she didn't have the strength. Whatever bravery, whatever curiosity had propelled her to this cabin in the woods had long since gone.

Just who did she think she was, tackling the supernatural? Who did Annie think she was, having so much confidence in her? And Keme when he'd said, *You're one of us.*

Who am I?

The answer came back at once, courtesy of the rasping voice: "You're useless!"

As the pounding continued, Shady sank back down again. She was shaking, moaning, any words that now left her lips incoherent.

She was useless. Weak. And this thing would feed on her, as it had fed on Wapun and Hurit. She was fodder, nothing more.

The door, the construct, whatever it was, couldn't hold against such fury, surely? It would cave and she'd be dragged out, back into the maelstrom and all who waited in it. She could imagine it now, so many clawed hands upon her, digging deep, turning warm blood into ice.

And Mandy would oversee it all, her glass eyes victorious.

There were so many sounds: her babbling, the banging on the door, the crying, the laughter, and the screaming, the humming having started up again, becoming more insistent.

"Shady Groves. Pretty little Shady Groves."

And then finally another sound.

A sound at odds with all the others.

The last sound she'd expected to hear.

A sound that confused her further.

The sound of her cell phone, ringing.

CHAPTER TWENTY-THREE

"Shady? Oh, thank God, you've picked up at last!"

"Mom?"

"Yes, it's me. Of course it's me! Shady, what's going on?"

How could she tell her? How could she *begin* to explain?

"Oh, Mom, it's so good to hear your voice!"

"And yours, sweetheart, and yours. We're on our way."

"What?" She had to ram a hand against her other ear to hear properly.

"I said we're coming to find you, your dad and me."

"But…you'll never find me!" Not here, suspended as she was.

"Oh yes we will," Ellen replied, her voice determined. "We know roughly where you are, and as soon as we get close, I'm sure this tracker thing will spring into action."

Tracker? An app? Is that what she was talking about? Set up an age ago, her parents insisting on it in case of an emergency. Shady shook her head as she listened to the continued pounding on the door, the handle rattling now; whoever was on the outside had noticed it at last and twisted it this way and that, the closet door valiantly resisting, but still she worried for how long. To be talking about an app under such circumstances, to even be able to use her phone, seemed surreal, abnormal. *No, what's happening out there is abnormal,* Shady reminded herself, plus this was about as big an emergency as you could get. Even so...

"Mom, tell Dad to stop. Turn the car around and go home. You can't come here."

"We've just made it over the border of Canada. Believe me, Shady, there's no turning back."

"Oh, Mom, Mom." Shady's head fell forward at hearing the same words Ray had uttered, and that she'd agreed with wholeheartedly, being used against her. Her parents had to do as she'd said and keep away—"here" was wrong, very wrong—but the fact that they were on her trail, just as she'd been on Mandy's, that they loved her that much, was not only humbling, it was inspiring.

Of course they love you. They're your parents!

Were they? Because sometimes—the family joke aside—she wondered. Keme's words came to mind again, when, just before he'd left her at the cabin, he'd insisted once more that his People were her People too. *And because they are, I'm letting you do this. Because you can.*

Mysteries. The world was full of them. You couldn't hope to understand them all. But with some...you had to at least try.

"Mom, who am I?"

As she said it, the noise that surrounded her died down, as if what was out there was also keen to know—although why, she couldn't fathom.

"Mom?" Shady prompted when there was no immediate

reply.

"Shady, this isn't the time."

"I have to know."

Still Ellen resisted. "On our last call, you told me you were heading to Saskatchewan, going north of Saskatoon, but how far north, exactly? Come on, honey, we need—"

"MOM!" Shady didn't mean to shout at her mother, but she couldn't help it, her own need for answers overriding all else. "Why am I like this? Why? Did I—" she found she was swallowing hard "—did I inherit this ability from someone? A woman that sings?"

"A woman that sings?" The shock in Ellen's voice was all too obvious.

"Yes, in my dreams, and lately she's been in my thoughts as well. There's a woman who sings, and it's that song I told you about, almost my namesake, 'Shady Grove.'"

"Oh my God!"

"Mom?"

"You're talking about Kanti."

"Kanti? Mom, I know that name. What does it mean?"

"She who sings. That's *exactly* what it means."

Yes, yes, it did, Shady knew that too, courtesy of the dream she'd had, the woman who'd come out of the mists, who was so like her with dark hair and dark eyes, although her face—her beautiful face—was cracked. But to hear it confirmed, and by her own mother, rendered her as shocked as Ellen. Kanti wasn't just a word, she was someone to her, someone…special.

"Who is Kanti, Mom?"

"Shady…"

"Who is she?"

"Look, you're in some kind of trouble—"

Shady didn't deny it. "I am, but I still need to know."

There was another silence, one that threatened to explode if an answer didn't fill it.

"Mom!"

The humming had started again, the notes not as she'd heard them before but discordant. A mockery, that's what it was, heaping scorn upon her.

"Mom, she who sings…Kanti…is she…? Is she my real mom?"

The words were out. She'd said it! And with it came relief and more fear.

"MOM, WILL YOU PLEASE ANSWER ME!"

"NO, SHADY!" her mother screamed just as loud as she had. "She was not your mother. She was…oh God, she was mine."

The humming grew louder, with the aim of distracting her? If so, she had to ignore it, had to focus on one thing and one thing only: the truth.

"Kanti was my grandmother?" Her *maternal* grandmother, someone whom she'd never met, along with her maternal grandfather; both had died, apparently, when Shady was young. That's what she'd been told. What she'd *always* been told. "So how come I recognize her?"

"She…she held you when you were first born. She sang to you, that song, on…on account of my married name. She said it was apt, it suited you. Said that's what we should christen you."

"Because of that?"

"And because you were born as the sun was setting. That much is true."

Born into darkness.

Damn whatever it was for putting that idea into her head, for soiling something precious.

"Kanti," Shady said, still trying to drown out that wretched humming and how it set her nerves on edge. "That's a Cree name."

There was further astonishment in her mother's voice. "That's right! She was Cree."

"Which means…"

"That I am. That you are."

"But you're so fair!"

"Apparently, my father was fair."

"Apparently?"

"I didn't know him, Shady. I *never* knew him." Her mother's voice had become choked, as if she was crying. "And nor did my mother."

"What? How's that possible? I don't understand."

"She was raped, Shady! You wanted to know the truth, well, there it is. She was raped."

Shady could hear her father speaking her mother's name, trying to comfort her, no doubt, but it seemed the floodgates had been opened as more words from Ellen came pouring out.

"My mother was broken, Shady. The rape broke her, how society treated her broke her, and in some ways, *I* broke her because I was a permanent reminder of the atrocity that had happened. In looks I must have taken after him, but it was more than that. Kanti and I…we just…we couldn't bond."

"Oh, Mom, I'm so sorry."

"I am too, Shady, I am too. But you know what? More

than all those factors combined, it was her gift that broke her."

"Her gift?"

"Her ability to see, to sense, just like you can."

"Her gift," Shady repeated, her heart hammering as wildly as ever. "She wasn't just fey…"

"And neither are you. I know that, your father knows that, but we—"

"Played it down."

"For your sake. Only for that reason."

"Do you have the gift?"

"No. I don't. More evidence that I must take after my father." Aside from grief, something else was in her mother's tone—bitterness, but bitterness that was justified.

"How did her gift break her, Mom?"

"Shady, that's enough—"

"How?"

Ellen's sigh was ragged. "Because of the *type* of thing she could sense and see. I think she tried to fight it, tried to break free, but whatever it was had a hold on her. What she was like before it happened, the rape I mean, before she realized the full extent of people's prejudices, I have no clue, but afterwards, the woman, the mother that I knew, was weighed down by darkness, to the point where she…became it. It took over. And it broke her."

Shady remembered the face she'd seen with the crack running through it.

"How did she die?" Shady had to steel herself for the answer.

"By her own hand. She hanged herself."

The moment that horror was revealed, the horror

outside began again, in earnest—the pounding as hard as ever, the humming as discordant, that terrible sense of glee, that reveling in another's tragedy, mist beginning to seep under the door now, forcing entry.

Shady Grove, my little love...

Shady gritted her teeth. The voice that whispered wouldn't know a thing about love.

The mist began rising. Shady swore at seeing it, clutching the phone as Hurit had clutched Mandy, pushing herself as far back into the wall as she could. "Shit! Shit! Shit!"

"Shady, what's happening? What's that noise? Speak to me. What's going on?"

"I...I..."

"Shady!"

"I don't know. I don't know what's going on."

"Where are you?" She could barely hear her mother anymore; she sounded exactly what she was—so far away. "I said, where are you?"

"In a cabin in the woods."

"Where's Annie? Where's Ray?"

"I...I don't know that either."

The mist was climbing up her ankles, a clingy, sinuous, and determined thing, as treacherous as floodwater and cold, the reek of it alone enough to render you immobile. It would choke the life out of her just as life had been choked from her grandmother; it was intent on doing that.

"Okay, okay, think, Shady. Focus. How many miles north of Saskatoon are you? Are you in a town? What's it called? Come on, come on, please, you gotta tell me exactly where you are. Dad's putting his foot down, okay? He's kicking ass here. We're on our way, I swear to you, and we will find you. You're not alone. Don't think you are. You are *not* alone."

And yet she was, just like Hurit was alone, as defenseless.

"You're not defenseless either!"

Shady started. What? What had her mother just said? Had she managed to pick up on what she was thinking, she who declared she wasn't fey at all?

"Listen to me, Shady Groves, you are not defenseless. Believe it. Please."

"But I am, Mom! I don't know what's on the other side of this door, but it wants to destroy me."

"Don't let it! Shit, will you listen to me? Don't let it! Not you too."

"How do I stop it? I don't know how to!"

"You have to try, Shady."

"How?"

She was so cold she could feel herself growing numb. How did you fight something as powerful as this? Hatred, which this thing was so full of, was always powerful, both in her world and in this world too, the in-between. She was losing any will to fight, could feel herself giving up, just as the child had. If she did that, would she linger, as the child had lingered? Would she always remain?

"Shady! Shady! Are you still there? Shady!"

"Yes…" Barely a whisper; she'd be surprised if her mother could even hear her. "I'm still here."

"Oh, thank God. Thank God."

"Mom…"

Her hands too frozen to hold the phone anymore, she let it drop, watching as it crashed to the floor. Tears poured down her face, for Wapun, for the child, and, in truth, for herself and the miserable fate she couldn't escape. She thought of Annie and Ray; like her parents, they wouldn't have abandoned her, just as Wapun wouldn't have left Hurit. Which meant they'd been *made* to leave her, something that struck new terror into her heart, that they may have been harmed in some way. Evil came in many guises, in the form of lovers and strangers and sometimes, with all pretense stripped bare, a raw, naked, sour thing.

She was going to die here. Whatever death meant.

Born into darkness, she was being delivered back into it.

Poor little Shady Groves, sweet little Shady Groves, useless little Shady Groves, the only thing you need to see, you need to understand, is where being different gets you.

The mist continued its onslaught, the stench both putrid and intoxicating. The pounding on the door had fallen into a rhythm as discordant as the humming, as the screaming and the laughter.

And somehow, someway, her mother's voice cut across it all and reached her even though she was sinking deep, deep inside herself, becoming as lost as the child.

"Shady, what if...what if...you *weren't* afraid?"

It was the last thing she'd expected her mother to say; there was just no sense in it. How could she *not* be frightened of what was happening? If Ellen were here in her place, she'd be terrified, so what was she saying? Was she asking her to *pretend* she wasn't? Like it was that simple?

"Listen to me, just try it." From the dropped phone, Ellen's voice sounded tinny, the line crackling in a threatening manner every now and then.

Rather than dismiss further what her mother was saying,

Shady leaned forward and inclined her head, too curious not to.

"I know you're scared," Ellen continued, "of course you're scared. You told me you were even before you started on this journey. Heck, *I'm* scared, for you. I…I don't actually think you can be more scared than I am right now; it's not possible. Shady, if I lose you too…

"But I won't lose you, I refuse. And so I *mustn't* be scared. I must believe you'll be all right. With all my heart. And you must believe you're going to be all right too. Because you will be. Remember who you are and the kind of people you come from. That kind of heritage is powerful, it's ingrained, and it's nothing, *nothing*, to be ashamed of, although I was. I was ashamed of everything to do with my background, ashamed of how I came about, of my mother and all the ways in which she was different. I was glad when she died, Shady, I was. But it also broke me, the unfairness of it. I was so scared I'd be someone like my father, but then, but then…I met *your* father, and I knew I wasn't a bad person. He knows all there is to know about me, and he still loves me.

"It's taken me years to heal, to accept everything, and just now, in this car, traveling to find you, I've had to heal further. I've had to forgive my father entirely, forgive my mother entirely too, and I've had to forgive myself. I've had to find pride in my heritage, believe that a People closer to nature can be closer to all things, the good and the bad, although it's good that prevails. Somehow. Someway. Good has prevailed in my life, Shady, and it will in yours. All you have to do is let go of your fear, your hurt and horror. Let it all go. And remember who you are. You're Shady Groves, my beautiful, brave Shady, born as the sun was setting in the sky."

"Mom, the place I'm in, it's called—"

"Shady…Shady…"

"Mom?"

"Shady, can you hear me? Shady…"

"Mom!"

As if someone had swung a scythe, the line was cut.

Almost entirely encased in the mist now, feeling it sink beneath her skin, into her bones, her joints, her veins, and sinews, freezing what was there just as she'd feared it would, she nonetheless forced her hands to work, flailing at first, reaching out for the phone.

At last she found it. Grabbing it, she held it close to her face. No reassuring light came on. She pressed a button, then another, stabbing at them. The battery was drained. Dead. But she wasn't. Half dead, maybe, but not wholly. If she wanted to prevent the latter, then she had to act, she had to do something before this mist buried itself too deep inside her, before it devoured not just her body but her spirit.

Although crystallized joints screamed with the effort, Shady forced herself to her feet.

What if you weren't afraid? That's what her mother had said.

An intriguing concept.

Standing facing the door, she heard the handle once again turn, turn…

She couldn't rid herself of fear, not just like that, but she could do something else with it—turn it into anger, *righteous* anger, which was just as potent. She could focus on where she came from, where people like Wapun and Hurit came from, imagine what it felt like to have something you loved snatched from you, your land, your beliefs, *everything*, to be denigrated by some to the ranks of subhuman. And because you were nothing or no one, you wouldn't be missed if you disappeared; you'd be, as Wapun's lover had said, just one less to worry about.

Oh, yes, yes, she could do this. She could let such injustice bolster her, fuel her limbs with adrenalin, fill her body with purpose. These were her People, a proud People, noble. The First Peoples. And they'd been wronged. If a woman went missing, you looked for her. If a child died alone and her body was left to lay there year after year, you wrote about it, you shouted it from the rooftops, you raised the question of how and why it could happen. A rule applicable to everyone. Regardless of race or creed.

This journey had not only been about discovering who Mandy was, Shady realized; it was also about discovering herself and her own family. And yet all she knew was just the tip of the iceberg.

Imagine it's him out there. Wapun's so-called lover. Imagine what you'd do to him.

Oh, she could imagine well enough. Grabbing the twisting handle, she held on to it.

"Asshole," she breathed before yanking the door open. "I'm coming for ya."

CHAPTER TWENTY-FOUR

If she'd expected the mist to have disappeared, she was wrong. It was still there, as heavy as before, and there were still things in it, but they were keeping their distance...deliberately? Were they shying away from her and what she'd become? Something colder than them?

She could call out the child's name, Hurit or Emma, or she could do something else—find Mandy. Drag her out from wherever she was hiding. And then what?

She'd tear her apart. She'd rip her damned head off.

She'd do that because what had been in the doll had finally burst its banks. But it might well use Mandy again, and she couldn't allow that to happen. She had to ensure it had no safe harbor. After Mandy, she'd destroy the cabin, burn it down. Whatever hellish energy continued to churn could then take its chances out there in the true wilderness, where people barely dared to venture and thus gave little to feed on. Let it pit itself against other energies, *better* energies, energies that would render it as vulnerable as Wapun and Hurit had been. Its reign was sure to be a short one. Why? Because history aside, this land was simply too beautiful, too pure, with no trace, no hint of ugliness at all.

In the end, surely beauty would triumph and evil starve.

"So, Mandy, where the fuck are you?"

Despite such poor visibility, Shady refused to stumble. She walked with determined strides, her head held high, blood rushing through her veins, no longer intimidated by this thing.

"I'll find you. And when I do…"

As before, something tried to touch her. Immediately, she cast her arm out and threw whatever it was from her. It happened a second time, and she repeated the action.

"You weak, pathetic things," she snarled. "I will burn you."

No screaming, no voices. Was that a whimper instead?

Her heart soared to hear it.

"You prey on weaker things to cover the fact that you're weak too. It's the vulnerable you seek out, that you've always hunted. If someone dares to retaliate, look at you then, you shrink. Ow!"

Shady lifted her hands to shield her face, her mouth open as she blinked several times. She'd crashed into something solid. Another wall! A cabin wall that she could see clearly enough, the dark wood of ancient trees that had been used to create a home. Finally, the mist had gone. Quite suddenly, quite dramatically. Parameters were back in place. She looked downward; rubble and roots covered the floor, the only smell that of damp and neglect, faint compared to what had been there. Expelled from the in-between, she was once more in a world she recognized.

Which was a good thing, wasn't it?

Quickly, she established which room she was in— Hurit's bedroom, the far side of it, exactly where she'd been before, as if she'd never left that spot and traveled so far. *What the hell?* Her eyes moved to the patch of ground she'd lain on with Mandy, the spot where Hurit had died. Mandy wasn't there. Where was she? Where were Annie and Ray?

She started running, out of the bedroom and along the hallway to the front door. It was ajar, and she had to pull hard to open it farther.

The sight that met her caused a cry of relief.

Annie and Ray were halfway along the snow-covered path, so near and yet so far. They stood with their backs to her, talking animatedly to one another, as if distressed.

Annie's cell was in her hand; shaking it, she then shook her head. Ray was holding his phone up to the sky, trying to get a signal, perhaps? He lowered it and started tapping at the screen. Who was he calling? Keme? If they were distressed, there was no need. She was safe. Quite safe.

About to call out, to let them know, a sound distracted her. Only slight. A floorboard creaking, from just behind her. She hated to take her eyes off her companions in case they disappeared again, but she couldn't not turn, couldn't not investigate. *Too curious for your own good.*

Her movement was measured, slow but dogged. Facing into the cabin, she gasped. Hurit stood before her, not the product of a vision; she was standing there in real time, as solid as she'd been before, as was the doll she clutched to her belly—Mandy, of course.

"Hurit," Shady whispered before taking a step forward.

The child was too quick for her. She darted out of the living room and down the hallway.

"No wait, I'm coming. Hurit, wait."

Shady hurried after her but came to a stop in the

hallway. Hurit's bedroom was on the left and Wapun's on the right. Which one had the child favored?

"Hurit, I'm not here to harm you. I only want to help."

Before reacting further, Shady forced herself to think. The mist had just suddenly disappeared, evaporated as if it had never been. Initially, however, when she'd strode out of the closet, it had been there, though something about it had changed. It hadn't been quite as…confident as before. It might even have been fearful. She was astonished. Did no one ever stand up to the darkness? Did everyone just…give in?

No, no, they didn't. That wasn't true. So many people were brave. They fought for what they believed in. All through history people had done that. There was example after example, each one that she'd learned about in the pages of books taking on new meaning—their victories, their triumphs more significant than she'd realized. The darkness would abate, but not forever. It recovered its strength, and it came back. History books showed that too, the battle beginning anew. If that was the case, where had the darkness temporarily withdrawn to within this cabin? The doll again? As it had done before. The one that Hurit held in her hands.

She had to prize the doll from her, but then what? What of Hurit?

One step at a time. Annie was outside; she'd come back in soon, she'd know what to do.

Just take it one step at a time.

"Hurit, where are you, darling? You're lost, I think. You're sad. You miss your mommy, don't you, so much. Is that why you're still here? Because you're waiting for her?"

Another creak of the floorboards, from deep within Wapun's room.

Shady took a deep breath and turned toward it. A ghost. A spirit. She'd never seen one before, only in her mind's eye, not like this, an entity as real as she was.

The girl was trapped. Just as Shady had been trapped. A little girl who'd known a loving home and then one filled with obsession and fear. How long had it taken her to die in these rooms, alone? How long had she called out before she'd been answered? Where had she hidden all this time since? And Wapun, what had become of her? Where had the man taken her, *buried* her? What was his name? Because if they had a name...

Wapun's door protested slightly as Shady pushed at it. Keeping at bay another rush of fear, she ventured inside. There the girl was, still very much a corporeal thing, at the room's only window, overlooking the rear of the property, staring out of it.

Shady could feel the child's longing, and not only that, how much the doll meant to her. A thrift store doll, it was the one constant in her life. But the doll was no longer constant; it had changed, was different now, not something to love at all. How could she make her understand that?

"Hurit..."

Immediately, the child swung around to face her, and Shady couldn't help it; she took a step back. The expression on her face! It contained such a mixture of emotions, some to be expected—bewilderment, of course, fear, even acceptance of her dire fate. But there was also determination.

Hurit was *not* going to let go of Mandy. Mandy was

hers.

There was movement behind Shady, but she didn't turn, not this time. She didn't dare break the contact she had with the child.

"Shady! Thank God, you're okay! You're alive! There was this mist—it came out of nowhere. We couldn't find you, only each other. You just…disappeared in it. It's a miracle we found our way out of the cabin. I never thought we would. I've managed to call Keme—"

Shady held up her hand. As relieved as she was to hear Ray's voice, she couldn't reply.

It was Annie who understood this. "Ray, wait. Something's happening."

Free to focus on the child again, Shady began to cajole her. "Sweetheart, you don't need Mandy, not anymore. You've got us now. You've got me."

The little girl simply hugged the doll harder, its cracked face staring outward, its eyes fixated on Shady, boring into her, and so damned black.

Shady dared to step forward, tentative steps, baby steps, praying all the while the child wouldn't take fright and fade away despite how solid she appeared. No matter the wretchedness of her situation, Hurit suited her name well; there was beauty in her features, although her mussed black hair and tear-stained cheeks lent a certain wildness.

"Your mother isn't coming back, Hurit. But I think…I think she's waiting for you."

Vehemently, the child shook her head.

"No, no, she's not somewhere dark, somewhere damp and lonely. She's not in pain anymore. She would have gone to…to…"

"To the light," Annie whispered. "She's gone to the light, and Hurit should go there too."

"Can you see her?" Shady whispered back, desperate to know.

"We know there's something there," said Ray. "But that could be because you've told us."

Auto-suggestion at play. "But Mandy's there too. Surely you can see her?"

"Mandy's on the ground," replied Annie.

She wasn't. She was in Hurit's arms. Again, what they saw was different.

Shady then questioned the child. "Can you see the light?"

The child continued to gaze at her.

"Hurit, look around, can you see it? That's where your mom is. Where your dad is too."

What about him?

The child hadn't opened her mouth, yet the words hit Shady like a wrecking ball.

"Him? Not your father?"

Again, there was a violent shake of the head.

Shady swallowed. "Do you mean the man?"

The bad man.

The bad man, the murderer. Shady shook her head as hard as the child had. "No, no, he wouldn't be there."

Where is he?

"I don't know," Shady confessed. He could still be alive for all she knew.

Nikawi…

"Your parents miss you so much. They want you to be with them."

Nohtawi…

"They're in the light, Hurit," Shady reiterated. "If you look for it, you'll see it." She pointed to the window that the child had been staring out of. "Perhaps it's out there?"

The child turned her head toward the window but only briefly.

"You can't stay here," Shady continued, "not anymore. There's just…too much darkness here."

Were those tears on the child's face? Yes, they were, tiny shimmering droplets.

"Oh, Hurit." How Shady wished she could rush forward, wrench that terrible doll from her and envelop the child in her arms. She'd give her all the love she'd missed out on for so many years. Make her remember what it felt like. Could she do it? Should she try?

She took another step, and another. The child remained where she was, which was good; it was encouraging. But she wasn't relinquishing her hold on the doll, not at all. Shady had to try to make her understand that she couldn't take something like that into the light with her. It was no more than an anchor, dragging her down, keeping her in limbo.

She'd find a way to destroy it, as she'd resolved to do, but not with Hurit looking on.

Still she drew closer. Still the child remained.

"Keep talking about the light." Annie's voice reached her again. "It's all about the light."

Shady did as she was asked. "There's so much peace in the light. And you deserve peace, little Hurit, beautiful, beautiful child. You deserve it so much."

Just a few steps from her now, Shady knelt, wanting to maintain eye contact at all costs. Being this close to the child felt incredible. And yet being close to the doll made her skin crawl. The temptation to reach out and tear it from her arms, to cast it aside, remained, and it took everything in her to resist it. She had to move Hurit on, but what more could she say?

And then it hit her, *exactly* what she had to say.

"I'll find your mom. Not her spirit—she's where I've said she is, in the light—but I'll find her body."

The child's eyes widened.

"Shady, be careful," Annie murmured from behind, and Shady could feel her tension, Ray's too, but what else could she do? Leave this place, leave the child here? That wasn't an option.

"I'll find her, Hurit. And I'll see justice is done. And in the light, somehow, someway, you'll know I've done that. You'll just…you'll know."

The tears had stopped as the child listened.

"I'll do that for you, Hurit, willingly, gladly. But you need to do one thing for me." No, that was wrong. "Hurit, it's *two* things I need."

The child's gaze was still so intent.

"I need the bad man's name, and I need Mandy."

Contemplation! There it was! The child considering the bargain.

"You *cannot* take Mandy into the light with you."

Was her grip beginning to soften?

"Give her to me. I'll—" she took a deep breath "—look after her."

Hurit was listening! She was! The doll not as close to her belly as before.

"That's it, that's right, you're doing great, Hurit."

You'll look after her?
Shady nodded.
Promise.

Shady faltered. How could she tell her a lie? But she had to. A white lie for a blackened thing.

"I promise."

The child was reaching out; she trusted her, something Shady felt both elated and guilty about. In the end, all that mattered was that she got the doll away from her and her spirit was released.

Shady reached out too, not wanting to hurry the child but desperate to separate the two, the yin and the yang, the opposite sides of the coin.

Look after her.
"Yes, yes, I will."
Mandy. My Mandy.
"I'll keep her safe."

Shady was touching Mandy now, her fingers closing around her waist once more, the doll's white dress so crumpled, so…*dirty*. It was almost done. Just the man's name and then Hurit could fly.

"I'll find your mother, and I'll find him."

The child smiled, actually smiled. And then her smile disappeared as suddenly as the mist had.

"Hurit? What's—"

Faster than a viper, the child snatched the doll back, and her mouth twisted with horror instead.

CHAPTER TWENTY-FIVE

The room was full of people. So many of them. An impossible amount. Blackened shapes that intermingled, that churned as the mist churned. There was also Annie, Ray, and Keme—she was sure of it, he'd arrived—as well as one other she recognized, but the rest of them, who and what they were, she had no clue. In among them she couldn't see Hurit, not anymore…or Mandy.

God, it was cold. It was freezing, the same cold she'd experienced in the closet, the kind that warm clothes couldn't protect against, that was beyond natural—signaling, then, the return of the darkness, which hadn't been hiding at all, but biding its time yet again.

"Everybody"—it was Annie's voice Shady could hear—"gather together. Ray, Keme, Shady. Don't scatter. Come close. Here's my hand. Grab it, all of you, and come close."

Shady couldn't move; she was simply too cold, her body shaking.

"Shady, come on!" Annie urged. Keme had reached the older woman, so had Ray, but Ray had his eyes on Shady, about to break away.

"Stay there!" she managed to instruct him. "I'm fine. Annie's right, stick together."

His eyes were fit to pop, Annie's too, and Keme's. What

was happening here? Who were these other people? No, not people, not exactly. They were indistinct, masses of them.

And the one she thought she recognized, the one who didn't mill about, who hadn't reached out for the others either, who was she, with her long hair and eyes so dark?

"Kanti?" Shady whispered. "Is it you?"

The woman neither moved nor opened her mouth in reply. She just stood there, fixated on Shady, the dark shapes that surrounded them becoming a swarm.

"Shady!" Ray shouted. "I don't know what the hell's going on, but come on, come here."

"I don't know where Hurit's gone," she yelled back. She was no more than a few feet from her friends, but as when she'd had her visions, there seemed to be such a divide between them, with yet another gulf separating her from Kanti.

Keme had closed his eyes and was chanting, his voice barely audible but firing words out, the kind meant to encourage further protection? Certainly, there was desperation in them.

She inhaled. Was that smoke she could smell? In competition with all that was putrid.

Annie's voice was more anxious than ever. "We have to get out. Now! Someone's lit a fire. Keme, Keme, listen to me, was it you?"

As if coming out of a trance, Keme answered her by shaking his head. Ray also denied it.

Fire. Shady had wanted to burn this cabin down. But she had no matches on her, no lighter. It wasn't her who'd done it. Was it the darkness itself, mocking her intentions?

There could be no fire. Not with Hurit here. The fire

had to come *after* they'd sent her to the light. Without the only walls she'd ever known around her, she'd be left yet more vulnerable.

"NO!"

Shady's scream was enough for Ray to break from his companions and rush to her, his hands grabbing her shoulders, intending to drag her out, perhaps, but she managed to shake him off.

"I'm not leaving without Hurit."

"Hurit's dead!"

"And yet she's still here. Don't ask me how, but she is. She can't be left, not again."

"The smoke's getting thicker," Annie countered. "We've got to leave!"

Shady turned to her. "You leave, you and Keme and Ray. I will too, but not yet. I can't."

The woman who was Kanti, Shady's grandmother, started to sing, her mouth at last gently moving with the words to a song Shady knew well enough by now, that she thought she'd been named after: *Shady Grove, my little love, Shady Grove, I say, Shady Grove, my little love, I'm bound to go away.* As if on a loop, those words repeated in her head, the shapes surrounding them flooding over to the woman, encircling her but not touching her. Not touching her because she stood tall and straight, her face not cracked but staring outward and in itself a fiery thing.

"Jeez," Shady whispered in awe, "will you look at that?"

Ray was frowning. "What is it, look at what?"

He was still intent on forcing her to move, but she refused, just as Kanti refused, and because of that, the black shapes wouldn't touch her either.

Annie and Keme were retreating, Keme helping Annie, who'd lost her glasses in the panic, who was coughing and retching. Even so, she had strength enough to call back to Ray and Shady, to plead with them. "Enough now. Know when you've done enough!"

"Shady," Ray pleaded too, and she tore her eyes from Kanti to look at him, at the face of a man with crazy red hair and a penchant for Taylor Swift, a brave man who'd accompanied her into the unknown, who'd never scoffed at anything she'd said, who believed in her.

"I'm not leaving," she repeated. "You can. But I'm not."

Had her grandmother just smiled at her words? Had the black shapes quivered?

Shady found she was smiling too. "I am *not* bound to go away," she said. "I won't abandon Hurit."

For a moment Ray simply stared at her, and then his gaze seemed to adjust, to look beyond her. "Who's that?" he said. "Is that her? Is that Hurit?"

Shady spun around, and as she did, she noticed that all the shadows in the room stopped and turned too, no longer endlessly milling or chaotic but becoming focused, laser sharp. There, indeed, stood Hurit, the doll no longer in her arms but on the floor where Annie and Ray had said it was.

Shady's heart lurched. Poor child! There was no disguising the horror in her soul.

With no time for tentative action, Shady hurled herself forward. "Don't be afraid. Please don't. You can't show them you're afraid. Because if you do…if you do…"

Ray was right behind her, coughing as well, his breathing becoming more and more labored. He wasn't the only one following—so were the blackened shapes, heading straight for the child.

A few feet separated them all from Hurit, no more than that. But who would reach her first?

"What if you weren't afraid?" Drawing on her mother's wisdom, Shady made sure that her voice at least filled the void. "What would these...these *things* do then? They can't feed on you, that's for sure. If you're not frightened, they can't touch you or harm you. They can't keep you here, in this cabin in the woods. Hurit, don't be frightened. Please. You *can't* be."

But the little girl had spent so long frightened, it was all she could remember. The warm, loving home that had once been hers too distant a memory.

"Even so," Shady cried, "it's *still* a memory, when you were happy, when you weren't afraid of anything. That memory is part of you!"

She reached the child first, then had no choice but to turn her back on Hurit, to shield her from the onslaught. Facing Ray, facing them, she could also see the flames that licked lasciviously at the doorway, that would soon come closer. She saw Kanti, singing still, staring at her, giving her potency: *I am bound to go away. But you are strong, stronger than me, you can do this.*

"Keep away from her," Shady screamed at the shadows, gaining more strength from Kanti, a woman whom Ellen had thought life had broken. Maybe. But in death she was different. "I know what you're doing, targeting the child because...because you can taste her fear. You coward! That's all you are, you and your kind. You can't touch me now, or my grandmother, just Hurit, because you think she's an easy target. Leave her alone! Let her be now. She's suffered enough."

Her words didn't halt the masses. If anything, they multiplied further.

Shady faced Hurit again. The child was still there, but she'd taken a step back, closer to Mandy. And Shady knew right then, without a doubt, that that was her hiding place too, deep, deep in the heart of a doll she loved, that she trusted more than anything. Hers was the crying she'd heard, that others had heard too, such a heart-wrenching sound. Hurit's. Trapped. And so, so scared.

"You're going back in there, aren't you?"

Now closer to Mandy, the child had become barely visible.

"You're going back in there?" Shady repeated.

A slight nod.

"And so is the darkness." It would chase her, disappearing through the crack in the doll's face, a metaphorical gateway, an entrance into other realms, but would it find her? Not if she hid well enough. The doll had protected her up until now, and it would do so again.

Mandy, a conduit for both good and evil.

And Shady had promised to look after it.

"And I will," she whispered. "I'll look after Mandy because I'll look after *you*, until you're no longer afraid. And despite the darkness that surrounds you, I won't let go."

The child seemed to flicker, to become whole again.

Shady caught her breath. Hope leapt when she thought hope had died. Was she going to change her mind and not hide after all? Flee to the light instead, where only peace awaited?

"Hurit?"

Hal Fenton.

"What? I don't—"

Bad man.

"Bad man? Oh God, the bad man." She'd been so desperate for Hurit to fight back, she'd forgotten him entirely.

You promised.

"Yes. Yes, I did. I'll find him."

Before her eyes, Hurit faded to nothing, the darkness that surrounded them vanishing too—and Kanti, with her sweet, silent singing.

There was a resounding crash, more deafening than thunder. A beam fell across the door, cutting off their exit, the room filling with smoke that was becoming mist-like, another maelstrom that would find its way inside their lungs and be the thing to kill them.

"The window!" Ray shouted, dragging his jacket off his body as he ran toward it, wrapping his arm in it, and smashing the glass there.

He wouldn't take no for an answer, not this time, she knew; he'd drag Shady out if she resisted him again.

But she didn't.

Dropping to her knees, she snatched Mandy up and held her close. For a moment she cradled her, staring into her eyes. As predicted, Ray grabbed her, clearly expecting her to fight back.

"This place is going to collapse," he said. "We leave now or we die."

We *die*... She wasn't going to abandon Hurit, and Ray had no intention of abandoning Shady either. No obvious Native blood in him, but he was noble all the same.

"It's okay," she assured him. "It's all right. I *am* leaving." She looked again at Mandy, committed the name Hal Fenton to memory. "I've got everything I need."

CHAPTER TWENTY-SIX

The minute Shady and Ray left the building, escaping through the cracked window that the child had stared out from, it was as if the cabin started to implode, raining timber upon timber down upon its rotten self, sending it all crashing to the ground in a spectacular display of fury.

They managed to stumble a safe distance away and noticed Keme and Annie hurrying toward them, stark relief on both their faces that their friends had escaped, gotten out of there. All four then stood and stared at yet another destruction, but one that felt good, that felt necessary.

"Shady, thank goodness. Ray, you're all right. I—" Annie started coughing, the smoke still irritating her throat despite the cold, fresh air. Ray reached out and rubbed at her back, trying to soothe her. Shady couldn't as she was clutching the doll so tightly.

Annie finally managed to speak again. "You've got the doll." Not a question but a statement, not even an accusation in it, only relief.

"I couldn't leave her in there," Shady replied. "Not now that I understand."

Yet another timber crashed to the ground inside the cabin, and as the first of the threatened snow began to fall in an effort to cleanse further all that had festered there,

Annie squinted at Shady. She held her gaze, and then slowly a smile transformed her, as it so often did, into someone not solemn, not grave at all, but who had an ever-youthful spirit.

"I suspected there was more to Mandy than just pure evil," Annie said, striking a strange balance between seriousness and tongue-in-cheek. "Evil doesn't cry."

They were simple words that told a simple truth. Yet, as Shady stood there—so tiny in such a vast expanse but within her a world of emotions, just as Mandy contained a world within her too, as the cabin had been the world to Hurit and her family—she couldn't help but cry.

Rather than rush to console her, the other three let her have her moment, Annie solemn once more, as were Ray and Keme. Soon, Ellen and Bill would arrive. No need for them to use their tracker; she'd phone them in a while, let Keme give them guidance to his cabin. Because that's where they'd go after here, where they'd convene and she would tell them all, including her parents, what she'd learned—the story of Hurit, Wapun, Hal Fenton, and, of course, Mandy.

* * *

They left the cabin to burn to the ground, not doing any damage to anything but itself. By then, the snow was much heavier and the flames not as furious, what needed to be done almost achieved. Nature would finish the job.

They'd report the fire, of course, along with their suspicions surrounding Wapun, but first they needed to rest, to meet Shady's parents, to get their heads around all that had happened.

Ellen and Bill were welcomed into the cabin, their relief palpable at seeing their daughter unharmed, both sets of eyes also traveling to the doll beside Shady, something in them hardening as they gazed on her, yet they remained silent.

Privately, Shady would tell Ellen about Kanti, how she'd been there, no longer broken but brave and strong, standing against the darkness and encouraging her granddaughter to do the same, to not let it break her. Ellen had said there'd been no connection between herself and her mother, no true bond. She'd blamed the circumstances of her conception for that, but there was a connection between Kanti and Shady. Kanti had named her not just because of her surname and the song but because it was indeed apt. She could see what her grandchild was: a child of the shadows, someone who was not just fey but could walk between worlds. A daunting realization, but if Kanti were by her side—if Ray was too, and Annie—not as daunting as it might otherwise be. And Ellen had let her mother name her only child, which she'd surely done because there was a connection after all, because she loved her mother, and her mother, regardless of everything, loved her. Yes, there would be further discussions about their shared history—there was so much Shady wanted to know—but that was for later, much later. One step at a time…

"Who started the fire?" Shady wanted to know.

"I brought some sage sticks with me, for the purpose of cleansing." Keme looked baffled but not sorry. "It was never my intention to start a fire, but perhaps one spark was all it took."

"It was a fire waiting to happen," Ray said, and Annie agreed.

A fire perhaps not started at the hands of humans—not this time, as it had been with the twins--but by the gathering elements. Just another thing to marvel at.

"Are you intending to bring that doll back to the house, Shady?" Ellen was still clearly not keen.

"Mom, I have—"

"She can bring it to the museum," Annie said, saving the possibility of further pleading.

Shady turned to her. "Really? You'll keep her there?"

"It's what we agreed, isn't it?"

"The thing is, Annie, I need to keep her close."

"Then come and work for me."

"Work for you?" Shady gasped. "At the museum?"

Annie nodded. "I can never keep staff. As you can imagine, it takes a certain type of person to fit the bill, and I can't continue to run it on my own. I'm getting on now, getting tired, if I'm honest."

"Do you actually get any visitors?" Ray asked.

Annie flared her nostrils at him. "Yes, young man, I do! Plenty pass through Mason, holidaymakers and the like, and they stop, keen to know at least a little something about local heritage. I also offer tea and coffee in the summer months, and, as it's the only drinks stop for miles, that's usually a great draw." As Ray contemplated, she added, "I've explained this to Shady, and I'll explain it to everyone here: There are certain things in my museum that *should* be seen, that shouldn't be left alone in the dark. Just as little Hurit should never have been left alone. Things that can flourish when kept in the light rather than fester."

"I'd love to work at your museum," Shady blurted out.

"I can help out too," Ray added. "Well…if you like. I'm in between jobs."

From having feigned indignance, Annie smiled. "Okay then, it's a deal! I'm sure I can find plenty to keep you both busy. Wages aren't wonderful, mind; I can only afford to pay so much. It's not as if you'll be able to climb the property ladder anytime soon, but—" and here she paused, held Ray's gaze and then Shady's "—I'm sure you'll agree, there's plenty of job satisfaction, at least."

She was right about that. Their quest to understand Mandy had uncovered not one death but several. Credibility could never be given to murders that the doll had played a part in, however. And Shady had to admit, a certain amount of culpability on the victims' part had to be taken into account, their imaginations embellishing when really none was needed.

Was it really Mandy's fault the twins had started the fire? Despite so many warnings, kids played with matches all the time. Would they have done so anyway, eventually? As for Cora, Greta Hollick was right—she was a law unto herself, intent on breaking the doll, only sensing the evil in her. Yet when she'd finally sensed something else, it had rendered her unable to cope, hence why she'd given her to Bryan. When you hurt so much yourself, the last thing you needed was more pain piled on top. As for Lena, she'd wanted to love Mandy, she *had* loved Mandy, but with her mind failing her, playing tricks on her, it was all too easy for love to turn to blame.

And though there had to be more owners they still didn't know about—possibly more deaths—what Annie had said, what Shady had thought, stood: they knew enough. They knew that before Hurit, for years and years, Mandy had just been a doll, even if the likes of Kate Jane had thought otherwise.

As for the likes of Hal Fenton, as Shady had suspected, he was still alive and living not more than ten miles from the cabin in the woods that had once been home to a happy family. Not that he'd been the first one to wreck it; fate had done that in snatching Wapun's husband, Hurit's father, from them so suddenly. It had left them open and vulnerable, exposed to the worst kind of humanity—a man like Fenton, whose obsession with Wapun would take a lethal turn.

His crime was more than thirty years old but not a crime in the eyes of the police, only a missing persons case, now closed. According to the sheriff of Dupont County, anyway. It was Annie who got that "lazy, good-for-nothing piece of crap" sheriff, as Keme described him, to sit up and take notice of what they were saying about Hal Fenton.

After grabbing some sleep the night of the fire, they'd woken to do a bit of research. Keme had taken to the snowy roads in his truck to ask around and about if anyone had heard of Fenton. Most people shrugged, said they hadn't, but one person had, one person said, "Hal? Sure, he's a rough type, lives down by Muldoon Creek. Used to drink at the bar in Dupont, though, when he was a young man. Still goes there from time to time. Sits at the end of the bar, head hanging low, talking to no one, grunts if you happen to pass the time of day with him. Like I said, rough fella."

Bingo! They'd gotten evidence he was still alive.

But that son-of-a-bitch sheriff still didn't want to know.

"If there ain't no body, there ain't no case," he said.

Downcast, Shady and Ray turned to leave, but Annie continued to stand there. Still missing her glasses, she put her hands on her hips and squinted furiously at him.

"The point you're perhaps missing here, Sheriff, is that there *will* be a body, Wapun's or Carol Anne's, as she used to call herself for the benefit of you white folk, although God knows why she felt she had to pander, why any of them feel that way. I mean, just look at..." She only just stopped herself from insulting him further; instead, she changed tack. "Think of it: if you go out there and question Fenton about Carol Anne, if you find there is a link, that there was indeed a murder, a body that can be found...because if he did kill her, she won't be far away. She'll be in the trees nearby or alongside the creek, which is, what, ten miles away? If he confesses, if you solve the mystery of what happened to her, you'll not only avenge two deaths, the media will get hold of the story and they'll write about it. I'll make sure of that. You'll get the credit."

"I will?" From lazing in his chair, the sheriff straightened.

"All of it. I'm not interested in any *fame*"—how she stressed that last word, the sheriff's dull eyes beginning to glow that little bit brighter—"only justice."

"But what if Fenton outright denies it? After all, this was a long time ago, and without a confession I don't have the manpower—"

"When you ask him, remember this: bullies can be such cowards."

Annie was absolutely right. The sheriff went to see Hal Fenton. He questioned him, accused him, and Hal Fenton, stunned he'd been found out thirty-four years later, crumbled there and then in front of him and confessed. Like all dark things, he had no real substance.

But perhaps—and the nice part of Shady hoped that this was so—there was relief in his confession. Because surely the weight of murder hung heavy.

News came a couple of weeks after they'd reached home that the remains of a body had indeed been found down by Muldoon Creek, with further testing identifying it as Wapun's. The media screamed out loud about the story, loving the angle Annie had fed them about an age-old wrong righted—*two* age-old wrongs, that of a mother and her innocent child. The Cree community, stretching for miles and miles, came together to give Wapun a burial unique to their culture, honoring her in the way she deserved. Something else the media made a splash about, with Annie, Ray, and Shady in attendance—and of course Mandy, sitting on Shady's lap, facing outward, her glass eyes taking it all in, not missing a thing…

Job satisfaction? Oh yes, Shady agreed, there was plenty of that.

EPILOGUE

In the museum, Mandy was confined to a glass case, the key to which was kept in the safe, only Annie, Ray and Shady aware of the combination.

No longer in the basement, the doll had pride of place, located where the windows allowed at least a modicum of natural light. And, if this should falter on grey days, on stormy days, the lights were left on anyway, a habit of Annie's and damn the expense.

Not that money was an issue, because Mandy had made the press as well, the doll that the child had lain with for so long, her only companion. Cannily, Annie had also let it be known that the doll resided in Mason Town Museum, as run by herself, Shady Groves, and Ray Bartlett.

As she'd intended, that had brought people to the museum in droves, and they just kept on coming, all because of Mandy—hence, the glass box she sat in so that no one could touch her, be...*affected* by her, although what people did with their imaginations was up to them.

Annie also charged for entry now. She had to if she were to keep the concern going. Just a modest sum, but it made a difference.

"It's a double-edged sword," she said when explaining the reasons why. "We have to keep this museum going, not just for the benefit of Mandy but other artifacts like Mandy, because they're in here and they're out there. You know that now as well as I do. You *understand*. And a cold hard fact is we need finances. I have money of my own, but it's not an infinite sum. It won't last forever, and so what I've done is essential if our work here is to continue long-term.

"Mandy will, of course, attract Annabelle and Chucky fans, visitors wanting to be thrilled by the prospect of a haunted doll and fancying a scare of their own, no matter how brief. It'll be something to tell their friends about, that they've seen her, that they felt a chill when they looked into her eyes. They'll feed on the myth; they'll bolster it. But—" and here she'd inclined her head, her eyes such a rich shade of brown "—Mandy will also attract those who sympathize with her, who feel sadness and sorrow for the child who clung to her, who died alone, Hurit, and that will balance out the thrill seekers. That will feed *her* and perhaps, in the end, encourage her enough to not just fight back but to break the attachment."

"It's always about balance, isn't it?" Ray murmured while listening.

"It's about the shade and the light, and a perfect rendition of each," Annie replied, holding Ray's gaze before her eyes moved over to Shady.

She means us, thought Shady. *She means Ray's the light to my shade.*

And perhaps he was, this boy who had a knack for being there at the right time—and a knack for something else too, something that had clicked with Shady only recently. When he'd first been there for her, as she'd come sprinting out of the mall, and he'd taken her for a drink to calm her down, she'd wondered how much to tell him about Mandy and what had been happening to her since their first encounter. She'd been agitating over an explanation, and in response he'd told her she didn't "owe him anything." At the time, that's exactly what she'd been thinking: that she *owed* him.

One day, as they were both manning the desk at the museum, Annie enjoying a day off, she questioned him about this, about whether he'd read her mind.

"It's just a coincidence, Shady," he said, a grin on his face, his cheeks reddening.

"And yet you saw the child too, didn't you? You saw Hurit?"

"I don't know...I thought I did, but now... Maybe it's our old friend, auto-suggestion."

She didn't challenge him further, but she didn't believe him either, not entirely. People entered each other's lives for a reason, both good and bad. While she had no doubt that he was in hers for only good reasons, what she did question was his acceptance of his own ability. Just as there'd been something about Mandy, there was something about Ray, and, deep down, Ray knew there was something about Ray—perhaps that's what he'd been trying to tell her that time in the hotel lobby, back in Canada, just before the bartender had interrupted them. She'd said it was amazing he hadn't been fazed by anything that had happened so far on their journey, and he'd replied, *I am...a little. But only a little. You see—* Perhaps being friends with Shady and Annie was destined to bring that something to the fore, a knack, a sixth sense, a calling that wouldn't, *couldn't*, be denied.

Time would tell.

That particular day, Ray had to leave the museum early

as it was his mother's birthday. Shady told him to go right ahead, that she was okay to lock up. He hesitated as he always did when she told him this, but she was insistent. Annie was visiting a friend, but she had no such hesitation in leaving Shady alone to lock up; she knew what Shady wanted, which was to spend time alone with Mandy once all the visitors had gone, time that was precious—to both of them.

Waving Ray off in his mom's Ford sedan, which he was borrowing until he could afford his own car, she then turned and closed the door behind her.

To be alone in the museum was always a strange feeling, but over the few months she'd been working there, she'd learned how to tune out residual emotions from other objects that tugged at her attentions so she could focus only on Mandy, on the good in Mandy, on Hurit.

With the light in the sky having faded, there was only electrical light to rely on, but that was okay, that was good enough. Light was light, after all.

Earlier, she had retrieved the key to the glass case from the safe and put it in the pocket of her jeans. She now inserted it into the lock, her heart hammering slightly.

Because of Hurit, she wanted to hold the doll, to cradle her in her arms as you would any child that had been hurt. She'd remind her that her mother was at rest, both in body and spirit, that she was waiting for her in the light, and that all she had to do to find her was to open her eyes and look for the light, start heading toward it. But in holding the doll, shivers still raced up and down Shady's spine because she was also holding the darkness, the energy that searched relentlessly for a lost spirit because it wanted to devour it, something that would easily shatter.

"Be strong, Hurit," she whispered. "You left Mandy once, and you can do it again. The darkness won't chase you into the light; that's another promise I'm willing to make. It won't because it can't, it doesn't belong there. Only you do, Hurit, only you."

Sometimes, and neither Annie nor Ray were aware of this, Shady wouldn't leave the museum at all. Instead, she'd head out to her car, gather some bedding from the trunk, bring it back into the museum, and bed down for the night on the wooden floor, taking Mandy again in her arms.

Ellen and Bill didn't know she overnighted in the museum either; she'd tell them she was staying at a friend's or at Annie's or even Ray's, their eyebrows raising at the latter, but they didn't overly question. She was an adult, and although she lived with them still, they were finally treating her as one, respecting her, proud of her, particularly Ellen, at how she was evolving.

This was one of those nights because perhaps tonight would be when Hurit dug deep.

"You can do it, Hurit, you can fly. You're not alone. I'm rooting for you. Many, *many* people are rooting for you."

As the hours ticked by and the silence grew heavier, her gaze deliberately avoided the corners of this vast room, where, despite the lights, shadows managed to pool, to shift, to creep closer.

That way lies madness...

Kanti was proof of that.

But madness can be overcome.

Kanti was proof of that also.

Shady's parents would certainly think she was mad for

doing this, maybe even Annie and Ray. Because it was always in the small hours, when sleep refused to come, that she'd sometimes lose control of her imagination, that she'd see not just those shadows creeping forward but feel Mandy move in her arms, feel her *squirm*, those cherub lips of hers curling…

Kanti, help me.

And Kanti would. Kanti would sing. Shady would hear her above the creaks, above the many groans an old building made, above a sudden scream or the faint but heart-wrenching sound of sobbing. Kanti's voice was low but always clear.

Remember who you are.

She did; she was part of Ellen and Bill and Kanti too.

The best of us.

That's what Kanti would say.

You're the best of us.

Shady would also recall Ellen's words, words that had, in effect, saved her:

What if you weren't afraid?

If she wasn't afraid, the darkness would retreat.

Hurit, don't be frightened. If you're brave, nothing can hurt you.

Not even the gathering energies.

When Shady at last fell asleep she had no idea, but morning came and woke her, the doll in her arms still, same as she always was, nothing changed about her at all.

It was early—six a.m. Annie would be there at eight. Time to get up, get washed, have a strong coffee, brush her teeth, change into fresh clothes, and return her bedding to the car, make it look like she'd arrived just ahead of Annie.

Before doing all that, she put Mandy away, her eyes watering because she was *still* Mandy, still the darkness, still Hurit—something to be wary of and something to love.

If I love you hard enough...

Perhaps that was all she could do. Be patient and love her—keep that love pure. Reaching for the dead was her job now, undoing the damage done, dreams of teaching English shelved. There was so much to learn still, a lifetime's learning, in particular that results didn't always come easy.

It was while she was brushing her teeth in the bathroom's small sink that a text came through, someone else up early too.

After she'd rinsed her mouth and dried her hands, she picked up her phone to see the text was from Gina, the woman the secondhand mirror had belonged to, the mirror Shady had buried.

She sighed as she read it, but she wasn't surprised. Not really. Just as she'd thought earlier, results didn't always come easy. *Permanent* results.

The four typed words proved it:

The nightmares are back.

As much as I love writing, building a relationship with readers is even more exciting! I occasionally send newsletters with details on new releases, special offers and other bits of news relating to the Psychic Surveys series as well as all my other books. If you'd like to subscribe,
sign up here!
www.shanistruthers.com

Printed in Great Britain
by Amazon